RUTLEDGE TRAILS THE ACE OF SPADES

A Western Story

WILLIAM MacLEOD RAINE

SAGEBRUSH
Large Print Westerns

Published in Large Print 2009 by ISIS Publishing Ltd.,
7 Centremead, Osney Mead, Oxford OX2 0ES
United Kingdom
by arrangement with
Golden West Literary Agency

British Library Cataloguing in Publication Data
Raine, William MacLeod, 1871–1954.
    Rutledge trails the ace of spades
    1. Western stories.
    2. Large type books.
    I. Title
    813.5'2–dc22

ISBN 978–0–7531–8259–8 (hb)

Printed and bound in Great Britain by
T. J. International Ltd., Padstow, Cornwall

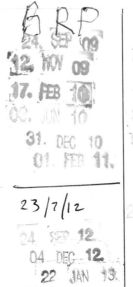
Please return/renew this item by the last date shown

worcestershire
c o u n t y c o u n c i l
Libraries & Learning

Will B To B

RUTLEDGE TRAILS THE ACE OF SPADES

RUTLEDGE TRAILS
THE ACE OF SPADES

Persons this *Story* is about —

JIM RUTLEDGE,
steel-muscled young Texan, is about to make his first drive alone with the herds up the trail from Texas. He refuses to be worried by his father's fear that old Devil Dave is about to settle a long-smouldering grudge against the Rutledges.

CHANDLER RUTLEDGE,
Jim's father, is temporarily stove up with a bad leg, and it doesn't make it any easier for him to know that Devil Dave and his hellion sons are out to get the Rutledges.

DEVIL DAVE MOSS,
who looks like an evil spider, isn't aiming to forget that he was once driven from the state by Chandler Rutledge.

ELLEN LAWSON,
18, a pretty, vigorous redhead, suddenly finds herself head over heels in love with Jim, although she is sure that she has several reasons for persuading herself that she hates him.

PETE MOSS, Devil Dave's arrogant, fiery son, usually gets what he wants, and what he wants at the moment is Ellen.

SAM MOSS, who shares his father's hatred of the Rutledges, runs his brother a good second in devilish doings.

BUCK ROE, Devil Dave's right bower, is as cool and hardy a ruffian and rustler as even this wild country can show.

STEVE LAWSON, Ellen's wild, reckless brother, says he doesn't want trouble, but he continues to run around with the Moss outfit.

JOE SHEAR, king-sized marshal, boasts 23 notches on his gun, and he has stored against himself terrible reservoirs of hate.

ALLISON MANDERS, sheriff, openly Shear's enemy, is an officer with a well-earned reputation for fearlessness.

MAMIE DUGAN, an actress, has a dusky beauty and an Irish spirit which give her extraordinary fascination. She seems to possess dangerous knowledge which she keeps to herself.

MART BROWN, a restless-eyed gambler, operates, with his brother, Bart, a crooked house. Shear aims to drive them out of town.

JACK BARTON, a young puncher with the Rutledge outfit, owes his life to Jim, and Jack is not one to forget it.

DOC AUBREY, a middle-aged man with a precise, oracular way of speaking, is glad to fulfill a rather strange request made by Jim.

RUTLEDGE TRAILS
THE ACE OF SPADES

List of Chapters —

CHAPTER
ONE

"Play Yore Hand Close to Yore Belly."

The old cattleman rasped a bristly chin and gazed dubiously at the long slim youth beside the bed.

"No other way to it, son. I've got to trust you to take these herds up the trail. This doggone busted leg knocks my plans galleywest. And there's nobody I can send but you. Can't even let one of yore brothers go along. They're too young yet."

"Don't you worry, Dad. We'll make the riffle, Sim and I."

Chandler Rutledge frowned resentfully at the limb stretched stiffly in front of him. "'Course I had to let myself get stove up right when we were gathering for the drive, after sitting around and wearing out the seat of my pants all winter swapping lies with the neighbors. Probably I've been piled fifty times by a bronc before and no damage done. I never saw the beat of such luck."

Every visible inch of Rutledge looked the old-timer. The shrewd blue eyes in the bronzed face, the broad heavy shoulders beneath the flannel shirt and open vest, the back of the leathery neck divided into geometric figures by deeply indented lines which gave the skin a resemblance to the cracked surface of a sunbaked mudhole, all proclaimed him indigenous to the Southwest. Unless appearances deceived, he was a man of forceful action.

"A stove-up old donker," he continued in bitter complaint. "I got to lie here and let you take the trail herds through. The contract calls for delivery first of July."

Jim did not permit his face to show the glimmer of a smile. "You always claimed you were waiting till you broke yore leg to read that book *Ivanhoe* Aunt Nellie gave you," he suggested.

The cattleman grinned wryly. "Dad gum yore impudence, boy, if I was on my feet I'd sure work you over for that. How old are you, anyhow?"

"Twenty-one coming grass."

"Which means you are two-three months past twenty. You're too young for this job, son."

"I'm a grown man and I've been up the trail before. There's nothing to lose sleep about."

"It's not the drive I'm worried about so much, though that's a man-size job. You can wrestle with storms and stampedes and bank-high streams — you and Sim together. Sim's faithful, and he knows cows. You can depend on him for that. The old squaw-humper has got cow sense — and then you've said it all. You'll have to be the boss of the outfit. Don't get too far out of touch with his herd — especially when you're going through the Red River country, for it's lousy with thieves. They'll stampede yore herds; they'll run off yore saddle stock and set you afoot a thousand miles from home."

"Not if I can help it," Jim replied.

Rutledge ran his eyes again over the trim figure of the youth. Jim was built like the Greek god Hermes — slender, supple, and graceful. His form was modeled on long lines deceptive to the casual glance. Long rippling muscles, true as steel, flowed beneath the smooth skin. His body was resilient as rubber, enduring as a hickory withe. When he moved there was something pantherish in his stride. Unlike most cowboys who have spent a large part of their lives in the saddle, he was only slightly bowed in the legs.

"I'm not saying you won't do to ride the river with, son," Rutledge explained. "But I got no right to expect an old head on young shoulders. If you get yore tail in a crack I don't know as I can blame you. What's worrying me is that when you reach the end of the trail yore troubles may just be starting." He hesitated before he continued: "Those cow towns are full of bad characters — gamblers and desperadoes and riffraff from the railroad construction gangs. I saw eight men killed in Newton one night. 'Course that was in the old wild days before they got tamed, but someone rips loose onct in a while yet."

Jim knew that his father had not yet freed his mind. He had something specific to say.

"Let 'er rip," the young man answered lightly. "I expect we'll be in our own camps attending to our business."

3

"Play yore hand close to yore belly, Jim. I'm not scared you won't be Katy-on-the-spot if trouble starts, but — don't let it start if you can wiggle out of it." Rutledge blurted out the name of his fears. "I'm thinking of the Moss gang."

The son nodded. "Knew you were. Well, what about 'em? Up to date they've been all bark and no bite, though you've watched for 'em each year on the drive."

"Don't fool yoreself, son. Dave Moss has got sharp teeth, and so have those hellion sons he's raised. They'll get you if they can. I've had luck so far that the only time they made a play we drove 'em off. But it wasn't so lucky that we had to kill a nephew of the old man when they jumped us last year. He'll be waiting for you somewhere sure as hell's hot. I know him. And he's slick as a greased pig. Dave's an old fox. When he sets a trap and baits it you'd never guess it for a deadfall. I've always figured some of the younger brood pulled off that attack on us and upset Dave's plan. Mostly his schemes work out."

"I never got the right of that Moss business, Dad. You drove 'em outa the state, didn't you, after they robbed the S. & G. train?"

A film of wariness robbed the cattleman's face of expression. "That was the way of it," he said shortly.

"I reckon they lit out before you got a chance to run 'em down."

"I reckon."

"Couldn't you bring 'em back?"

"No."

4

"I don't see what kick they had. You being sheriff, they surely didn't expect you to lie down on yore job."

Chandler looked through the window, eyes opaque as a blank wall. "Dave's not what you'd call reasonable." He paused for a moment before he continued, choosing his sentences carefully. "He'd been my friend — in the old days before he went bad. Fought beside me under Price in the war. He figured I'd kinda wink at the robbery — not get on the prod too much."

"Then he didn't know you," young Rutledge said with a grin. "If he's so wise I don't see how he come to make such a fool mistake as that."

The cattleman filled and lit a corncob pipe. "Well, look out for him. Play close, like I said. Keep to yore camp much as you can and stay out of the towns. You'll have to give the boys some rope, of course. But ride herd on them close as you can. They're a good bunch of waddies, but you know cowboys when they hit town. Sho! What's the use of me jawing. If you get in a tight you'll have to work yore way out by yoreself."

"Looks thataway," Jim agreed cheerfully. The worries of his father did not reach him. He was at the start of a great adventure and he anticipated nothing but success.

From a table beside the bed Chandler picked up a small package wrapped in oilcloth. He gave it to his son. "Don't open this, boy, unless you should get in a jam with the Moss gang. I'm not sure it would help you any, but anyhow you'd understand where you're at."

"I'll not open it unless I have to," Jim promised.

Briskly the cattleman came back to the order of the day. "Do you reckon to get through road-branding today?"

"Just about."

"Then I'd push off in the morning. Tell Sim I want to see him tonight after supper."

Sim Hart was a short heavy-set man of forty with a head as bald as a billiard ball. His legs looked like parentheses. He wore a cotton shirt, a vest without buttons, and striped trousers with the extremities tucked into high-heeled cowboy boots.

He grinned at Rutledge and asked, "How they comin', boss?"

"Jest tolerable. I hate to be tied here while the herds go up the trail. I'm counting on you to watch over Jim, Sim. If he gets into trouble I know you'll be right beside him. If it wasn't for knowing that, I wouldn't let him go, contract or no contract."

"Sure. Everything will be all right. I recollect onct when I went up the Chisholm trail with the buffalo wild and woolly —"

"Keep yore eyes on the boy, Sim. I don't want anything to happen to him, even if I've got four other lads and three girls."

"Bet yore boots."

"Take the upper ford at Wolf Creek. There's no bottom to the quicksand at the lower one."

"That's right, Chandler. I remember —"

"You'll have charge of one herd, Jim of the other. He'll boss the outfit. Give him yore advice when he asks for it, but do as he says."

"Suits me down to the ground."

"Everything ready for the start? Wagons greased — saddles all fixed up — cockle burrs outa the horses' manes and tails? I hate a lousy-looking outfit."

"All slick as a whistle."

"Good! Then you can shove off bright and early. Drift the herds along easy. Plenty of time. You won't have to drive 'em hard."

Sim dealt in ready-made phrases. "Bet yore boots," he said again.

"Keep yore eyes peeled for Dave Moss and his outfit. I feel it in my bones that you're gonna hear from him somewheres on the trip. If you cut their trail send for Jim right off. The idea is to duck trouble long as you can. The best way to do that is to be ready for it all the time."

"Keep yore powder dry an' give 'em merry Christmas if they come a-shootin'," Sim suggested. "Make yore mind easy, boss. Maybe I'm a mite slow in what you might call strategy, but when the stampede's on I don't allow to stay in the drag."

"What I'm trying to drum into yore head, Sim, is that stampedes which ain't are the kind I'll be pleased to hear about."

And again Sim answered cheerfully, "Bet yore boots."

CHAPTER
TWO

Not Even a Cigarette
for Breakfast

Jim made an early start. The herds had already been tallied and all the last details supervised. He sent the wagons ahead to pick up a bill of groceries waiting for them at Lockhart. The cattle moved slowly forward in a long loose line guided by the point men. Young Rutledge took charge of the lead herd and let it string out for half a mile or more. He knew that the best trail drivers never pressed the stock except when necessary, but let the animals saunter on as though under no restraint. Long of leg and horn, the steers were fleet as deer. Startled into a stampede, they could make a tremendous lot of trouble.

The second herd under Sim Hart followed several miles behind the first. Sim had been up the trail half a dozen times and knew every bad spot in it as a Latin teacher knows the difficult passages in his Virgil.

They made a good drive the first day and bedded down not far from Lockhart. Supper finished, the first guard took the herds and the other riders settled down around campfires to tell yarns and listen to them. Both

8

Jim and Sim Hart made a round of their respective herds to make sure that the cattle were resting easily. They left the riders circling the bedding-ground in different directions and softly singing range songs to let the longhorns know they were friends and not enemies. It was a night of stars, quiet and windless, such as every trail driver has known many times.

Water and feed were plentiful, and Jim noticed with satisfaction that after the cattle had been driven ten days they were in better condition than when they started. Scarcely a day passed without the sight of other herds, strung out in long snakelike formation, heading north by east in the same direction as the Rutledge outfits. They were making for Dodge or Ellsworth or Cheyenne as the case might be.

One day followed another without mishap. Round Rock and Fort Graham lay behind them. They crossed the Brazos to the left of Cleburne, passed Hell's Half Acre, and forded the Trinity. Fort Worth was then, as Sim Hart phrased it, "a little burg on the bluff where the panther lay down and died."

The troubles of the Circle R herds began at Red River Crossing. Swollen by the spring rains, the stream was running bank full. Young Rutledge and Hart rode along the river, looking for the best place to strike the swift current. It was beginning to rain, and presently the rain turned to hail. Icy bullets large as marbles pelted them.

"We'd better get back to the herds," Sim advised. "This is liable to start a run. Onct when I was workin' cows back in the piney woods and canebrakes of east Texas . . ."

Jim did not wait to hear the end of the story. He untied the cantle strings which held his oiled slicker and put on the coat as a protection against the stinging shots of hail. When he reached the herd he found the cowboys hunched up in their saddles but circling the cattle watchfully to prevent a break. The longhorns were drifting before the storm.

The hail pounded down for an hour, then stopped as suddenly as it had begun. Jim left the waddies to turn and bring back the animals while he cantered back to make sure that Sim's herd had not stampeded. Already the sun was shining and there was not a cloud in the sky. He caught sight of the foreman at the point and Sim joined him.

"All right here. They're quieting down fine. You still figurin' on crossin' tonight?"

"I reckon. I'm going to swim over and see how it goes."

"Let Jack Barton do that. The gray he's a-straddle is a right good swimmer. You don't want to start babying yore punchers."

"All right. We'll let Jack go," Jim agreed reluctantly. He was still young enough as a trail boss to prefer to take risks himself rather than to ask his men to face them. But this he knew was a weakness to be overcome.

Barton stripped to the skin and removed the saddle from his mount before he rode into the stream.

"Ouch! It's cold," he shouted back.

The hail had chilled the water to the temperature of a mountain brook fresh from a snowbank.

Jim watched the man anxiously. He could see the gray was having trouble. The animal was in the deep water where the current ran swiftly. It seemed to have stopped swimming. Barton slipped from its back just as the horse went under.

"Got a cramp from the cold water. Jiminy, Jack'll never make it," Sim cried excitedly. "What the blue blazes you doing, boy? Come back here, you crazy fool."

Jim had plunged into the river and was heading straight for Barton. The gray had disappeared beneath the rushing waters, but the head of the cowboy still rose and fell and rose again as he struggled with the icy torrent. Young Rutledge shouted encouragement to him. Barton was making little headway. It seemed to Jim that the strokes of his arms were growing feebler. Any minute the red head might vanish never to reappear.

The rescuer gave his cowpony a loose rein except for an occasional touch of guidance. "Go on, you Buckskin. You're doing fine. We're close now. Keep a-traveling," he urged.

Jim lunged forward and down the saddle just in time to get a grip on the curly red hair of the sinking man. He could feel Buckskin faltering beneath the extra drag of the cowboy's weight.

The rider shook his foot from the wide wooden stirrup. "Grab holt, Jack," he ordered. "That's right. Can you hang on if I let go of yore head? Good. Stick to that stirrup, boy, like death to a hunter's heel." Rutledge slid from the saddle on the other side from the cowboy.

The ice-cold water chilled him instantly, but he knew they were out of the most rapid current. A dozen yards of swimming separated him from the shallow water near the farther bank. Presently his feet touched bottom. Chilled to the bone, Barton's fingers released their hold and he slipped back. Jim caught him beneath the arms and dragged him ashore. The man sank down, eyes closed, completely exhausted.

Jim shivered in the warm sunshine. First, he must light a fire to dry his clothes. The sun did not yet have its summer heat and would not be enough to steam out the moisture. He gathered slivers of wood from a tree that had been struck by lightning. In the pocket of his shirt was a small oilskin package of matches. Within a few minutes he had a fire roaring.

Jack Barton looked at him and grinned. "You were sure enough Katy-on-the-spot, Jim. I come mighty nigh not cuttin' the mustard as it was."

"You all right now?"

The cowboy edged closer to the fire. "I'm still a leetle mite trifling and some shivery. It was a right cold bath, if anyone makes inquiries."

Jim stripped to the skin and draped his clothes on logs and brush around the fire. "Reckon we'll have to divide 'em when they dry. We got to make a night of it here without grub, blankets, or tarp. How do you divide one pair of boots, one pair of pants, one shirt, and one vest between two suffering sons of Adam?"

"Gimme the shirt and the pants, an' you can have the boots and the vest," Barton suggested. "You forgot one saddle blanket. Too bad we ain't got a deck of cards. We could play freeze-out for first choice."

"We're liable to play freeze-out anyway, cold as these nights are. But we're in luck at that. It'll be warmer here than at the bottom of the Red."

They did very little sleeping. One side of them toasted and the other side froze. Barton complained that he had to turn as often as a turkey on a spit to keep both sides done the same.

"When I think that only yesterday I kicked on Doc's coffee!" Jim mourned.

"I'd give five dollars Mex for the makings," Barton murmured.

They had never been more glad to welcome the sun when it rose.

Barton looked across the river at the smoke rising from the chuck wagon. "What a chump a man is, anyhow! The boys are sittin' down to steak and flapjacks and hot coffee, an' there ain't one of 'em got sense enough to be thankful. Missing all that good grub reminds me of a young lady I onct kept company with. She usta sing a song about how waters broad between us roll since auld lang syne."

Two riders came into view, caught sight of the smoke of their fire, and rode down a long slope to their camp. The strangers were hard-looking specimens.

"What's wrong, boys?" one of them asked.

Jim explained their plight with no unnecessary detail. He did not know why the sight of these men made him

13

instantly wary, unless it was that he felt if they were honest men they had a right to sue their swarthy ill-favored faces for libel.

"What's yore name, young fellow?" one of them demanded.

"James Warren," answered young Rutledge. This was true as far as it went. His middle name was Warren.

"What outfit you belong to?"

"Taking a herd to Dodge for my father."

"Where from?"

"Near Cleburne."

"Got a big outfit?"

"About five thousand four-year-old beef steers."

"Who's in charge?"

"I am."

The man looked him over insolently and laughed sourly. "Sent a boy to mill, didn't they?"

"I wear man-size boots," Jim said quietly.

It was the turn of the other man to jeer. He was younger and taller than his companion. "I'd never of guessed it," he said.

Jim let that pass. He wanted information rather than a quarrel. "My friend's name is Barton — Jack Barton," he mentioned. "What can we call you gentlemen?"

Was there a momentary hesitation before the older man spoke? Jim was not sure.

"Buck Roe's my name. This is Sam Moss." He spoke harshly, as though in answer to a challenge.

"Pleased to meet you," Jim replied.

"Seen anything of the Rutledge outfit on the trail?" Roe asked abruptly.

Jim turned to Barton. "Didn't we hear the Circle R was about five or six days behind us, Jack?"

The cowboy took his cue at once. "Seems to me that old donker at Bolivar said so."

"Hmp! How many vaqueros you got with yore outfit, young fellow?" Moss asked with elaborate carelessness.

"Plenty," Jim said innocently. "We've been told this country here is lousy with cattle thieves. So we kinda came prepared."

"Fellow, who you talkin' at?" Roe wanted to know.

Jim looked at the mounted men in wide-open candor. Both of them carried rifles as well as six-shooters.

"Why, I thought you gents might give me a steer how to get through the Red River country without meeting up with these birds. If you live here I reckon you have to watch out for them mighty close."

"This country is no worse than any other," Roe growled.

"But it's no place for smart-aleck kids," added Moss, an edge to his voice.

Jim had been sitting with the saddle blanket across his knees. It chanced to be the turn of his companion to wear the trousers. There was a chill wind blowing and Jim rose to replenish the fire.

"Where are yore pants, fellow?" inquired Roe.

Rutledge explained with a grin. His manner was deceptively friendly, but it got nowhere with his visitors. Moss laughed derisively and spoke to Roe. "He can't cross a crick without losing his pants, by his own story."

The young man flushed angrily but said nothing.

"If he hadn't crossed the crick, as you call it, I would have been in Kingdom Come," Barton spoke up. "And if you've got to ride someone, mister, why, I'm the guy that left his pants on the other side."

Moss turned his horse to ride away. Over his shoulder he said audibly to Roe, "A couple of greeners, I'd say. Betcha they don't get half their herd through."

The Circle R men watched them go. At the top of the slope Moss waved a scornful hand. Jim's lids had narrowed. All the warmth had been burned out of his eyes.

"Glad to meet up with you, Mr. Roe and Mr. Moss. I certainly don't take a smile to either of you. But I'll give you one credit mark. You're like rattlesnakes and give warning before you strike. Well, cut loose yore dogs soon as you're ready."

Jim spoke to himself rather than to Barton. He had been made to look ridiculous and he was young enough to resent it hotly. In spite of his father's admonition he was ready for war.

"They surely go outa their way to make themselves unpopular," the cowboy agreed. "Say, I'll bet those fellows, come to think of it, belong to the Moss gang."

"Go to the head of the class, Jack," his trail boss said. "You guessed right first shot outa the box."

"They got fifty thousand dollars from the S. & G. robbery. By jacks, some fellows have all the luck."

"The wife and kids of the express messenger they killed didn't have much, did they?" Jim suggested.

"They're ornery devils," Barton assented.

16

"A while ago you were mentioning about guys not knowing enough to be thankful, Jack. I'll say you've got good cause right now. For if those two hombres knew I was Chandler Rutledge's son they would ride back and pump us both full of lead."

Barton stared at him in surprise.

CHAPTER
THREE

Rustlers' Gulch

The wind died down and the sunshine warmed the land. Jim donned the trousers, saddled Buckskin, and set out to find a crossing-place for the herd. He found one a couple of miles from the camp. Near the upper point of an island the stream had widened above a bed of gravel to comparative shallows. Buckskin found it necessary to swim for only one short stretch. Moreover, the water had already lost the icy chill given it by the hailstorm.

He met Sim Hart on the opposite bank.

"Looks like a good place," the foreman said. "How's the bottom?"

"Gravel. Couldn't be better. We'll throw 'em over right away. First off, though, send one of the boys across with Jack's clothes, some grub, and the makings. He hasn't even had a cigarette for breakfast."

"Must of been cold in the night."

"Some."

"Onct when I was a line-rider in the Panhandle —"

"We had two visitors," Jim interrupted. "Ever hear of a gent named Buck Roe?"

The foreman stared at him. "I'll say so. I've known that cow thief for twenty years. He's Dave Moss's right bower. You ain't tellin' me you've seen Buck Roe?"

"Buck and a friend of his called Sam Moss. They drapped in to say 'How-d'ye-do?' and to warn me Dad was sending a boy to mill."

"Golly! You tell 'em who you were?"

"I did *not*. When Roe asked about the Circle R trail herds I said they were a week back of us. But this means we've got to keep our eyes skinned. They good as told me they were after our stock."

Jim ate a sandwich hurriedly while one of the cowboys roped and saddled a fresh horse for him. He rode back to the ford and watched the leaders of the first herd go into the water. They took it with very little hesitation. Inside of three hours both herds had crossed in safety. They covered ten miles before night.

After they were bedded down, Jim took extra precautions about the night guard. He warned the riders to be very careful, and he made sure that they carried revolvers. Twice during the night Jim rode out to the sleeping herd to make sure that all was well.

Before daybreak the men were fed and as early as possible the cattle were in motion. Jim rode at the point to give the direction. He made a long day of it, for he wanted to get out of the danger zone quickly. Evidently the Moss gang did not know the Circle R herds were in the immediate vicinity. There was a chance that he might slip past without trouble, though he hardly dared hope for such good luck. Roe and young Moss had probably been sent to look their outfit over and had contemptuously decided they were easy prey.

The sky was heavy with clouds, and before darkness fell the rain was pelting down. Thunder rolled up and distant lightning played across the sky. Jim doubled the guard, for this was stampede weather. An hour later the full force of the storm was upon them. Cannon crashed in the heavens, and the lightning played around the horns of the cattle. At the ears of the horses phosphorescence gleamed. The herd was disturbed and uneasy, but as yet had made no break. The animals were on their feet ready for whatever might take place.

Jim met one of his riders, a Swede named Oscar Helgeson. "We'll be lucky if we get off without a run," he said to the cowboy. "Never saw so much fox fire in my life."

Helgeson drew the slicker closer about him. "Y'betcha, boss. It's a helluva night."

From the other side of the herd came the sudden unexpected flash of guns. A zigzag of lightning lit the night. On the elevation where the two men had drawn up to talk they could see and be seen in the storm-tossed night illuminated by the momentary glare. Jim got a swift snapshot of four or five horsemen firing into the ground close to the edge of the herd. Darkness closed over the scene. There was a wild surge of bellowing beef. The stampede was on.

It headed straight for the hillock where Jim stood. He wheeled his horse and quirted to escape the rush. For a few minutes he was dominated solely by the instinct for self-preservation, but after a time he drew to the outside of the galloping herd. From this position he tried to point in the leaders, but they were still going too strong for him. He fired twice in front of them to check the run, without being able even to deflect the course of it.

The longhorns in the lead came to a hill. Some swung to the left and some to the right. Jim went with those that took the left. Half a mile beyond this point they poured into the brush with a rush like the charge of cavalry. When they emerged from the mesquite Jim knew there had been another split. There were no more than a hundred or a hundred and fifty in the bunch he was following.

He saw the flash of a revolver in front of him. Someone was at the point trying to swing the four-year-olds into a mill. Rutledge throttled his impulse to shout a greeting. He must find out first whether this was friend or foe. Urging his horse forward, he drew close to the rider. The storm had died down, and from behind scudding clouds a moon showed.

The man at the point had taken off his slicker and was waving it in the face of the leaders. Jim recognized York Evarts, one of his father's men. He swung in beside the cowboy and presently they forced the steers to turn. In a few minutes the bunch was milling.

"They certainly pulled off a big show," York said, wiping from his face the blood drawn by the scratches of mesquite thorns. "I'll bet by morning there will be Circle R longhorns scattered in twenty bunches all over this Red River country. They sure went high-tailin' into the night lickety-brindle."

"They were stampeded by cow thieves," Jim explained. "I've got to get back to round up the outfit. This bunch has had all the run it wants. Hold 'em till morning, then drift back toward camp. Likely you'll run into some of the boys with more cattle they've gathered. Keep an eye open for strange waddies."

He left York to watch the cattle and rode in the direction in which he thought the camp was. The run had not followed a straight line, but even in the rush of it Jim had tried to check up on directions. He struck a match and looked at his watch. The time was half-past one.

After riding some distance he knew that he was lost. No use going farther. He might travel away from instead of toward camp. Dismounting, he tied his horse and waited till the light of early dawn sifted into the sky. Close at hand there was a small hill. He rode to the top of it. In a draw not a hundred yards from him a bunch of cattle was feeding. They carried the Circle R brand.

Jim was sure the camp was to the east, and he headed the stock that way. After he had driven them less than a mile he came into a wide valley where he could see two riders following another herd moving in the same general line as his own. He examined his revolver, thrust it back into the holster, and cut across to them. They might be his own men. They might not. He had to take a chance. If his guess as to the position of the camp was correct these must be Circle R riders.

He was right. The men were a Mexican vaquero, Juan Perez, and the cook, Doc Simmons. Jim gave orders to throw his bunch in with their own and follow him toward the camp.

The sun was riding high before he reached the wagons. He was relieved to find them and their contents safe. It had occurred to him that the raiders might have doubled back and burned the outfit while the men were engaged in rounding up the stampeded stock. Three of his cowboys were with the wagons. They had brought back between three and four hundred longhorns with them.

Jim distributed rifles to them. "Stick right here," he said. "Don't leave the wagons under any circumstances. If any strangers show up, hold 'em off and don't let 'em get close."

The dust of another bunch of cattle drew nearer. Jack Barton was driving them. As soon as he had thrown them with those already recovered, Jim told him to ride back to Sim Hart's herd and tell the foreman to send ten of his men up to help round up stock. Rifles were to be issued to the others to guard the herd and wagons.

Barton cocked an eye at him whimsically. "Did anybody say anything about breakfast?"

"Not yet. Tomorrow morning, if we're lucky." Jim relented enough to add, "You can stay with herd number two and get some grub there."

Jim roped and saddled a fresh horse and started out again at once. He had imperative business that would not wait. Whoever had stampeded the cattle had not

23

done so for the fun of it. Without doubt the raiders had
rounded up a bunch of steers and would be driving
them hard to get the animals holed up before losses
could be checked. Jim meant to cut their trail if he
could, then ride swiftly back for reinforcements.

There was no way for him to know in what direction
the rustlers would drive the stolen cattle, but there was
a low line of hills to the northeast that invited him. If
they could be reached by the thieves, the gather could
be cached in some hidden draw until night. A drive to
any other point of the compass would carry the risk of
meeting some trail herd. Therefore logically the outlaws
should push for the hills. His deduction might be based
on false premises, but it seemed to Jim his best bet. He
cut across country straight for that broken line standing
against the horizon.

The young trail boss rode rapidly. Since the day
when his father had first lifted him to the saddle of a
cowpony he had worked with stock. He could read
much desert lore that a tenderfoot would have missed.
His eyes watched for signs of a bunch of longhorns
recently driven this way. They swept the landscape to
pick up the dust of moving cattle.

The hills drew nearer. They were not far distant
when he caught sight of a drift of dust to the west of
him. His heart jumped with excitement. Unless his
guess was wrong he had found the thieves who had
stampeded the herd.

What Jim did was characteristic. Having discovered
the rustlers, most men would have turned back for
help. But Jim wanted to know more before he went for

his friends. He meant, if possible, to get close enough to identify the thieves.

In the hills ahead of him was the mouth of a canyon. As he came closer he saw that it was a pass leading into the heart of the ridge. The dust cloud was moving toward it. Marks of hoofs were plentiful in the sand at the edge of the little creek. It was a reasonably safe bet that through this cut the rustlers meant to drive their gather.

Jim rode up beside the brook. Just beyond the mouth of the gulch its walls lifted to make of it a rocky gorge. A wooded draw twisted down to the bed of the stream. Dismounting, he led his horse up this and around a bend into a clump of cottonwoods. Here he tied the animal.

Climbing the bluff that made one lip of the gorge, Jim found a place among the big boulders where he could look down on the pass below. His intention had been to lie concealed while the rustlers and the stolen herd filed through, but a plan shaped itself in his mind that was appealing in its simplicity and its audacity.

Running back to the place where his horse was concealed, he returned with the rope that had been tied coiled to the saddle. From a pocket he took a piece of cord and tied it securely to the trigger of his revolver. To the end of the cord he fastened the lariat. The six-shooter he weighted down with heavy rocks to hold it in place, then drew the lariat around a boulder and tied one end of it to his ankle.

Already Jim could hear the bawling of the approaching cattle. The first stragglers appeared at the mouth of the canyon. He took position behind a large flat rock and waited for the rustlers to show up.

Clearly the thieves felt they had reached safety. They rode carelessly, bunched together, at the tail of the drive. As far as Jim could make out, there was only one rifle in the party and that was in a scabbard beneath the leg of one of the riders. The men were talking loudly and cheerfully. They had done a good night's work, for they had with them a bunch of about three hundred and fifty Circle R longhorns.

Buck Roe and Sam Moss rode side by side. Three long-bodied youths in chaps, dark from the tan of many summer suns, brought up the rear.

Jim rose, rifle at shoulder, from the place where he had been crouching. "Throw 'em up!" he ordered sharply. "No monkeying. We've got you covered."

The outlaws pulled up, taken completely by surprise. What they thought is not a matter of record, but without question they felt they were trapped. It could not have occurred to any of them that one man would attempt such an enterprise.

"Who the hell are you?" growled Roe.

"I'm the boy that was sent to mill, the smart-aleck kid who lost his pants. Remember me, don't you? None of that you redhead. *Get* 'em up."

"How many of you are there?" demanded Sam Moss.

"Plenty," Jim called back. "And we'll stand no shenanigans. First man pulls any funny stuff we'll drill through and through."

From the point of view of the rustlers the situation was bad. It was not only that these fellows had the drop on them. They carried rifles as against six-shooters, and the distance was too great for any accuracy with forty-fives. In the event of a fight the men in the cut would not have a chance. They could be picked off without any serious danger to the men in the rocks.

"What's the idea holding us up?" Roe asked sullenly. "What's the idea in stealing our cattle?" Jim retorted. "We're not stealing 'em. We picked up this bunch to hold for you — figured you musta had a stampede."

"We did," Jim said grimly.

"You ought to know."

"By jings, we'll shoot this out," the redheaded boy cried with an oath, and he reached for his revolver.

The crack of Jim's rifle sounded. The redhead slumped down in the saddle. Simultaneously Jim moved his leg sharply, twice. Two shots rang out from the rocks a few yards away.

One of the rustlers whirled his horse to run.

"Stay where you're at," Jim cried. "Or we'll drop the whole outfit of you."

Buck Roe's hand fell from the butt of his revolver. "What d'you want, fellow? I done told you we weren't stealing yore dogies. What's eating you?"

"Keep going right on up this canyon — all of you. And stay up there. We'll keep this pass guarded till night and drop any visitors without argument. Now hit the trail quick!"

Sam Moss flung up a doubled fist toward him furiously. "We know who you are, fellow. You're not foolin' us any Lie, you did, lie to us. You're one of Chan

Rutledge's damn litter. We aim to get you right one of these days."

"Says one cow thief real sincere," jeered Jim. "Now having declared intentions, keep moving, Mr. Moss."

By way of emphasis Jim jerked his leg again. Since he was standing behind the boulder the motion was concealed from those below. A pistol shot rang out.

"No more firing," Jim ordered, "unless they run on the rope."

The rustlers put their horses in motion, one of them supporting the wounded man. They pushed through the cattle toward the head of the gulch.

Roe stopped and turned his horse. He lifted his defiant eyes toward Rutledge, cool and unhurried, as hardy a ruffian as even that wild country could show. He knew he was an inviting target, and he deliberately ran the risk of being shot down.

"Yore say — so now," he called out, spacing his words deliberately. "Better kill me now, fellow, for if you don't, sure as taters grow in hills I'll bump you off some day."

He waited there, straddling the horse in impudent contempt, then swung round and moved slowly after his companions.

Jim watched them go up the canyon. He could see them for a distance of nearly a quarter of a mile before a bend cut them from sight. Then, swiftly, he got to work.

Running to the horse among the cottonwoods, he swung to the saddle, cantered down to the brook, and circled the cattle. He headed them the other way and pushed them out of the canyon. Once in the open, he drove them hard. It was possible the rustlers might turn to check up on the cowboys who had recovered the cattle. Possible but not probable, Jim thought. One of them had been wounded, and their first concern would be to get him to a place where he could be looked after. Moreover, they would hesitate to challenge the supposed rifles of the vaqueros with their six shooters.

None the less he kept the cattle moving. The outlaws were wild and undisciplined, and anything might be expected. Many times during the trip back to camp his anxious eyes swept the plain behind the herd. When he caught sight of three riders loping toward him from the distant wagons his relief found vent in a loud "Hi-yi" of greeting.

Sim Hart was one of the riders. "The boys are all in, Jim. We better tally yore herd, don't you reckon? Where'd you get this bunch? They look sure enough gaunted, like they been driven hard."

"Got 'em in a canyon back a ways. Buck Roe and the Moss boys gathered 'em for me."

"Quit joshin' me, boy," the foreman grinned.

"I'm not. It's like I said."

Hart became pop-eyed with amazement. "You're not tellin' me that — that —"

"I found this stock with them. Roe said they were holding the bunch for me. So I talked it over with them and brought the gather back."

"You — talked it over with Roe?" Sim gasped.

"With him and some of his friends," Jim said, his eyes dancing. "They were too busy to come back with me, so I hustled the stock along alone."

"But — but —"

Barton interrupted Sim. "Lemme get this straight. The Moss gang had rounded up these longhorns and then turned 'em over to you. That the way of it?"

"Correct," Jim assented.

"Then all I got to say is you're either a doggone liar or you can make oration so good we'd ought to send you to Congress. Are you claimin' they didn't put up any argument? Just let you take 'em?"

"Not much of an argument."

"No gun play a-tall?"

"I didn't say that."

"How many of the Moss crowd?" the third rider asked.

"Five."

"And they let you get away with the steers? And nobody hurt?"

"I didn't say that either," Jim smiled.

"Looky here," burst out Sim. "You tell yore story pronto, boy, or someone is gonna get hurt right here."

Jim told it, to an appreciative audience that listened wide-eyed to the tale.

Jack Barton slapped a dusty sombrero against his chaps and sent a cloud into the air. "By hokey, we'll call that canyon Rustlers' Gulch," he cried.

And to this day Rustlers' Gulch is its name.

CHAPTER
FOUR

"They're After Me."

Ellen was in the kitchen making dried apple pies. Her sleeves were rolled up to the elbows, showing arms firm and muscular beneath the soft skin. The sunlight poured in through the open window. It was late June, and a day to make one glad of life. The girl felt the lift of it, for she was a fine vigorous young creature in tune with the universe. Lustily she sang, "Good-by, My Lover, Good-by," though she had no lover and was intent on escaping rather than achieving one.

Sounds came from outside, the *clip-clip* of a horse's hoofs, the slither of gravel at an abrupt halt, the spacing of light quick steps. A man stepped into the room and closed the door behind him. He was breathing hard. His eyes made a swift survey of the room and came to rest on Ellen.

They saw a girl still in her slender teens. Even in his haste he noticed, oddly enough, the little patch of flour on one temple below the cascades of red hair.

"You alone — in the house?" he asked quickly.

His eyes had the look of a hunted man, not fear but wariness and a grim resolution to meet the threat of danger.

"Yes," she answered.

She looked at him with startled eyes, an odd excitement drumming in her veins.

"They're after me," he said.

"Who?"

"The Moss gang. They jumped me this side of Fisher Hill."

"What do they want with you?"

He took the wide-rimmed hat from his head and looked at two small holes in it, one through the side and the other through the crown. The dilated eyes of the girl lifted from the hat to the man. Her heart was beating fast.

"They — did that?"

He nodded. "It'll be here — the finish. Clear out."

Her heart stood still. She went white to the lips.

"In two-three minutes now," he added quietly.

The girl's gaze flashed to the window. Over the crest of the ridge a quarter of a mile away were coming riders, three or four of them, headed straight for the house.

She asked no more questions, wasted no words.

"This way," she told him, and opened the door into a small bedroom.

It was her own room. A frock and a nightgown in the closet, a pair of shoes peeping out from beneath the bed, scattered hairpins on the home-made dresser informed him of this.

"Up there," she said.

His eyes followed the sweep of her hand. Above the rafters was a floor of puncheon extending over two thirds of the room.

"My horse is back of the house," he mentioned.

"I'll take care of it. Wait there till I come for you."

Her blanched face and troubled eyes betrayed the girl's inquietude. She was fighting to control the fear in her.

The young man smiled reassuringly, then swung himself by a rafter to the puncheon floor separating the room from the roof. Looking down, he watched her pass into the kitchen. She moved with the light lank grace he had observed in antelopes and other untamed creatures of the wild.

Ellen ran out of the house and pulled herself to the saddle of the gelding that waited in the shade. Its head drooped. Sweat stains discolored shoulders and flanks. She dug her heels in and forced the horse to a trot. There was a grove of young cottonwoods fifty yards from the house. She left the horse among the trees and scudded back to the log cabin.

When the first of the pursuers flung himself from his horse and strode into the kitchen, Ellen was trimming with a knife the dough from the edge of the pie tin.

"Seen anything of a fellow passin' this way?" the man demanded brusquely. "Not five minutes since. Couldn't have been longer."

He was a tall, long-bodied man, with straight black hair, so dark that his swarthiness suggested Indian blood.

"A man passed the house, Sam. Went down into the cottonwoods. Looked like his horse was played out."

He gave a whoop, the shout of a hunter in at the kill. "Bet yore boots his bronc was played out. We had him

33

cut off from town and from his camp. He's our meat now." Sam Moss called the good news to those outside. "We got him, boys. The damn scalawag just went down into the cottonwoods. His horse was wore out, Ellen says."

"We better go slow, boys," Roe advised. "Like enough he's in the cottonwoods now waitin' for us."

"Either that or high-tailin' it down the crick. One of us better circle round the draw an' cut him off from below," a third man said.

"You're whistling, Pete. Then we'll know we've got him," an eighteen-year-old lad chimed in.

Sam Moss laughed, cruelly and vindictively. "We've got him, Dave. Don't you worry yore head about that. I aim to collect Mr. Rutledge pronto."

Ellen stood in the doorway. Her troubled gaze moved from Sam Moss to his brothers Pete and Dave. It came to rest on the youngest of the three.

"Who is this man, Dave?" she asked.

"It's the fellow who shot Steve. We'll even up that right now, Ellen," the boy boasted.

"The man who shot Steve?" she echoed, her brown eyes wide with surprised distress.

"Fellow called Jim Rutledge," Sam added. "Come on, boys. Buck, you an' Dave head him off below and Pete an' I will crowd him down to the crick."

Pete dismounted to join Sam. The other two rode away to cut off the flight of the hunted man.

The two Moss brothers moved cautiously toward the cottonwoods.

"He's got no rifle with him this time," Ellen heard Sam say to his brother. "If we don't get too close we can pick him off easy an' never give him a chance."

The excitement had died down in the girl and left instead a sick depression. She turned back into the house. Before passing into the bedroom, she glanced through one of the kitchen windows to make sure those outside were still moving toward the cottonwoods.

The man whom she had saved dropped lightly from the puncheon ceiling as she came into the room. His eyes were eager with admiration.

"You did fine," he said. "I was scared yore face would give you away."

She did not respond to his enthusiasm. "Is yore name Rutledge?" she asked abruptly.

"That's my name — Jim Rutledge," he replied.

"You shot my brother Steve." Her eyes blazed anger at him.

He stared, for the moment dumb with surprise.

"Six weeks ago," she added. "Down the trail."

"Yore brother? Jiminy!"

"And you come here and beg me to hide you."

"Is yore brother a redheaded young fellow?"

"What had he done to you? Why did you want to kill him?" she demanded.

"I didn't want to kill him. And I didn't either. He's riding around good as ever, ain't he?"

"Why? I want to know why. What had he done to you?"

"He was reaching for his pistol. And they were five to one against me. What could I do? Why does he run

35

around with a bunch of cow thieves if he don't want to get in trouble?"

She flinched at that. It was an unexpected thrust, but he knew it had got under her guard.

"You had Moss cattle in yore herd," she charged.

"Not one," he denied. "They stampeded my herd and I found the rustlers driving away several hundred Circle R steers. If yore brother was one of the thieves —"

"You can't say that to me," she cried wildly. "It's not true. It's not true. You'd better go. I don't want you here."

He laughed, grimly, the sardonic recklessness of his face in strange contrast with its boyishness. "I sure came to a good place to hole up. Well, sorry I disturbed you, miss. I'll be movin' along."

"Wait," she cried, barring the way. "What are you going to do?"

"What would you advise?" he asked, his eyes mocking her.

"You can't go — yet."

"Why not? Is yore brother out there with the gents looking for my scalp?"

"No."

"Then why worry? If I bump off anyone it won't be him."

She was furious at him. He stood there jeering at her, as though life and death were trifles. He did not plead with her to save him, yet he knew that if his enemies caught sight of him he was lost. His head was up. His eyes were steady and unafraid.

"I think you're — hateful," she cried in a low voice.

"Then that's all there is to that," he mocked. "Why don't you call out and bring yore friends the rustlers back? I reckon they're still within hearing."

"Because —"

"Because I might get one of them before they got me. I might, too. Is that rifle hanging up in the other room loaded?"

"What rifle?"

"The one I saw in the other bedroom as I came in here with you. I may have to borrow the loan of it."

"No. You're not going to make more trouble. Give me yore pistols and get back up where you were."

"I hate to refuse a lady, but I wouldn't feel dressed today without my guns," he drawled. "I'd do 'most anything else for you. Shoot a rustler or two, say. I'll tell you what. You go collect the weapons from that Moss bunch of law-abidin' citizens first. Maybe then I'll give you mine."

His ironic laughter rang harshly on her ears. She hated him for his callousness, for the cool hardihood with which he defied her even though he was at her mercy. He was quite capable, she felt, of taking the rifle from her brother's room and walking out to confront his foes. Anything but that. She knew by the wild beating of her heart that she had to save him, no matter who he was or what he had done, regardless of the anger his insolence stirred in her. She did not ask herself why this was so. If she had asked, she could have given no other answer except the universal one that bloodshed was horrible to her because she was a woman. Yet that would have been only the partial truth. Contradictory emotions fluttered in her bosom. She was both fascinated and furious. Her little fists were clenched below pulses drumming in her wrists.

"I suppose you're what they call a killer," she flung at him.

"That's the story yore side is telling, I reckon," he said, bars of gray steel radiating from the pupils of his eyes. "Let it ride at that, if that's what you claim."

"You wound my brother. You come here and ask me to hide you. You treat me like — like —"

A sob of indignation choked her words.

"How do you want me to treat you? First off, you blame me because I had to shoot up yore brother to save my own life. Then you claim I make trouble when this bunch of outlaws jumps me and I have to ride hell-for-leather with them pumping lead at me. After we've stood 'em off for six weeks coming up the trail. They're a bunch of highwaymen. That's plain talk, miss, but you asked for it."

"My brother's no highwayman."

"Then he's trailin' with the wrong crowd. You'd ought to have him wear some kind of uniform, so's when he starts shooting at me I'll know he's Miss Redhead's brother and not interfere with his fun."

"That's yore story. Course you can *say* anything. I don't have to believe it — and I don't. I know Steve. He's not like you."

"I've said my say. Take it or leave it."

"I know what I think," she cried. "But that doesn't matter now. I don't want any killing around here. Go back into the loft — or take Sam's horse while he's down in the cottonwoods and ride away."

He had already considered the second alternative. But there was an objection to it. If he did this his enemies would know he had been concealed in the house, and the girl would be left to bear the brunt of their anger.

"You've got my company," he told her. "While I'm here you can put me anywhere you say."

He swung up to the rafters and vanished above.

Hours later the Moss brothers and Roe returned to the cabin sour with disappointment.

"We found his horse wore out like you said, but the fellow got away," Dave explained. "Must have gone down the crick an' slipped into the hills."

"Can you fix us up with dinner, Ellen?" asked Sam.

"Of course."

While Ellen made dinner for them they washed up and discussed the escape of Rutledge.

"Saw he couldn't make it on the horse an' slipped off into the brush," Roe said. "Funny we couldn't find his tracks anywhere."

"That bird shows us up every time we bump into him," Pete Moss said sulkily. "He's had the laugh on us ever since single-handed he took several hundred head of longhorns away from five of you lads. Glad I wasn't among those present that day."

Pete was a slender youth of twenty-two, dark like all the family, with straight black hair and beady eyes. In

39

bearing and manner was a suggestion of impatient arrogance.

"If you'd been there you'd have done like the rest of us," his brother Sam told him sharply.

"I wonder," murmured Pete impudently. "Maybe I would have had guts enough to back Steve's play instead of stickin' my tail between my legs."

"What did it get Steve?" asked Roe. "Not a thing. Me, I know when to make a gun play an' when to stick up my hands."

"I reckon the time to stick 'em up is when one guy rounds up half a dozen," Pete sneered.

Ellen came to the door. "Dinner's ready," she called.

After they had eaten, they rode away. Pete lingered behind the others. He came and stood close to Ellen while she gathered the dishes.

"Girl, have you found the right answer for what I told you the other day?" he asked roughly.

"Yes, Pete. The right answer is the one I gave you then and always have given." She looked at him, color flooding her cheeks. "I wish you wouldn't speak about that today. Please."

"Well, I will. I'm tellin' you that you got to come to my way of thinking. I get what I want. You're my girl, an' that's the way it's going to be. Understand?"

"I'm not yore girl, either," she told him indignantly. "You can't bully me, Pete Moss. I'm a free-born —"

There was a scuffle. He pinioned her hands and kissed her in spite of her struggles. As soon as he released her she struck hard at his face, furious with resentment. A stain of blood showed on his lips.

He drew his hand across his mouth and looked at the crimsoned fingers. "You li'l wildcat," he cried in exasperation. "I'll sure pay you off for that."

Pete snatched at her wrist. She tried to twist it free, fought with all the strength of her lithe, muscular young body. He laughed with savage delight at her efforts.

"Fight, girl," he urged. "I like mine wild. Pete Moss is the lad can tame 'em. When you've quit rarin' around I'll take a dozen kisses."

Unexpectedly the girl relaxed in his arms, her gaze fixed over his shoulder. A voice shocked Moss like the touch of a live wire.

"Why, Mr. Moss, that's no way to treat a lady," it drawled reprovingly.

Young Moss whirled, to face a man behind a gun. The gun was a very businesslike revolver, and the end of the barrel was jammed against his stomach. The owner of the weapon was a stranger to Pete, a brown young fellow in the garb of a cowboy.

"Who are you?" Moss asked angrily.

"Me? Oh, I'm only the boy Dad sent to mill — Jim Rutledge. Better stick up yore hands, Mr. Moss. It'll be safer — for you. Then you won't get wrong notions. That's right."

"How did you get here?" Pete blurted out. He was chagrined, very much so, and quite uncertain of what was in store for him.

"Came in the door while you were so busy. Saw yore outfit ride away and thought maybe I could borrow a horse somewhere."

"Where you been the last two hours?"

Rutledge laughed derisively. "You'd never guess, Mr. Moss. Hidden in a cottonwood not more'n a hundred yards from here. Lying up close to a big limb. You and yore friends passed so close to the tree I could have dropped on you."

"We looked up in the trees."

"You didn't look thorough enough. And maybe it's lucky for one or two of you that you didn't . . . Now let's talk turkey. First off, I'll take yore popguns. Good! There's an old saying, Mr. Moss, that a fair exchange is no robbery. Yore friends have taken my horse. So I'll take yours."

The black eyes of Moss fastened to the light gray ones of the trail driver. Nobody could have read fear in those savage focal points of defiance, though the owner of them was still in doubt as to whether the man behind the gun meant to kill him. He and his friends had fired at Rutledge a dozen times. They would have shot him down callously if they had caught him. He had no right to expect from the Texan a better fate.

"And now, Mr. Moss, we'll say good-by," Rutledge concluded.

Good-by might mean one of several things. Pete Moss still glared silently at the other man, waiting for the definite word about to be spoken.

"I hate to set you down afoot so far from home," the Texan explained, "but I reckon it's got to be thataway."

"What d'you mean?" asked Moss.

"You're taking a walk. It starts right now."

"Where?"

"Suit yoreself. North, south, east, or west. Anywhere from here."

On a tide of sudden furious anger Moss flung out his last word, a challenge against the future. "I'll not forget this, fellow."

Jim followed him to the door and sat down on the step. He watched the defeated man go clumping in his high-heeled boots across the plain. Moss took the same direction as the other three.

"I reckon it'll be quite a while before he catches them," Jim said with a chuckle.

"He'll never forgive you," Ellen said.

"That should worry me a lot."

"You can't laugh at a Moss."

"Any more than you can at a wolf."

"Pete's no wolf. He's got a good side to him," she defended.

"That sounds to me. The whole Moss tribe are poison to me if you want to know."

"They're vindictive, I admit. I wish —"

"What do you wish?" he asked, after her sentence had died away unfinished.

"That men weren't such — beasts." A flood of color swept the girl's face to the roots of the red hair.

Jim had no answer for that. He stepped inside and picked up the rifle Pete Moss had left.

"Tell him I'll leave this at Wright's store," he said. "I'll keep the horse till they bring back mine."

He moved to the cowpony and appeared to be busy with the stirrups. Presently he turned. He smiled at Ellen, and the smile was warm and friendly.

"Moss is not the only one that won't forget. I'll remember how you hid me. If you hadn't they would have collected me sure."

The long lashes dropped over the brown eyes. "That's all right," she said, much embarrassed.

"What I said about Moss don't go with all my enemies. I'll be worried till one of them forgives me," he said.

Her eyes shyly lifted to his. Again excitement set her pulses hammering. Something stirred in her heart, an emotion alarming and delightful.

She wrenched her gaze from his, turned, ran into the house, and slammed the door behind her.

Jim swung to the saddle and turned the head of the horse toward town.

CHAPTER
FIVE

Twenty-Three Notches on His Gun

Jim crossed the bridge and rode up into a town humming with activity. The traffic on Front Street was so heavy as almost to form a blockade. The crack of the mule-skinners' whips cut into their lurid language. Cowponies stood at hitch-racks close to the sidewalks. The freighter jostled the tenderfoot, gamblers shouldered cowboys and railroaders. For this was the end of the long Chisholm Trail, the point where the last frontier met and shook hands with the civilization of the Atlantic Coast. The meeting place was a turbulent one. It roared with the lusty voice of hardy youth released after months of hardship in the saddle.

Swinging from the back of the horse in front of a billiard hall, Jim noticed a man watching him. The man moved forward. "Where'd you get that horse, young fellow?" he demanded.

Jim took his time to answer. His gaze swept and appraised the questioner, decided at once that this was someone of importance, though perhaps not as consequential as he himself thought. The stranger was an eye-filling spectacle. He stood about six feet two, straight as an Indian, broad of shoulder and lean of loin. Physically he looked a perfect specimen. Long thick hair fell in curls to the black coat and framed a handsome pallid face. If there was any weakness it did not lie in the features but in an expression of smug satisfaction. He looked too sure of himself. Young Rutledge guessed that he was one of the gunmen for which this section was notorious.

"I'll answer that soon as I know where you come in on the question," Jim replied.

The long-haired one flicked back the lapel of his Prince Albert broadcloth coat. A star was pinned to his vest. "I'm marshal of this man's town," he announced.

"Good enough. I borrowed the horse from Pete Moss."

"Borrowed it? Young fellow, did Pete know you borrowed it?"

"Sure he knew it. He was there."

"And let you have it?"

"Yes, sir."

"Hmp! What might your name be?"

"James Rutledge."

A flicker of surprise and interest animated the cold eyes of the officer. "You're the bird who shot Steve Lawson. I reckon I'll put you under arrest," he said.

"For wounding a rustler in self-defense when I was one against five?" asked Jim, meeting him eye to eye.

"You can tell that to the judge."

46

A big voice boomed a greeting that was almost a shout. "'Lo, Jim Rutledge! When did you get in, boy? Yore herds come through all right?"

Jim was thankful for the sight of that huge man rolling across the street to shake hands with him. Harrison Pendleton was one of the best known of the Texas trail drivers. He was a bluff, hearty old-timer, one whose word was as good as another man's bond. Everywhere he went he made friends.

"They're on the trail a couple of days back," Jim said. "Yore herds get through in good shape?"

"Two of 'em. I got two more on the trail." Pendleton wrung the boy's hand and turned to the marshal. "Joe, like you to meet a chip of the old block — Chan Rutledge's son Jim. This is Mr. Shear, boy. You've heard of him."

Heard of him? Who hadn't heard of Joe Shear, gunman and killer, whose Colt's .45 had twenty-three notches on it? Jim looked at him with wide-open eyes.

"Glad you showed up, Mr. Pendleton," Jim said. "I'm in a little jam. Mr. Shear wants to arrest me for wounding a rustler who was running off cattle of ours that had stampeded."

"I heard about that. One of the Moss gang, wasn't he? I reckon I can fix that with Mr. Shear for you, Jim."

"His story don't hitch with the one I heard, Mr. Pendleton," the marshal said brusquely. "You don't know the facts, do you? Not there personally?"

"No, Joe, but I certainly would have liked to have been there. A fellow don't often get a chance to see a kid hold up five outlaws an' take from the skunks the stock they were rustling."

"We got nothing but his word for that," the officer said.

"His word is good with me, Joe," the cattleman said cheerfully, throwing a huge arm around the shoulder of young Rutledge. "Lemme tell you what I did see him do on the way up from Texas. I was throwin' a herd across the Canadian an' one of my point men got brushed off his horse by a limb of a tree. He swam ashore, but the horse had hopples tied round his neck an' one of 'em got caught on the limb. All that buckskin could do was swim round an' round till someone got him loose or till he drowned. Well, Joe, this boy here swam his horse over there an' cut that buckskin loose. How he did it beats me, for the animal was thrashin' around something terrible. Jim's there both ways from the ace, take it from me."

Shear was annoyed. He had reasons of his own for wanting to arrest this lad, but Pendleton's open championship of Rutledge could not be ignored. The cattleman was too powerful and too popular for that. He could rally half the drivers on the trail to his side.

"If you want to answer for him, Mr. Pendleton, and guarantee he'll be here when he's wanted, why, I expect that will be all right," the marshal said reluctantly. "I've had orders to arrest him. So I've got to know he'll be on hand."

"Who gave you orders, Joe? Sounds to me like someone is trying to run something on you."

The light gray eyes of the killer narrowed. "Nobody will try to run anything on me, Mr. Pendleton. It's not considered safe." Shear paused to let this sink in. "The friends of this boy Steve Lawson have asked the authorities to arrest Rutledge. They claim he had a lot of their stock in his herd and they asked for a cut to check up. 'Nothing doing,' he said, and went right to a gun play."

"Who are these friends of Lawson?" the cattleman's heavy voice drummed out.

"Ranchmen along the trail. They've been bothered a lot by drivers picking up their cattle as they pass through the country. They have a right to check up any herd they suspect."

"Nobody asked to inspect our herds," Jim said.

Shear turned bleak eyes on him. "So *you* say. Your story doesn't get to first base with me."

"It'll all come out in the wash, Joe," the cattleman roared heartily. "Bet the drinks will be on you, for you'll find I'm right about this boy."

"That's not all, Mr. Pendleton," the marshal continued. "I find him riding a horse belonging to Pete Moss. He claims Pete loaned it to him. Is that reasonable?"

Surprised, Harrison Pendleton turned to the young Texan for information. "What about that, Jim? Some mistake, I reckon."

"That's another story. I had a run-in with the Moss gang again this morning. They jumped me while I was coming to town and kept on my tail for thirty miles.

Down the river they picked up fresh mounts and ran my bronc ragged."

The marshal cut in on Jim's tale. "And then Pete Moss said, 'Take my horse, Mr. Rutledge, since yours is wore out.' It certainly sounds to me." Shear laughed, in heavy irony, without mirth.

"I hid in a cottonwood and they didn't find me," Jim went on. "Afterward I found Pete Moss by himself and got the drop on him. So I borrowed his horse."

"The name of that in this country, young fellow, is horse stealing," Shear said harshly. "I reckon you know what happens to horse thieves."

"They had taken my horse with them and left me afoot. What else could I do?" Jim asked.

"I never yet knew a bird like you who didn't have some explanation of how he came to get the bronc in question," commented the officer with a thin lip smile. "Usually they met some guy who sold it to them. You go them one better. Held up the owner and took it from him. You've got a nerve, fellow."

Pendleton's laugh could have been heard a block. "You're off on the wrong foot, Joe. I'll admit it's not a reasonable story, but I'll bet a four-year-old against a plug of tobacco that it's true. The joke is on Pete Moss, I'd say."

"Is it?" asked Shear coldly. "Now I wonder."

"You know what the Moss outfit is."

"Why, yes, Mr. Pendleton. I know Dave Moss and all his boys. I've never seen anything wrong with them. The more I think of it the less I like this young man's story. I'm arresting him right now."

"All right, Joe. You're the doctor. I'll go along and see if I can arrange bail."

"I'll take your weapons, Rutledge," the marshal said. Jim turned his arms over to the officer.

"I'd ought to throw you in the calaboose," Shear added. "But I'm willing to accommodate Mr. Pendleton. We'll go right down to Judge Drachman's office and put it up to him."

The three men walked side by side down the street.

CHAPTER
SIX

Joe Shear Makes It Twenty-Four

The Marshal took the inside of the walk, his prisoner next to him.

"No trouble about fixin' this up, Jim," the cattleman said. "I know Drachman."

"I'll be much obliged," Rutledge replied.

From the Cowboys' Retreat a man came through the swing doors and stopped to speak with someone standing by the curb. With a laugh he turned toward the three men who were approaching. He was slight and neatly dressed. His wide hat was tilted to a rakish angle.

"Didn't know Doc Brown was in town," Pendleton said. "Running a game, I reckon."

Shear did not answer. "Take this," he said urgently, a knife edge to his voice, and thrust into Rutledge's hands the rifle he had recently taken from him.

Events happened so fast Jim's brain could hardly record them. The man with the tilted hat recognized Shear. His stride faltered for a fraction of a second. Then he came on, the barrel of his pistol flashing into the light. A heavy arm, flung around Jim's neck, dragged him into the street. Two shots rang out, almost together. A third followed. The slight man staggered, clutching at his heart. As his knees sagged under him and he pitched forward, he tried to raise his weapon to fire again.

Pendleton released the boy.

A little curl of smoke rose from the end of the marshal's revolver. He stood, crouched and wary, eyes on the fallen man. The expression in his face was demoniac.

From every direction men poured toward the battle ground. Shear ironed out his face to its usual impassivity.

"I had to do it, gentlemen. He's been threatening me. Mr. Pendleton will tell you he drew his pistol before I did."

"Soon as he saw you," the cattleman assented.

"You'll testify to that, too," Shear said to the prisoner.

"He didn't wait," Jim admitted.

"It had to be him or me, one. He's been laying for me. So have his brothers. It's come to a showdown. I aim to drive Bart and Mart Brown out of town. They're running a crooked house."

A doctor pushed through the crowd and examined the man lying on the ground. "Dead," he pronounced.

"Wouldn't have it any other way," the killer said. "I'd have ducked this if I could, but he kept asking for it."

"Shot through the heart," the doctor added.

"Kept crowding me — Doc and his brothers, too," the gunman went on. "Wanted to run this town. I told 'em no, not while I was marshal. Joe Shear stands for law, gentlemen."

The body of the dead man was carried into a saloon and put on the floor, to remain there until the arrival of the coroner.

The crowd around the saloon continued to swell. Among the later arrivals was a heavy-set man in corduroy trousers, flannel shirt, and gray Stetson hat. "Let me through," he said curtly to those on the edge of the throng.

"Sure, Sheriff," someone answered good-naturedly. "Make way, boys."

"Gangway for Mr. Manders," another called out.

Allison Manders reached the heart of the press. Shear was still explaining himself as a vindicator of the law. He was anxious to make this clear, even while his vanity sunned itself in the respectful awe his exploit had imposed upon those around him.

"What's the row?" asked Manders.

He was a hard-faced man with a well-earned reputation for fearlessness. His jade eyes fastened on the marshal.

"Had to bump off a bad man who tried to kill me," Shear said, a challenge in his voice.

The officers were not friends. They belonged to opposing factions in city politics.

"Who?" Manders asked.

"Doc Brown. He came at me with his gun smoking."

The eyes of the two clashed. Manders made no comment in words.

"Where did they take him?" he asked Pendleton.

The cattleman hitched his thumb toward the swing doors. "Inside."

Manders turned and walked into the saloon. The marshal might make whatever he pleased of that square, uncompromising back.

"What about Jim here?" Pendleton asked the marshal.

Shear waved that matter aside with a gesture of the hand. He had more important matters on his mind now. Moreover, there was a chance he might need young Rutledge as a witness.

"Forget about it, unless Steve Lawson's friends push the matter. I understand you're guaranteeing he'll be here when wanted."

"Yes," assented the cattleman.

"Take your weapons into Wright's store and check them while you are in town, young fellow," Shear told Jim.

The young man nodded. He would check the rifle, but he had no intention of walking the streets without a revolver, well concealed but handy for use.

A man joined the two Texans as they walked away. He was a fair-haired lad in the early twenties. He wore the chaps, hickory shirt, and wide hat of a cowboy.

"Never saw the beat of it," he said, the excitement of what he had just seen still quick in his blood. "Shear is sure chain lightnin' on the draw. Doc

55

pulled first, looked to me. An' at that Shear took time to aim. Then, bingo! All over. Plumb spang through the heart."

Pendleton spoke the usual formula of introduction. "Jim, this is Jerry Denver, one of my riders. James Rutledge."

"Glad to meet you," the youths murmured in unison, and they shook hands.

"First time I ever saw one of these noted killers in action," Jim said.

"Me too," Jerry replied. "An' I want to tell you I'm ridin' 'round the gents. Can't any of 'em have a difficulty with Jerry Denver long as his legs are what they are. Say, did you notice how Shear an' Manders gave each other the glare, kinda like two strange dogs sizing each other up? My advice to Mr. Sheriff would be, lay off that guy."

"Is there any trouble between them?" Jim asked.

"I wouldn't say trouble exactly. It's known they don't like each other. Manders runs with the Brown crowd, known to be unfriendly to Shear. Story is they're after his job as marshal. He's been talkin' about closing their place, the Green Parrot. So folks say. Can't prove it by me."

"You'd ought to join an old ladies' sewing circle, Jerry," his employer drawled. "You'd certainly be at the head of the class for gossip. You any good at tatting? Or making crazy quilts?"

"I keep my eyes open," the cowboy said, uncertain whether he ought to be offended.

"And yore ears. You been in town 'most a day, an' I'll bet my boots you can tell who's going to run for sheriff next time."

"They're gonna run Shear. His crowd is. The other side will back Manders again."

The cattleman slapped a heavy hand on his thigh, letting out a whoop of laughter. "By jings, he did know. An' I get this encyclopedia of universal knowledge for thirty dollars a month, Jim. Think of that."

"There's no law against you raisin' my wages, Mr. Pendleton," the cowboy intimated.

"If I was hirin' an editor for the *Trail News* instead of an ornery cowhand, I might. Or if you could rope a longhorn with yore tongue, Jerry."

"What about Doc Brown's brothers?" Jim asked. "Are they liable to make trouble?"

"If they've got the guts," Jerry answered promptly. "Me, personal, I've got my doubts. They're vindictive guys. That's their reputation. But Joe Shear has served notice on 'em to leave, an' I don't reckon either Bart Brown or Mart aim to commit suicide yet awhile. One in a family is enough."

Pendleton shook his head mournfully, speaking in a murmur as though to himself. "I'll never be able to keep him for thirty dollars. One of these circus sideshows will grab him off sure as flies stick in molasses."

"What say we go in to the End of the Trail an' wet our whistles?" Jerry proposed.

"Our whistles aren't as dry as yours, Jerry," Pendleton told him. "You run along. I got a few words to say to Jim private."

Jim waited for the older man to open up whatever subject was on his mind. Young Rutledge had a capacity for silence.

"How long is it going to take you to do yore business here, Jim?" the cattleman asked.

"Can't tell. Be two-three weeks anyway. Maybe more," Jim said.

"Be mighty careful, boy. I don't know any more ornery outfit than the Moss gang. They'll get you if they can. Better stay in yore own camp. An' when you have to be in town bring some of yore boys with you, good dependable lads that won't go hellin' off an' leave you."

"That's good advice," Jim agreed.

CHAPTER
SEVEN

Arrested

Unfortunately Jim could not take immediately the advice Pendleton had given him. His riders were with the Circle R herds two days back on thc trail. He had ridden ahead to meet the buyer, a young Englishman named Dane Sackville who had recently stocked a ranch in Wyoming. He was buying the Circle R herds to supply a contract he had made with an Indian agency.

Whether any of the Moss family were here Jim did not know. If they came to town, and nothing was more likely, Shear would be sure to tell them of his presence. The last thing the Circle R driver wanted was trouble. He hoped to deliver the cattle, get a check made out to his father's order, and return to Texas without damage to his men or to himself. Therefore he kept himself inconspicuous, not frequenting any of the saloons or gambling-halls where the outlaws would be likely to congregate.

Sackville was a pleasant and companionable man in the early thirties. He had come to the West because of a predisposition toward consumption. He took a fancy to Jim.

"You seem to know cattle, Rutledge," he said. "Is it a gift? I like the life, but I have had no experience. I'm gullible — haven't cut my eye teeth as one fellow said after he had sold me a blind horse. I don't suppose, you know, that anybody could saw off on you — that's the odd expression one of my cowboys used — a horse that can't see."

Jim laughed. "No, I don't think he could, Mr. Sackville. But that is no credit to me. I've been brought up with horses and cattle ever since I was born. I know their habits. It's not a gift and it's not brains. My foreman, Sim Hart, knows them better than I do — and in some ways Sim is a lunkhead. He has had more experience. That's all."

Sackville smiled wryly. "Mine is costing me a good deal. I'm a mark for conscienceless scoundrels who can tell a plausible story. They seem to feel I'm fair prey because I'm an Englishman, you know."

"I've noticed that," Jim admitted. "Not with you, but with others from across the water. Better get a good foreman and go slow for a time."

"Will you be that foreman, Rutledge? I'm not satisfied with the man I have. I don't trust him."

"Isn't that rather sudden, Mr. Sackville? You've known me just about six hours, and you've never even seen me with cattle. For all you know, I'm bringing our herds in gaunt as wolves and with their tongues hanging out. Maybe I'd better change the order of my advice. Go slow, and get a good foreman."

"I've talked with Mr. Pendleton. He recommends you highly. And, by Jove, I like your looks and your way of talking. I'll be fair with you. If I make money, so will you. They say there's a fortune in cows. Let's find out for ourselves."

Jim was not sure that this would not suit him very well. His father had plenty of other sons to carry on with him. The young man felt he could do better on his own if he had a good chance, and this looked like a very good one. But it was not a matter to be decided in a day.

"Let's sleep on that, Mr. Sackville," he suggested. "I'm pretty young. You may not feel the same about it in two or three days. Anyhow, I wouldn't be able to throw in with you until after I've been back to Texas and seen my father. I've got to finish the job I'm on now."

"Take your time. The offer is open. But I want you with me. If I don't get someone honest and experienced, I'm lost."

They walked out together to an adjoining restaurant. Jim chose a table in a corner, his back against the wall and his face to the door. Sackville had started to take that chair but he surrendered it at the Texan's request.

"Are you superstitious?" the Englishman asked.

"About sitting with my back to the door of a public eating-place in this town — yes," Jim answered grimly.

"Why in this town, if I may ask?"

"Because I have enemies. It's a long story."

Sackville was about to make a comment upon the lawlessness of this frontier country when he observed that Rutledge was not paying attention to him. His gaze was fixed on some point over the Englishman's left shoulder.

Looking around, Sackville saw that three men had come into the restaurant and were walking straight to their table. One of the three was the marshal Shear. The other two he did not know. Simultaneously he was aware that the Texan on the opposite side of the table had pushed his chair back. An odd sensation, like the patter of ice-cold feet of mice, ran up and down Sackville's spine.

"I'm going to arrest you, Rutledge," the marshal said harshly. There was a look of annoyance on his face, as though he were doing this against his own wishes.

Jim had risen. He did not look at the marshal but at the two men standing beside the officer. The men were Sam Moss and his brother Peter. His gaze held steadily to them. He knew that a critical situation had arisen. It was possible, probable, that within a few seconds guns would be roaring. Jim's first remark was characteristic. He spoke to Shear, though his eyes did not shift to the marshal.

"Mr. Sackville here isn't in this."

"All right. I don't want him. He can go," Shear said.

"See you later," Jim said to his new friend, without looking at him.

"What does this mean? I don't understand, you know," Sackville responded doubtfully.

"None of yore business. Hit the grit, fellow," Sam Moss ordered with savage impatience.

Sackville was not a timid man, but he did not know the factors that went to make up this situation. Shear stood for the law. If he had come to arrest Rutledge, there was apparently nothing to be done about it. Reluctantly he rose and drew back from the table.

"I'll take your pistol," Shear said to the man he had come to arrest.

"Just a moment, Marshal." Jim spoke softly, spacing his words, in a voice chill with menace. "Is it yore idea to take my six-shooter and let my enemies kill me? Because it's not mine."

"He's resistin' arrest," Pete cried exultantly.

"No," Jim denied. "Do you need all this help, Mr. Shear, to take me to jail?"

"No, by gum, I don't," the officer flung back angrily.

"Why bring it then? Volunteer deputies, I reckon. You can have my pistol soon as these fellows go."

To Sackville it seemed that all four guns flashed into the air at the same time and without warning. Shear's broad body leaped forward between the Moss brothers and their intended victim. His arm swung up and down. The long barrel of his revolver struck Jim on the forehead. The boy tottered back, clung to the wall a moment, and collapsed.

Instantly Shear swung around and faced the Moss boys.

"Don't you! Don't you!" he snarled, his face distorted by rage. "I'll pump lead in you both."

"He reached for his hogleg first," Sam charged.

"That's a lie. You came in here to kill him. Get out. Both of you. Sudden."

"What's eatin' you, Joe?" gasped Pete, taken aback at this surprising transformation. "He's no friend of yours, is he?"

"Get out." His eyes blazed at Sam Moss furiously. "And don't you monkey in my private business, young fellow, or I'll send you to hell on a shutter. That goes for Old Dave too. Tell him for me."

The brothers stared at him, uncertain how to meet this unexpected defiance. They dared not look at each other. The instant snatched for a consultation of the eyes might prove fatal. Sam made choice for both of them.

"All right, Joe. It's yore business to arrest this bird, not ours. But I don't get you. Thought you were our friend. No need to get sore about this."

"Friend, eh? I've heard about you callin' at the 'dobe house the other side of the tracks. Stay away. You hear me? Marked private property."

Sam's beady eyes narrowed to shining slits. "Since when, Joe?"

"From right damn now, far as you're concerned. I'm serving notice. Don't you try to blot the J S brand, fellow."

Once more Sam made his choice, and it was not for immediate war. He laughed heartily, without mirth. "Come on, Pete. Seems we're not wanted here," he said, backing toward the door.

Another moment, and they had gone.

The marshal called for water and a towel. He sponged the face of the unconscious man. Jim opened his eyes and looked at Shear.

"You hit me with yore gun," he complained.

"Lucky for you I did. Soon as yo're ready we'll drift to the calaboose."

Jim spent the rest of the day and the succeeding night in jail. He was released the morning of the second day. Sackville and Pendleton had made the necessary arrangements for bail. The charges against him included horse stealing, rustling cattle, and attempt to kill.

CHAPTER
EIGHT

Jim Is Shocked

You could hear Harrison Pendleton's voice, so Chan Rutledge claimed, half across the state of Texas. The hearty vitality of the man boomed out in it. When he had anything to say not meant for the entire world he had to resort to whispers.

He was whispering now, as he leaned across a card table in a private room of the Longhorn Saloon. "I don't get this straight, Jim. Something back of it. When we first met up with Shear two-three days ago he was in cahoots with old man Moss. I could see that. So could you. There's been some kind of a bust-up. Joe had no objection to you gettin' outa the calaboose. Fact, it looked to me like he was kinda helping us when we took yore case up with Drachman this morning. Why? What's been going on we don't know?"

Jim shook his head. "Shear's gun knocked me plumb out, but according to Mr. Sackville's story the marshal got on the prod considerable with his friends the Moss boys, especially with Sam. There's no doubt he saved my life after he wiped me with his pistol."

"Why? He could have got away with a resisting arrest story. It's been done a hundred time. As I understand it you had yore gun out. Plenty excuse to bump you off or let his friends do it." The cattleman put his forearms on the table and frowned ruminatively across at a steel engraving of an Eastern houri stepping coyly into her bath.

"You can figure it two ways," Jim said. "I've been told Shear is vain. Maybe he just wouldn't stand for anyone buttin' in to an arrest he was making. That's not an entirely satisfactory explanation, I'll admit."

"Gets nowhere with me."

"How will this do, then? He and old Dave Moss hadn't been gettin' along well, say. We'll put it that Shear was sore at him, an' this gave him a chance to explode. He sure enough read the riot act to Sam, according to Mr. Sackville. It was war talk, an' Sam choked the horn and chawed leather. Didn't want to be number twenty-five, don't you reckon?"

Pendleton looked at his watch. "I told Jerry Denver to report to me here at ten. Time he was coming. Thought he might pick up some news for us."

From the big room below there floated up to them the strains of a fiddle playing "Hogs in the Cornfield" and the sounds of feet shuffling in a quadrille. A door opened. Someone was moving up the stairs. On the off chance that it might be an enemy Jim's hand edged toward the butt of his revolver.

Jerry Denver walked into the room. His boots were muddy. Earlier in the day it had been raining hard.

"Find out anything?" his employer asked.

"There's nineteen saloons in this town," Jerry told him gravely, balancing himself as he swayed on his feet.

"And you've been in all of them. I can see that."

Jerry lifted a protesting hand. "Been roundin' up inf'mation."

"All right. Spill any you have."

"Ol' man Moss is in town. At the K.C. house. Four-five of yore Circle R boys rode in a while ago an' they sure been tankin' up, Mr. Rutledge. Had pleasure of drink or two with them myself. Right lively colts, I'd call 'em, an' it's their night to howl."

Jim made a gesture to rise. "I'll have to get after them right away. I can't have trouble now."

Jerry continued to unload his budget. "Young fellow you shot down the trail — redheaded guy called Steve Lawson — is in a poker game downstairs with Joe Shear. He's sure gettin' skinned plenty. Mostly the big games are off in private rooms, but this one started kinda small an' gathered moss, as you might say."

Jerry grinned. He had discovered that he was unconsciously a wit. "Gathered Pete Moss," he explained.

Pendleton looked at Jim. "Got that little difference patched up maybe," he said. "Such loving friends as Joe Shear an' the Moss outfit ought not to let any angry feelings disturb their harmony."

"Sam Moss isn't playing?" Jim asked.

"No, sir, I ain't seen Sam." Having proved himself a humorist, Jerry proceeded to leave no doubt of it. "If you want to see Joe Shear a lamb you better drap in downstairs."

Jim rose. "Not interested. Where did you see my waddies raising hell?"

"At the Green Parrot. But they're making the rounds. I dunno where they're at now."

"I'll go round 'em up," Jim said. "Much obliged for yore trouble, Jerry. See you tomorrow, Mr. Pendleton."

As Jim left the room the orchestra downstairs was playing "Old Dan Tucker." By the time he had reached the street the dance was over and the music had died down. He stood for a moment in the doorway, hesitating as to which way to go. He did not want to make a round of the saloons, for that would increase the chance of meeting his enemies. If Jerry had been a little less lit up, he would have gone back to get him as a scout to find the Circle R cowboys.

While he stood there, uncertain what to do, watching the stream of life that seemed to be tossed up and down the crowded thoroughfare, a woman crossed the road and passed through the swing doors into the Longhorn. Jim caught only one swift glimpse of her as she disappeared, but that was enough to startle him. Surely that quick animal grace, that light freedom of movement, could belong to no other woman than Ellen Lawson. Of course he must be wrong. He realized that. It could not be she. No good woman ever went into a dance hall. It was forbidden territory. And yet — he could almost have sworn that this was Ellen. The impression on his mind was so vivid that he could not escape it.

He pushed through the swing doors into the Longhorn. His eyes swept the big crowded room and did not find the woman for whom they sought. She had been swallowed up in that vortex of milling humanity.

The scene was one that could have been duplicated only on the frontier. Laborer and freighter, muleskinner and floater, moved to and fro. Hard-eyed professional gamblers presided at faro and roulette and chuck-a-luck games to fleece the cowboys released from the hardships of the trail and eager to spend what they had earned or double it. Dance-hall girls in short dresses wheedled drunken men to buy champagne for them. Passions showed themselves raw and uncurbed. Cold avarice and hot lust, the gay good temper of youth, wild recklessness, the weariness of cold cupidity, were reflected in one or another of the faces upon which Jim looked.

Then he saw the girl whom he had followed into the dance hall — and again the sight of her shocked him. For the girl was Ellen Lawson. She stood by herself, near the front of the room, trying to make herself inconspicuous. She was frightened, aghast at the garish place in which she found herself.

A man moved toward her. Evidently he was asking her to take a drink or to dance. She shrank back against the wall.

Jim shouldered a way through the crowd to her.

CHAPTER
NINE

Murder!

The man speaking to Ellen wore the costume of an Eighteenth Century buccaneer. His turban was Roman-striped. A scarlet sash, knotted around his waist, contrasted strikingly with the blue pantaloons. A black beard and long mustachios covered the face to the cheekbones. Over one eye was a green patch.

"Zounds, madam! 'Tis Blackbeard — the great Teach in person, king of all the pirate crew," Jim heard him say. "Tread a measure with him — and tell the story to your grandchildren."

"I — I do not want to dance, please," the girl murmured, distressed and embarrassed.

"But with Blackbeard," he protested in an assumed voice that came from the chest, and twirled the end of a mustachio fiercely. "Sink me, Blackbeard never takes 'no' from a lady."

Jim spoke in the vein adopted by the man. "Up anchor and unfurl sails, Blackbeard, or shiver my timbers! I'll sink you fifty fathoms deep."

The pirate was above medium height, slender, and not ungraceful of gesture. The single eye that turned to observe Jim was a very light gray.

71

"Blood and thunder, fellow! Who are you that throws a challenge at Blackbeard?" he demanded. "Would you walk the plank, young sir?"

"Make off, pirate, while the winds favor," Jim ordered. "The lady is mine."

Blackbeard threw out a hand in token of surrender, while the fingers of his other hand clutched in burlesque melodrama the handle of a knife fastened to his side.

"A day will come," he said darkly, bowed to the girl, and backed away.

"Who is he?" Ellen asked in a low voice.

"I don't know. It doesn't matter. There's a masked ball advertised at the Green Parrot. I reckon he's going there." Jim spoke impatiently, his mind pushing on to the question troubling him. "What are you doing here?"

At sight of him her eyes had flung out lights of gladness. She felt less helpless in this dreadful place. He would know what to do. But the stern note in his voice drenched the relief and was a counter-irritant to her shame.

"I came to find Steve," she said, on the defensive.

"You've got no business here," he told her harshly. "You ought to know that — in a place like this."

"I had to come," she answered sulkily.

"That's tommyrot. You can't be so dumb as not to know better than that. You ought to be shut up on bread and water for a week. If I was yore dad —"

"— you'd whip me," she finished for him. "Well, you're not. I don't reckon it's any of yore business why I'm here."

"You shouldn't have come. I'll take you out right now."

"No, you won't," Ellen replied, very quietly. She was looking at him with a surprisingly stubborn expression.

"You can't stay here. Women aren't allowed — not yore kind," he explained, curbing his annoyance.

"I'm not going till I see Steve."

"Why didn't you send someone in? Don't you know what kind of a place it is? Haven't you been taught anything?"

From throat to forehead the hot blood stained her face. "I've got to see my brother. He's here — gambling."

"Go outside and wait. I'll bring him to you."

"How can *you* bring him — with Pete Moss and Buck Roe playing there at the table?"

"I'll get someone to tell him you're outside waiting for him."

"He won't come, unless I can see him a minute myself."

Jim noticed that several men were watching them curiously. They were wondering what this girl, with the look of a shy innocent child still clinging to her, was doing in this gambling-hell where women never came except to earn a living. The Texan flushed. He was both annoyed and distressed. What were her people doing to let her come to such a place? Had she not been brought up to understand that there was a deadline no good woman could cross?

His fingers closed on her wrist. "We're going out," he said curtly.

With unexpected strength she twisted her arm free. "No. I've *got* to see him. I've *got* to."

The orchestra struck up a dance tune. It was a waltz. Jim came to an impulsive decision.

"Then dance with me," he said. "If he's here we'll see him at the other end of the room. You're not to make a scene if you do see him. I'll try to fix it so that you can speak to him a moment. But you must do just as I say."

"Yes," she promised eagerly.

As he took her in his arms he knew her nerves were at a high tension. She was afraid of this place. She had come into it with her heart in her throat, driven by some compulsion greater than the fear in her fluttering bosom. Why must she rescue her brother at such a cost? What was the imperative urge that drove her? Other lads squandered, with no great ill to anyone, what wages they had saved. Ellen must know that it was almost a rule for a cowboy to lose his money when he came to town. That was his reason for coming.

Jim was no expert waltzer. At the ranch hoe-downs quadrilles were the order of the day. Many of the cowboys went on the floor only for squares. But Jim discovered in himself a certain assurance when he guided Ellen across the room. Her lissom, slender body seemed to him light as a feather. He felt a curious exultation, even in the midst of his anxiety, at finding how good a dancer he was.

An irruption of men poured through the front door. They were cowboys on a tear. They lined up noisily at the bar. Between the shifting figures on the floor Jim caught a glimpse of Jack Barton and another Circle R rider, a wild young buckaroo called Cinders. They were, he guessed, gloriously drunk and therefore ripe for trouble. But just at this moment he could not take them in hand. He must get rid of this girl first.

At the other end of the room Jim saw the poker players. They were in a large alcove that formed a wing to the main hall. He recognized Joe Shear and Pete Moss. The redheaded lad facing him must be Steve Lawson.

Jim could tell by a sudden tautness of his partner's body that she had seen her brother. Steve was reaching for a stack of chips to push into the center of the table. He lifted his eyes and saw his sister. He stared at her in amazement, his jaw dropping ludicrously.

At that moment there came a crash of guns. The big lamp hanging from the ceiling went out, followed by the one behind the bar. The whole front part of the room was in darkness. A woman screamed. A raucous oath lifted above the clamor. Another shot rang out and shattered the lamp above the poker players. The entire hall was black as Pharaoh's Egypt.

Among the dancers there was a near-panic. They crowded toward the back of the room. Somebody stumbled against Ellen and the impact forced her from the arms of her partner.

Out of the darkness the reassuring voice of a bartender came. "It's all right, folks. They've gone. Shot out the lights an' lit out. We'll have candles right away."

Jim had been driven by the press into the alcove. His hand groped to find Ellen. A horrible sound, the intake of a breath that was neither quite a gasp nor a groan, shocked him to rigidity. A chill ran down his spine. Something dreadful had occurred. He waited, tense and expectant.

At the other end of the room a candle flickered. Simultaneously, there came the wild scream of a woman in terror. It rose from a spot not six feet from Jim. He moved toward the place, for he knew the cry had leaped from the throat of Ellen.

Jim found the girl and took her in his arms. She was shivering with fear. He could hear the teeth chattering in the head that lay against his shoulder. The fingers that clutched his neck were trembling.

The candles were lit, one after another. A bartender moved back to the card table with one in each hand. The flames flickered, blown by a breeze from the open window back of the players.

"We're getting lamps," he said. "Have 'em in a minute. Don't get impatient please, gents."

Somebody laughed, nervously. "All cowboys are poison, I claim. Ought to be a law against 'em."

Another man spoke. "If we find who they are, we'll run 'em outa town. Disturbing peaceable folks with their fool deviltry."

The bartender let out a cry of dismayed surprise. "Good God!" he cried, holding one of the candles above the card table.

One of the players was huddled down in his chair. A knife had been driven between his ribs into his heart.

CHAPTER
TEN

The Ace of Spades

Ringlets of black hair cascaded over the broad shoulders of the dead man.

Pete Moss leaped to his feet and pointed a trembling finger at him. "Cripes! It's Joe Shear," he cried. The man was laboring under an excitement he was trying hard to control.

From Moss the gaze of Jim Rutledge passed, with swift stabbing scrutiny, around the poker table. Buck Roe sat on the left of Shear. His leathery impassive face told nothing. Next to him was a man ear-marked as a professional tinhorn gambler. He had both the clothes and the manner. In the chair on his right was a brown-faced player who might be a trail driver or a cattle buyer. Steve Lawson completed the circle and was seated beside the marshal. The boy was colorless to the lips. He stared at his sister from a stricken face that seemed all eyes of guilty horror.

A harsh voice gave orders forcefully. "Close the doors. Let nobody leave the house. Get some lamps lit, Jimmy."

Sheriff Manders pushed to the front and took in the situation.

"Someone has killed Joe Shear," the bartender faltered.

"So I see. Who did it?" His hard gaze swept from one startled face to another.

Roe spoke, smoothly, evenly. "It was done when the lights were out, Allison."

Manders gave curt orders. "Those of you who are at the table or near it stay where you are. The rest of you quit crowding. I'll have to ask you, gentlemen — those who're not in the alcove — to get back and line up against the walls. I've got to have room here. I expect you all to see that nobody leaves the hall."

Another bartender came back to the poker table with a lamp. "There's not another lamp chimney in the house," he said. "I can borrow one from Brady next door."

"We'll get along with this and the candles," the sheriff replied. "Hold it over here, Tim. That's right. A little higher."

Manders leaned closer to the dead man, the balls of his thumbs on the edge of the table. He gave an exclamation of amazement. The blade of the knife, on its way to Shear's heart, had been driven through a playing card. The card was the ace of spades.

Over the shoulder of the sheriff Jim stared, aghast. He had just made a shocking discovery. It could not be true. It was impossible. Yet he knew there was no escape from the certainty of it, appalling though the thing was.

The sheriff realized that Shear must have had a split second's warning before death found him. His right hand rested on the butt of the revolver at his side. A notorious killer knows that the price of life is eternal vigilance. He suspects everybody, for his reputation has made him a mark not only for enemies but for other ambitious gunmen. The last conscious thought of the marshal had probably been connected with this instinct for self-preservation.

"Look, Allison." Buck Roe pointed to Rutledge. Triumph rode in the face of the rustler. It leaped across the table and struck Jim almost like a blow.

Manders turned and looked at the trail driver. His slightly protuberant eyes, hard as agates, fastened on Jim. On the brown neck of Rutledge were four red streaks.

The sheriff moved closer to him. "Blood," he said. "So it was you."

Instinctively Jim started to lift his hand to his neck. The officer caught his wrist and looked at the young man's fingers. He examined the other hand. Neither of them were stained. Manders frowned. Even if he had wiped his hands, there should be some trace of blood on them.

"No," Jim denied. But his voice carried no conviction. It had no ring of indignant innocence. He was trying to drive back a heavy weight of dread that pressed against his heart. If there was blood on his neck there could be only one means by which it could have got there.

The sheriff's gaze moved to the waist of the Texan. He pointed to the empty scabbard where a hunting knife usually was sheathed.

"Where's your hog sticker?" he asked.

The Texan had been expecting that question. There was no use lying. Jim had cut his initials on the handle of the knife. His own men would be forced to testify that it belonged to him.

"That's it," he said, pointing to the one still protruding from the body.

Roe gave an exultant whoop. "Caught red-handed," he cried with an oath.

There was an ominous murmur among those present. A duel after a difficulty was one thing, and a killing that resulted from it would be condoned. But this was coldblooded murder. Shear had not been given a chance.

"String him up," someone urged.

"Get a rope," another cried.

Manders was a fighter. He had been elected to office on his record. "There won't be any of that," he announced with instant decision. "This man is my prisoner."

"We'll show you about that, Allison," a voice in the wide doorway of the alcove flung back.

"Y'betcha. Right damn now."

"But he didn't do it," a horrified protest came in a woman's low contralto.

Jim looked at Ellen. He had not dared turn his eyes upon her before lest his glance call attention to the girl. Now everybody was staring at her.

"Why didn't you keep still?" he asked reproachfully.

Pete Moss cried out her name, taking a step toward the girl. "What you doing here?" he asked.

"Who is this girl?" demanded Manders.

"It's Ellen Lawson. She —"

Moss stopped. He was dumb with astonishment. On the right hand side of her print dress, about the thigh, was a rumpled spot stained red.

"How did that come there?" the sheriff asked.

Ellen shrank back within herself. All these eyes focused on her — eyes curious, accusing, clamorous as tongues — burned into her like branding irons.

Steve pushed Moss aside and stood by the girl. He was very pale. His face reflected fear. He put one arm around her shoulders.

"Where do you come in, young fellow?" Manders asked.

"She's my sister."

"Live here in town?"

"No. We have taken up a claim nine miles out."

"Not employed here, is she?"

"No, sir," Steve answered with resentful emphasis.

"Don't push on the lines, buddy. It's my place to ask questions and yours and hers to answer them. Now let her talk. How do you know this Texas man didn't kill Shear? Speak up, girl."

"Because —"

Her voice died away on the ancient woman's reason.

"Because what? There's blood on his face. His knife did it. He had a grudge at the marshal. What makes you so sure?"

"He couldn't have done it," she burst out. Then, with a little rush of eager words, she added, "My fingers left the marks on his neck. See? I wiped them off on my dress later."

"Yes, I see," Manders said harshly. "Are you confessing that you killed Joe Shear, miss?"

Her eyes opened wide with horror. She shuddered. "No — no — no!" she screamed.

"Don't tell me that your nose just happened to bleed."

"No, I — I'll tell you all about it. I was dancing — with — with Mr. Rutledge —"

"An old friend of yours, is he?"

"I never saw him but once before."

"What are you doing here, anyway?" Manders flung at her abruptly. "You're no dance-hall girl."

"I came to — speak to my brother on — on important business." Ellen's voice faltered. A tide of high color flooded her cheeks. She was twisting her fingers together in an agony of shy distress. Yet the look she flashed at the sheriff carried resentment. He had learned from her own lips within the hour the reason for her presence.

"Came to a public dance hall?" Manders was openly incredulous. "Why didn't you send for him?"

"I — I was afraid he wouldn't come. I — had to see him."

"We'll take that up later. Go on with your story," Manders ordered.

"I was dancing with Mr. Rutledge when the lights went out."

"What were you dancing with him for?" Pete Moss hurled at her angrily. "When did he get to be a friend of yours?"

The sheriff turned to him, with an elaborate politeness that masked exasperation. "Someone elect you major-domo of this roundup, Moss?" he asked. "If so, I'll drop out; if not, you keep out, please."

Pete gave way sulkily. "Shoot," he said.

"Much obliged." Manders spoke to Ellen. "Go on, miss."

"They shot the lights out — and everybody got scared and tried to crowd to the back of the hall. Somebody pushed against me, so that I got separated from Mr. Rutledge. I was shoved into the side room here close to the table. There was a — groan. Then I was jammed against a chair and — put out my hand to steady myself. It — it — it — my hand —"

Ellen's words died away. She leaned on Steve and for a moment the eyes in her white face closed. But she recovered herself without fainting.

"Yes?" the sheriff asked, watching her closely.

She shuddered. "My hand fell on — it."

"On the knife or the wound?" he insisted inexorably.

"On the — wound."

"What did you do then?"

"I screamed. After that I don't know what I did till —"

"Till what?"

"Till Mr. Rutledge found me."

"Where did he find you?"

"Why, where I was standing."

"And where were you standing?"

"By the table."

"Was that before the candles were lit?"

"I don't know. I'm not sure. About the same time, I think."

"Not before?"

"It couldn't have been before, because in the darkness he wouldn't have found me."

"I'm not asking for explanations but for facts, miss," the sheriff told her.

Ellen did not see to what his questions were driving her, but Jim Rutledge saw and so did Buck Roe. Both of them waited, in a still tensity, for her final answer.

"I don't think it was before."

"Anyhow, there he was beside you when the first candles were lit?"

The purpose of the quiz was clear enough to her now. He wanted to prove by her that the Texan was close to the murdered man when she first saw him again.

"I didn't say so," she protested. "And he was coming toward me from the main hall."

"How do you know that, since you're not sure the candles were lit?" Manders asked harshly. "Can you see in the dark?"

"I could hear him brushing past folks, kinda." .

"You mean you could hear someone," he corrected. "And I thought you just said you didn't remember anything till he was there beside you?"

"You try to make me say things I didn't mean," she cried.

"I want the truth," the sheriff told her sharply. "I don't want you covering for this fellow."

"I'm not. He didn't do it. I told you how it was," she pleaded.

"By your own story you don't know whether he did it or not. You got separated from him, and you were pushed to the table. The killing was done by someone mighty close to you. Soon as there is light you see him beside you."

"But he had just come into the small room."

"You don't know that. You think so. That's not evidence." Manders passed to another point. "Go on. When you saw him did you say anything?"

"No."

"Did he?"

"No."

"What did you do?"

Again a wave of pink beat into her cheeks. "I was frightened — horribly," she explained.

"I asked what you did."

The long eyelashes fell to the hot cheeks. Shame flooded her being. "I don't know. I — I think I was sorta faint — afraid I'd fall."

The mercy of being alone behind locked doors should have been given her agonized distress. Instead, she was surrounded by eyes.

"Don't you see?" Jim broke in. "She caught at me to keep from falling."

The sheriff whirled on him. "You stay out of this till you're called on to speak," he ordered roughly. "You'll get chance enough later."

"What's the use of ridin' her? She admits she was scared to death an' didn't hardly know what she was doing."

"I'm asking what happened — and I aim to find out, young fellow. That'll be enough from you now."

Manders brushed his interference aside with a push of his hand. "Well, miss?"

"Like I said, I was scared and — I guess I hung on to him." She spoke in a low voice, as though the words were being whipped out of her.

"Put your arms round his neck, did you?"

"Yes, I — had to hold to something."

"And the stains on his neck came from your hand?"

"Yes, it must have been that way."

"Did you wipe your hand on your dress afterward?"

"Yes."

"Sure it was afterward?"

"I think so."

Jim realized that Manders once more had scored a point against him. Her first instinct would be to wipe the blood from her fingers. Therefore presumptively Rutledge must have been with her almost immediately. That was the argument that would be made by the sheriff, and it was one that could not be denied weight.

Manders hesitated a moment. "That'll be all just now, miss."

"Are you right- or left-handed, Miss Lawson?" asked Jim.

"I'm right-handed," Ellen answered.

The question puzzled her. It puzzled the sheriff, too.

"What difference does it make?" he asked.

"A lot," Jim replied, and gave no more information.

"What's your name, young man?" the sheriff asked of Jim.

"James Rutledge."

"Where from?"

"Near Lockhart, Texas."

"Cowboy?"

"I've just brought a coupla herds of four-year-olds up the trail for my father."

"In some trouble about stealing a horse, ain't you?"

"No, I'm not," Jim answered, flushing angrily.

"Accused of it?"

"By a bunch of rustlers lookin' for an out," Jim said.

"Had some trouble recently with Mr. Shear, I understand?"

"No trouble. He did me a service."

Buck Roe laughed derisively. "We'll learn soon that this fellow an' Joe were thicker than three in a bed."

"The marshal knocked you cold with the barrel of his six-shooter, didn't he?" Manders inquired.

"To save my life from a pair of murderers," Jim said quietly.

"That's a lie," Roe flung at him.

"I'll prove it when the time comes."

"This Texas fellow was resistin' arrest for horse-stealing when Joe put him to sleep," broke in Pete Moss.

"Why do you talk about his stealing a horse, Pete, when you know he didn't?" Ellen cried indignantly. "Four of you tried to kill him and you took his horse. He had to take yours or be left afoot. Why don't you tell the truth?"

"I have so many volunteer helpers," the sheriff said with heavy sarcasm. "Looks like I won't have to do a thing myself."

"You want the truth, don't you?" the girl flamed. "You don't want to — to put this on an innocent man."

"Or woman," Manders added. "I thought perhaps if I asked some questions we might find out something. But I'm only the sheriff. Don't mind me."

"Go ahead, Allison. You're findin' out a-plenty," Roe said.

"Just two or three more questions, Rutledge, before I have the body moved," the officer went on. "Did you have that knife with you when you came into this place tonight?"

"Yes."

"Where did you carry it?"

"In this sheath attached to my belt."

Manders waited a moment for dramatic effect, then spoke very deliberately, pointing to the weapon. "Did you put that knife where it is now?"

"I did not," Jim answered.

More than one of those present, watching this tall, bronzed youth, whose eyes were so steady and yet so quick with life, felt a conviction that he could not have done this cold-blooded murder.

"Then who did it?"

"I don't know."

"Did you lend the knife to Miss Lawson?"

"No. She couldn't have done it."

"To anybody else?"

"No."

"How did it get from its sheath to Joe Shear's heart?"

"I'll tell you how, Mr. Sheriff," Jim made answer evenly. "When the lights went out and I was being pushed and crowded, the murderer slipped it out and drove it into Mr. Shear's body."

"Someone else, not you?"

"Yes, someone else." Jim had picked up a card from the table and his fingers were playing with it.

"And not Miss Lawson?"

"Not Miss Lawson."

"Fair enough," Manders said with honeyed sarcasm. "She tried to alibi you. Now you do as much for her. Turn about is right."

"Miss Lawson doesn't know I didn't do it, but I know she didn't," Jim said quietly.

"How can you know it — unless you did it yourself?"

"I use my brains, Mr. Sheriff." A faintly derisive smile twitched at the corners of his mouth. "It's written in blood for all of us to see."

"What is?"

"Her innocence."

"Put your cards on the table, Texas man, if you're not bluffing."

"She couldn't have done it — not if she is right-handed."

"She's right-handed," her brother Steve contributed.

"That's so — about her being right-handed, Sheriff," Pete Moss said sulkily.

Manders focused his attention on Rutledge. "You mentioned before — about her being right-handed. What's that got to do with it?"

"Everything. The proof that she didn't do it is that there was blood on the palm of her hand and on the front of her fingers. It might have spurted anywhere else, but the inside of the murderer's hand was entirely protected by the handle of the knife."

A murmur of astonished assent passed through the room like a wave. "By jiminy, that's true," Jimmy the bartender said. "Any lunkhead can see that, come to think of it."

Manders recovered prestige by his comment on Jim's deduction. "You're proving what don't need any proof, Mr. Rutledge," he said, a little scornfully. "It sticks out plain as Old Roundtop that a man and no woman did this."

There was an increase of respect in the way Jim looked at the sheriff. "I've been noticing that myself," he said.

"How do you know that?" someone asked.

Manders paid no attention to him. "Let Dr. Aubrey through to take care of the body," he ordered the crowd.

As the doctor pushed his way forward Jim stooped and picked an object from the floor.

"What's that?" demanded the sheriff quickly.

Jim held out his hand, palm exposed. Upon it lay a small piece of green felt.

The officer examined it and was about to toss the fragment of cloth away.

"Better keep it," Jim said. "You can't ever tell."

"What is it?"

"It might be an eye shade." Jim smiled sardonically. "The fellow who's lost it may offer a reward for its return."

CHAPTER
ELEVEN

Who, How, and Why

"We'll adjourn to the poker room upstairs," the sheriff said. "I want all of you who were in this room when the lights went out to go up with me."

"What for?" asked Buck Roe brutally. "You've got yore man, Allison. Take him to the calaboose — if the boys don't decide to hang him right away."

Manders looked hard at Roe. "That's what you'd like, Buck, I reckon. But it won't be thataway. Anyone who tries to take a prisoner from me gets bumped off. I aim to be sheriff of this county an' not just draw the pay. Understand?"

"Don't get on the prod with me, Allison," Roe advised. "It ain't supposed to be safe, even if you are sheriff. I don't want yore prisoner — not right now."

"Am I a prisoner?" Jim asked. "You've just got one thing against me you haven't got against every other man in the room, and that is my knife. What does that amount to? There's not a man present who couldn't have slipped it from its sheath and killed the marshal."

"True enough," Manders admitted. "That's why we're going upstairs. I want to ask each of you some questions."

Roe laughed, with harsh derision. "Once I knew a sheriff who figured he was elected to get criminals an' not let slick guys like this bird talk themselves out of a hole when they were caught in the act. But he died an' went to heaven, I reckon."

"If I'm so slick, why did I leave my knife there as a witness against me?" asked Jim.

"The candles came too quick for you, fellow," Roe flung back at him.

"It was a put-up job," Pete Moss chipped in. "Any fool would know that. Why, the birds that shot out the lights were Circle R cowboys, a bunch of toughs in the pay of this fellow Rutledge."

"That's so," assented the bartender Jimmy.

"These bad men come up the trail from Texas an' try to run the town. You fellows gonna let them get away with it? Can they kill yore marshal without any come-back?" Pete demanded.

"Not by a jugful," someone cried with an oath.

"Find the cause of this killing," Jim said quietly. "Who had it in for Mr. Shear? Not a man whose life he saved two days ago."

"Talk," jeered Moss. "He knocked you cold an' you swore you'd get him for it."

"I have witnesses," the Texan said.

"Where are they?" a voice demanded.

Manders asserted himself. "We're not trying Rutledge — yet. Move upstairs, you fellows, and let the doctor have this room."

As Rutledge followed Steve Lawson and his sister out of the Longhorn and up the stairway leading to the private rooms above he was grateful for one thing. Ellen Lawson had nothing to do with this. As the sheriff had said, the murder was marked as having been done by a man. The explanation she had given was a true one — as far as it went. The scream that had been born of her terror at the chance discovery in the dark was not that of a woman who had just committed cold-blooded murder.

But it might have been plucked out of her fear, out of her horror at finding a dread in her heart turned into reality. Had she come into the Longhorn to save Steve from the guilt of this very crime and had she arrived too late? What could have driven her to enter such a place except some such imperative impulse, an urge potent enough to overcome ironbound conventions? Jim remembered the guilty eyes staring out of Steve Lawson's blanched face.

This crime had been committed by somebody very cool or by somebody very impulsive. It was a murder of audacious nerve or one of sudden uncontrollable anger. Which? There was one bit of evidence left by the assassin that probably answered the question. This Jim tucked away in his mind for future reference.

The sheriff herded them into the upstairs room and closed the door. "Take a chair, Miss Lawson. Rest of you sit down, many of you as can. We'll be here quite a while. I want each one of you to tell his story, what he saw and heard downstairs."

"That's all right, Manders. No objections on my part, if yore idea is to get more evidence against this fellow Rutledge," Buck Roe said. "We got enough to hang him already. We know who, how, and why."

"We know how, Roe," the officer differed coldly. "But we don't know who or why — not for sure. At least I don't. Maybe you do."

"Meaning just what?" the rustler asked with narrowed lids, his drawling voice a warning.

"Meaning that you move too fast for me. You're an enemy of this young fellow. I'm not. Maybe he did it. Maybe he didn't. I'm here to see he gets fair play, and there can't anyone crowd me to prevent it."

Roe's sarcastic laughter was only a murmur, as though it was born of private mirth within him.

"Eeny, meeny, miny, mo, catch a feller by the toe. If he hollers let him go," he chanted.

It occurred to Jim that it might be well to carry the war into the territory of the enemy.

"Why don't you finish yore nursery rhyme?" he asked. "Roe matches up with toe for the last line."

"You finish it, Texas man," Roe suggested warningly.

"Some day I may. I'm not right sure yet who did this. My opportunity to know wasn't as good as yours, for I wasn't sitting close enough to hear Shear's heart beat."

"If you claim I killed Joe —"

"I don't. How do I know whether you did or not? A fellow may be a train robber and a rustler without —"

The sentence was never ended. The sheriff had Roe covered before the man could fire.

"I'll take that pistol, Buck," he said quietly.

"Can't any man say what he did to me," Roe snarled. "I wouldn't take it from Grover Cleveland."

Yet, reluctantly, he gave up the revolver. Manders was no man to run a bluff on.

"I hope this bird gets off," Roe added, furiously. "I want him for my own meat."

"You may get your wish, Roe. Anyone could have done this. There were a hundred men in the Longhorn when it took place. Joe Shear had more enemies than any man in the state. He had killed twenty-four men. Don't you reckon any of 'em left friends or relatives?"

"Oh!"

The exclamation fell from the lips of Ellen. She had just remembered that within three days Shear had killed a man and served notice on his two brothers to sell out inside of a week and leave town.

"How many of those friends an' relatives were in the Longhorn tonight, Allison?" Roe asked.

"I don't know, Buck. For the present we'll confine our inquiries to those present. You were sitting in the game all evening. Did you notice anything unusual before the cowboys shot out the lights?"

"Not a thing."

"Playing a big game, were you?"

"Pretty big. Draw. Table stakes."

"How was the game going?"

"Shear was a big winner."

"How heavy a winner?"

"Over a thousand, I'd say."

"Who were the big losers?"

Roe nodded toward young Lawson. "The kid here."

"How much were you in?" Manders asked the redheaded lad.

Evidently reluctant, Steve answered slowly. "I reckon fourteen hundred — maybe more."

"Oh, Steve!" his sister cried, shocked at the amount.

"Any other loser?" the sheriff asked Roe.

"Pete Moss was in two-three hundred."

"Any unpleasantness develop during the game?"

"N-no. There was a li'l argument about a pot. Pete thought Shear backed in too late."

"A big pot?"

"It ended up a big one."

"Who won it?"

"Shear. His ace full beat Pete's jack full."

"You were sitting on the right of the marshal. Did you notice anything unusual while the lights were out?"

"Folks were crowdin' back of us. I heard Joe groan. Then the girl screamed. Nothing else."

"Never had a quarrel with Shear, did you?"

Roe's answer drew a little laugh. "No, sir. I always figured Joe was a good man not to quarrel with."

Questioned by the sheriff, Pete Moss had very little to tell that threw light on the murder.

"What about the argument over the pot?" Manders asked.

"Nothing to that. I kicked on Joe backin' in after he had passed, but he bulled it through. By rights it was my pot."

"Had a little trouble with Joe the other day in a restaurant, didn't you?"

"No trouble. Joe got a little annoyed at Sam an' me. We all laughed about it later."

The sheriff turned to another of the poker players. The man was dressed in a loud checked suit. He had the cold immobile face and the long tapering fingers of a professional gambler.

"Anything interesting to tell us, Mr. Black?"

The man shook his head. "Nothing more than the others have told."

"You've been acquainted with Shear some time. Knew him at Newton, didn't you?"

The gambler's face was a blank. "Yes."

"Saw nothing suspicious tonight — that is, before the lights went out?"

"No."

"Ever hear anybody make threats against Shear?"

Black laughed. His laughter was metallic. "Folks didn't threaten him. Not safe. I've known a dozen men would like to have seen him dead, if that interests you."

"I'll get a list of 'em later. Did you see any of his enemies in the hall tonight?"

The protruding eyes of Black had as much expression as two large glass marbles. "I never see anything that's liable to make trouble for me, Mr. Manders," he answered.

"Meaning that you don't want to tell me?"

"Meaning that I'm not observant," the gambler corrected.

"Don't happen to be an enemy of his yourself, do you?" the sheriff asked incisively.

"I do not. I'm like Roe. I wouldn't be so careless in choosing an enemy."

Manders questioned each of the others present, but he elicited nothing new of importance.

"You may go for tonight, all of you but Rutledge. I'll expect none of you to leave town," the sheriff said at last.

"Just a moment, Sheriff," Jim said. "One thing isn't clear to me. Maybe some of these others here can help me out. The lights in the main hall were shot out by the cowboys, but not the one in the alcove room. They weren't where they could get at it. I'd turned to see what the disturbance was, so I didn't notice who fired the shot at the lamp in the little room."

"That's important," Manders agreed, looking around at the others. "Who was it?"

"I didn't notice," Ellen said. "I was looking toward the front of the house too."

Steve started to say something, but he changed his mind. Roe was looking at him.

"Some of you must have noticed," Manders urged.

"Must have been the cowboys," said the brown-faced cattle buyer. "I would have noticed if anybody in the room had fired."

Roe spoke. "Mr. Rutledge is right for once. It wasn't the cowboys."

"Who was it?" Manders asked.

"It was Mr. Rutledge himself. He didn't attend to that by deputy."

Jim's smile was a picture of ironic insolence. "Too bad you didn't think of that before I prompted you," he said, and at once handed his revolver to the sheriff. "Hasn't been fired, you'll notice."

"I've heard of two-gun men," Roe jeered.

"And my other gun?"

"Passed it to one of yore pals, probably."

"I see you've elected me guilty, Mr. Roe. Kind of you."

"You elected yoreself guilty, fellow," the rustler gloated.

"That's all now, gentlemen," the sheriff said. "I'll say good night. Mr. Rutledge, you're going with me."

In a low voice the Texan made a request of the officer. Manders hesitated. "What do you want to say to her?" he asked suspiciously.

"I'll say it before you."

"All right. Hop to it."

The sheriff beside him, Jim moved over to the spot where Ellen and her brother were standing.

"Will you get a message to Harrison Pendleton for me right off?" he asked.

Her eyes rested in his. She asked no questions, made no stipulations. "Yes," she said.

"He's stayin' at the Trail's End Hotel. Tell him what's happened tonight and ask him to go to the Green Parrot or send some responsible person there. I want him to check up on a man wearin' a pirate's costume — striped turban, scarlet sash, blue pants, and black beard. Say I want to find out everything I can about him. I'll be much obliged."

Steve felt the inferiority of youth. He ought to assert himself, and he did not know what course he ought to follow.

"I don't know as you've got any right to ask favors of my sister, Mr. Rutledge, or whatever you call yoreself," he blustered. "Our family ain't indebted to you any that I know of."

"Don't be silly, Steve," his sister said. To Jim she added, "I'll get yore message to Mr. Pendleton right away."

"I knew you would. Thanks." Jim smiled, and with that smile his face warmed to a boyish charm. "You're a right good li'l sport."

"If you are ready," the sheriff suggested.

"I'm ready." Jim walked out of the room with Manders.

CHAPTER
TWELVE

Jim Makes Deductions

At first sight few would have picked this Texas boy fresh from the range to untangle the twisted skein of this mystery. None the less his training had given him certain qualifications lacking in one more sophisticated. As a cowboy it had been necessary to deduce much from little. Written in the desert are a thousand stories for him to read who can. They have been stamped into the ground, chewed on its grass and brush, scraped against the bark of trees. Only an expert can know the tale they tell.

From the spoor of a bear he knew approximately its size. He could tell whether bruin was in a hurry, could guess where he was going and how hungry he was, might even be able to determine the state of his temper. From the tracks of vanished horses he knew whether they carried riders, were grazing unherded, or were being driven; how long ago, within reasonable limits, they had passed; and could even perhaps describe roughly some of the animals. His eyes had been trained to see and his brain to interpret. He could cut sign from details so indefinite that a tenderfoot would not have been cognizant of their existence.

No living creature, Jim knew, could be in any spot without leaving evidence of its presence. The spoor might not be visible to the untrained eye or indeed to any human eye. None the less it existed, to be seen and understood by anyone clever enough to read. Unfortunately, the most expert trailer can read a very little of what is printed on the desert plainly enough for its denizens to ascertain instantly. A dog can do better. A wolf knows the story stamped there much more surely than a dog.

The murderer of Shear had left behind him a score of evidences to betray his identity. Some of them were physical, some products of his mentality. Most of them were so subtle, so close to the border line of the unknown, that human intelligence could not decipher their significance or even realize their existence. But others must be less elusive.

There were, for instance, fingerprints on the handle of the knife if one knew how to observe them, marked as the individual sign manual of the assassin. Jim was sure of that, though he had never read *Pudd'nhead Wilson* or heard of Bertillon's method of identification. It was true because it must be true. This was, however, of no practical value to him, since the information was Greek as far as he was concerned.

But there were other signs — clues, they were called in detective stories — waiting to be picked up by any mind astute enough. These were to be found not only in the dance hall where the murder had been committed. They marked the progress of the killer from the moment when he had determined to make an end of Shear.

Jim had plenty of time to devote himself to rationalizing the case, for the sheriff had decided that for the present he would hold him a prisoner.

Premeditated murders resolve themselves into one of three kinds so far as motive goes. They are done for revenge, out of fear, or for profit. The chances were that in this case one of the first two reasons named had influenced the slayer.

Walking up and down his cell, four paces one way and four the other, Jim considered the most dramatic aspect of the killing. Why had the knife been driven through an ace of spades? Had that been done to throw the officers off the track? Not likely. In the blackness of the night the crime was difficult enough without the addition of that detail. The assassin had contributed that touch as a warning, or to satisfy his vanity, or as a spectacular postscript without which he would not have felt revenge complete.

Jim was glad of that ace of spades. It definitely proved to him that this was not a crime of impulse, and it determined within limits the character of the man who had done it. Nobody without cool and steely courage had killed a man like Joe Shear in the presence of a score of men and had deliberately added that gesture of defiance. The assassin was marked by it as one needing that flamboyant touch to taste the full flavor of his deed. There was a bare possibility that the card had been pinned to the body of the marshal by chance rather than design. Shear might have been holding it in his hand when the descending knife fell. But the odds were very much against this. Jim was convinced that the black ace was a symbol. It called attention to some secret common to the dead man and his slayer, a secret probably shared by others.

Undoubtedly Shear had many enemies. Not three men on the border had such a record as a killer, for the gunmen of the West had nearly all passed from the scene. Pat Garrett had accounted for Billy the Kid. A coward's bullet had finished the career of Wild Bill Hickok. The Texas bad man John Wesley Hardin had been metamorphosed into a Sunday school superintendent. Joe Shear had remained, an anachronism. Jim Rutledge knew that no man could kill twenty-four men in private warfare without storing up against himself terrible reservoirs of hate. Nor were the enemies of the marshal confined to friends and relatives of those he had shot. He had been an arrogant man, over-bearing even with his friends; and he had been attractive to women and attracted by them. That was his reputation.

Of the marshal's enemies many would be able to offer alibis unimpeachable. A good many were not within hundreds of miles. Others, even though in town, could prove by good witnesses that they were nowhere near the Long-horn at the time the crime was committed. Still others could be eliminated by the peculiar circumstances attending the murder. No weakling had done it, no man who was not very sure of himself.

Jim reserved the right to change his mind, but his first judgment was to reject Steve Lawson and Pete

Moss, just as it was to suspect Buck Roe and Blackbeard. Buck was a hardy devil, capable of anything. The pirate had a devil-may-care insouciance and an instinct for the dramatic that marked him as a possibility. And the light gray eye he had turned upon Jim had been warmed by no genial glow. It was a distinctly cold and penetrating eye, and unless Rutledge was a bad guesser it could be deadly.

The Texan had no proof that either Roe or Blackbeard had any cause for enmity toward Shear. He would have to look into that later. But the opportunity to commit the crime had been open to both.

For Blackbeard, too, had been in the alcove room, and he had been there after Jim met him and before the murder. The proof of that was the green patch Jim had picked up. After the felt slipped from his eye why had not the pirate recovered it? Why was the patch left on the floor? The answer to that stood out like a sore thumb. It fell after the lights were out. Blackbeard had been in the card room when the murder was committed, *but not there when the bartender brought the candles.* What imperative urge had driven him to disappear so swiftly? Jim could think of one, the clamorous desire within him not to be among those present when the lights were carried in.

How had Blackbeard got out of the Longhorn? By fortunate chance Manders had been passing when the lights were shot out. He must have just missed meeting the Circle R cowboys as they ran from the hall. It was not likely that Blackbeard could have reached the front door through all that milling mob in time to escape before the sheriff ordered all exits closed. There was a back door, but that would not be easy to reach quickly. And there was the open window of the card room. Of course. Convenient and within easy reach. It was a safe bet that Blackbeard had vanished through it.

Jim pulled up abruptly in his stride. His eyes focused on a moth circling around the lamp chimney. But that was not what he saw. He had been struck by another possibility, an angle of approach to the mystery that might change the whole problem.

CHAPTER
THIRTEEN

Jim Becomes an Amateur Detective

Harrison Pendleton came down the corridor booming a greeting at the prisoner.

"How is it comin', boy? I'll be doggoned if I ever did see such a hellion to raise cane. It's outa one jam into another with you, an' each one worse than the last."

The jailer let him into Jim's cell and locked the door on him. "I'll be back after a while," the man with the keys said.

"You haven't said it all," Jim added, after he and his friend were alone. "I haven't been to blame for a single one of the jams I've got into. Luck has got a pick at me, looks like."

The big cattleman seemed to dwarf the room. He sat down on the bed, and it creaked like the cabin of a ship in a storm.

"Tell me the whole story," Pendleton ordered.

Jim gave the facts briefly.

Pendleton nodded. "About the way I heard it. Only I didn't know how you came to be with the girl, an' I hadn't heard a mention of the fellow in the fancy dress being present. I was wonderin' why you wanted me to keep cases on him."

"Did you find out anything about him?"

"Darned little. Sure enough he'd been at the Green Parrot, but he had left before I got there. Several folks remembered him, but he was masked an' they didn't know who he was. Say, boy, that girl of yours, Miss Ellen Lawson — she's a fine girl, all right."

Jim flushed. "She's not mine. I hardly know her."

"Just well enough for her to put her arms 'round yore neck," Pendleton said, grinning at him. "Well, all I got to say is, if you don't make her yours, an' you're a fair sample, the crop of young Texans ain't what they used to be when I was high-steppin' it. She grades 'way up."

"I knew she'd get my message to you," Jim said, dodging any discussion of the question raised.

"She came with that redheaded boy you winged down in the canyon. I could see he was against coming. He acted kinda sulky an' reluctant, but she spoke her li'l piece right out in meeting."

"She's like that," Jim agreed.

"Well, let's get down to brass tacks," Pendleton said, dropping his voice to a whisper. "Who killed Shear?"

"I don't know. It was done in the dark. Nobody could see. I reckon they're sayin' I did it." Jim made the last statement with the rising inflection of a question.

"Some say you did. Some ain't so sure. If either Bart or Mart Brown had been in the Longhorn at the time they'd get the credit for it."

"They had motive enough," Jim said reflectively. "Shear had just killed their brother Doc an' he'd given them a week to light out and leave a prosperous business."

"Prosperous, hmp! The Green Parrot is a gold mine. If they'd made a forced sale they wouldn't have got a fourth what it was worth. But Shear had put it up to them. They either had to fight or get out. Bet yore boots they had motive a-plenty."

"Were they at the Green Parrot when you got there?"

"Bart was. Mart came in a few minutes later."

"Say where he'd been?"

"I didn't talk with him."

"What kind of fellows are the Browns?" Jim asked.

"Tough nuts. 'Far as that goes, they might have hired some fellow to kill Shear," the cattleman said.

"I mean, what do they look like? Is one of 'em a kinda tall, slim, graceful guy, with a gift of easy gab?"

"That's Mart. You've met him?"

"Light cold gray eyes?"

"Yes, sir."

"I reckon Mart must be my friend Blackbeard."

"Might be," agreed Pendleton. "You can take it for sure that neither Mart nor his brother are the kind to lie down an' then crawl off with their tails between their legs when Shear cracked the whip."

"Are they the kind to come right into the open an' fight it out with him?"

The cattleman narrowed his eyelids in thought. "Well, they would if he crowded 'em to the wall, but I'd say they would prefer to do business another way," the

109

big man drawled. "Shear was a dead shot. It was pretty near suicide to go up against him even-stephen. I'd expect the Browns to play for a better break than that."

"This masked ball at the Green Parrot would give them a mighty good break. We'll say they wanted to get at Shear without being recognized by him. One of 'em, Mart probably, rigs up like a pirate. He has a turban pulled down low over his forehead. A patch covers one eye and a false beard all the lower part of his face. He could stroll right up to the marshal without being known. Say he went into the Longhorn to shoot Shear. He asks Ellen Lawson to dance, so he can get up to the other end of the hall kinda casual like an' size things up. Maybe he figured he would move up close an' watch the poker game, the way some other fellows were doing. When he was standing just where he could get Shear good, probably as the marshal was studying his cards, he would go to fannin'. No jury would convict him."

"No," Pendleton agreed, "not after Joe had threatened them and killed their brother Doc."

"But it doesn't happen quite like Mr. Blackbeard expects. The lights go out. That gives him an even better break. He moves toward Shear, bumps into me, feels my knife, takes it, does the job, and lights outa the place. How does that sound to you?"

"He wasn't in the Longhorn, then, after the candles were lit?"

"No."

"Any evidence he was there when yore lads smoked up?"

"Yes." Jim told him about finding the green felt patch.

"It certainly looks like Mr. Blackbeard did the trick," the cattleman admitted. "Is it yore idea that he shot out the light in the card room?"

"That's a sticker," Jim said. "I don't see how he could have done it without someone in the room seeing who did it."

"That goes for anyone in the room."

"That's so," the young man assented. "And someone fired the shot — either someone in the room or out of it."

"One of yore Circle R lads from the big hall?"

"No. Some guy standing outside the window of the card room."

"What would his reason be for that, unless he was in cahoots with Blackbeard? And that's not reasonable. If the two Brown brothers were there they would be in the room together taking an equal chance."

Jim shook his head. "It doesn't exactly dovetail with my theory. Still, I'd like to know if someone was standing out there by the window. It rained most of the day. There must be footprints. Just a chance they are still there. Depends on the amount of travel. Would it be too much to ask you to get Dr. Aubrey to go with you an' take measurements or even plaster casts of any prints there may be? I hate to impose on you, but —"

"Forget that, boy. But why Aubrey?"

"He's a friend of my father, and I know that last year he had plaster. He fixed up a busted leg for one of our boys. You'll have to slip up on this job, so folks won't

111

notice what you're doing. I don't want to advertise that we're on the trail of this killer. I'd say not to tell anybody."

"That's right. I'll get a wiggle on me right off. Chances are that if any tracks were left on the ground they've been messed up. I'll measure any that are there, but don't count on me to get any plaster cast of 'em. Maybe Doc Aubrey can do that."

"We may be barking up the wrong tree. Someone in the game may have killed Shear. Whoever did it was a hard cold proposition. That seems to let out the two young fellows Pete Moss and Steve Lawson, though either of the two might have been sore at him. He was winning their money, and Pete had just had a row with him. What's more, both of 'em looked so darned guilty they gave themselves away. Well, maybe not guilty, but mighty concerned."

"How do you know one of 'em didn't do it?"

"I'd be surprised if either of 'em did. That ace of spades marks the character of the murderer. He's a cool devil. These lads are both hotheaded. The Lawson boy boiled up an' tried to shoot me when I had the drop on him. Pete is the same way. No, sir. I can't see either one of 'em in it."

"But you said they looked guilty. Don't forget, young fellow, that theories haven't got a thing to do with this. Someone with a grudge at Joe stuck a knife in him. That's all there is to it."

Jim looked through the barred window, considering the situation. Then he shook his head decisively. "No, Mr. Pendleton, that's not all there is to it. You're older than I am, and you've had a world more experience. I'm only a kid. Don't think I'm trying to act like I know it all. I'm not. I don't know how to put it exactly, but it's as if the killer had burned his brand into the thing he did. Tell me one thing. What makes you so sure I didn't do it?"

"Because I've known you since you were knee high to a duck. Because you're a white man an' don't stick knives in the dark into yore enemies — if he was yore enemy, which he wasn't."

"All right. Just what I'm trying to get at. The fellow who did this is a certain kind of guy. You or I couldn't have done it. We're not killers — not bad men. But Buck Roe could have done it, if he had a grudge at the marshal. It's up to us to find out if he and Shear had quarreled. Then there's that fellow Black, the tinhorn gambler. He had known Shear back in the old days at Newton. We'll have to look him up, too. He's a cold, fishy-looking proposition. Either Roe or Black are capable of it."

"Did either of 'em look worried or act nervous?"

"Not a bit." Jim laughed, wryly. "An' both the kids playing did. But there was a reason for young Lawson lookin' scared. He'd seen the blood on his sister's dress, and I expect that was a knockout."

"I reckon you'd like to alibi that boy, Jim." The cattleman grinned. "But I'll admit that I've seen a liar on the witness stand who looked like he was tellin' the truth and an honest man so doggoned flustered you'd swear he was a perjurer."

"That's it exactly," Jim assented. "I wouldn't expect the fellow who killed Shear to give himself away. Don't forget that ace of spades. The one thing that sticks out like a white mule in a cavvy is the fact that the fellow who did it is a villain with guts enough to put up a front."

"I reckon you're right. Say, you don't suppose old man Moss could be back of this? He's in town. If he had quarreled with the marshal and had a reason for shutting his mouth —"

"That'll have to be looked into, too. According to what that Englishman told me, Shear hinted as much the day he knocked me out. And that brings up Sam Moss. The marshal called the turn on him and bawled him out in the restaurant."

Pendleton slammed a hamlike fist down on the table and whispered eagerly across it to his friend. "Why couldn't Sam be Blackbeard?"

Jim considered and rejected this. "I don't think so. Blackbeard was a smoother proposition. Better educated, I'd say. He mentioned his name was Teach. I wouldn't expect Sam Moss to know any more'n a jack rabbit that Blackbeard's real name was Teach. If I hadn't just happened to have read it somewhere I wouldn't have known it myself. Then, too, the fellow used highfalutin words — book words that wouldn't be like Sam. He said 'Zounds!' and 'Sink me!' and he asked Miss Ellen to tread a measure with him."

"Hmp! You're right. That lets Sam out. He didn't do it. We'll check him off, since he wasn't present."

"Will we?"

"Got to. If he wasn't at the Longhorn, he's out. No two ways about that."

"Yes. If he wasn't there."

"If he was there someone would have noticed him, wouldn't they?" Pendleton asked, a little impatiently.

"Maybe not. I've a fool notion someone may have been there who wasn't seen."

"Had an invisible cloak, I reckon," the cattleman suggested with sarcasm.

"Something like that. Oh, well, it may be a crazy idea of mine. I'll keep it under my hat, so you won't laugh at me. There's another thing you can do, Mr. Pendleton, if you will. Find out for me whether that ace of spades came from a red or a blue deck, and see what kind of design it had on the back."

"All right. Why?"

Jim took from his coat pocket a playing card, the five of hearts. "I helped myself to this while Manders was questioning us. It is one of the deck they were playing with when Shear was killed."

He turned the card over. It had a red back.

"I get yore point," the big man said. "You want to find whether it was from the same deck?"

"Yes. If the ace of spades was from another deck, the killer must have had it in his pocket waiting for a chance. That would cut out even a possibility that someone stabbed Shear impulsively without figurin' beforehand on doing it."

Pendleton's whisper wheezed from excited lips. "Boy, you'll make one of these detectives yet. You're right it would. An' that's not all. Maybe the ace was a kind of a

115

sign. Might have meant something we don't know a thing about."

"That's likely enough, too. Wish I could get to work myself checking up on some of these suspects. But I can't — not for a few days. Could you loan me Jerry Denver to do some snoopin' around? He's the sort of Simple Simon I need, a gabby interrogation mark, but not half such a fool as he looks."

"Sure. I'll send him to you. Well, I'll go hunt up Doc Aubrey. I don't go much on that footprint stuff, but you're the lad in the calaboose. It's yore say-so."

They called the jailer and Pendleton boomed a request at him. "Hank, you treat this boy right. I know him. He's my friend. Give him good grub an' see he has the makings and anything else he wants."

The jailer nodded dryly. "Sure I'll treat him right. I don't have a first class ace-of-spades killer like him in my hotel every day. I've got orders from the sheriff to look after him proper."

"Does Manders think he did it?"

"I dunno what he thinks. Allison lives under his hat mostly. He don't generally explain what he's thinking."

"He's given me a square deal from the first," Jim said. "That's the important thing. Wouldn't let Roe get heavy and convict me before I had a trial."

"Good! Well, I'll get busy. So long, boy."

The big cattleman went rolling down the corridor.

CHAPTER
FOURTEEN

Jerry Denver Bowlegs In

Jerry Denver came, received instructions, and departed. Ellen Lawson sent a message to Jim that she wanted to see him or some reliable friend of his; she had been twice to the Trail's End looking for Mr. Pendleton, but could not find him in. The cattle buyer Dane Sackville visited him to talk over the matter of the delivery of the Circle R herds.

The sheriff himself brought the Englishman to the cell occupied by young Rutledge.

"You're certainly busier than a bumble bee," the officer told his prisoner sarcastically. "I'd ought to charge you office rent. Six callers yesterday, and I don't know how many today. This is a jail, not a Fourth of July picnic. Maybe you haven't thought of that."

"It's right good of you to let me see my friends," Jim said, and his warm smile thanked Manders. "You've given me a square deal from the start."

"So *you* say. Buck Roe probably has a different idea."

"His idea was to have me hanged first and study the evidence afterward."

"He did seem to be set some against you." The sheriff looked at Jim with lifted eyebrows that suggested he was willing to listen to reasons if any were offered.

Jim nodded to the cattle buyer. "Take the chair, Mr. Sackville. The law has the first call on my time." He turned to Manders. "We had a difference of opinion down the trail about the ownership of some cattle. I had the drop on him then, but he threatened to bump me off at a later date. Those were the words he used — said he'd bump me off for sure."

"He's out for revenge, you think."

"Yes, but I have other thoughts, too," Jim drawled. "He sat on Shear's left, nearest to his heart."

"Do you know they had ever had any trouble — Shear and Roe?"

"No, I don't. But there's evidence that Shear and the Moss family had had a difficulty recently, an' Roe is old Devil Dave's right bower."

"What evidence?"

"There was some talk in the restaurant the day Shear arrested me. I had been knocked cold and didn't hear it. But Mr. Sackville was present."

The cold eyes of the sheriff rested on the cattle buyer. "What took place?" he asked.

"The two brothers, Peter and Sam Moss, were with the marshal when he came in to arrest Rutledge. They were primed for trouble, I thought. Revolvers were drawn, and Mr. Shear jumped between them and this young man here. It all took place so quickly I could hardly tell what happened. But Shear struck down

Rutledge and whirled on the brothers. He said they had come in to kill our friend Rutledge and he drove them out of the place. I never saw a man look as — as venomous as Shear when he talked to them."

"What else did Shear say?"

"He used an odd expression to the older brother, the one they call Sam. Said he would send him to hell on a shutter if he monkeyed in his business. And he added, the marshal did, that this was applicable to old Dave too."

"Hmp! Fighting talk, that. How did the Moss boys take it?" asked Manders.

"They backed toward the door, and one of them said he thought Shear was their friend."

"Anything more said, Mr. Sackville?"

"Something about some property of Shear's at an adobe house — cattle, I presume, because the marshal mentioned the J S brand. He told Sam Moss to stay away and let it alone."

The sheriff smiled. "I've a notion that property wasn't cows," he said. "What you have told me is important, Mr. Sackville. It may have a bearing on this case. I've about made up my mind, Rutledge, to turn you loose for the present. Me, I don't think you killed Shear. But that knife is certainly against you. A good many responsible cattlemen have offered to go bond for your appearance when wanted. I'll be criticised if I let you go, but I reckon I can stand it. I'm going to sleep on it another night before I decide. Now I'll leave Mr. Sackville alone with you."

Sackville had come to tell the young trail driver that he and Sim Hart had made a tally of the two herds and found a full count.

"You brought them through in good condition and I am ready to take them over today if that suits you," the buyer said.

"It suits me bully. Glad to get them off my hands. I'm going to be right busy trying to clear up my name for a few days, looks like. I never did see so many trails tangled up as there are in this Shear killing. He seems to have been a man who made enemies about as easy as most of us eat. I'll bet there are fifty men in this state with a good reason for hating him."

"You didn't feel anybody slipping your knife from its sheath?"

"A dozen people jostled me in the dark. I didn't even guess my knife was gone till I saw it in the body of Shear."

"Hope you succeed in finding the man. I suppose you want the check made out to your father?"

"Yes. I'll mail it to him today."

"I've been thinking, Rutledge, that you ought to send for him. You're pretty young, you know, to be here without him, accused of murder."

Jim grinned, his jaw set. "He's the last man in the world I want to see just now. I aim to rough through alone, with the help of such friends as I've got here. He gave me this job to do because he figured I was a full-grown man. I reckon we're gonna find out whether I am or not."

Sackville offered assistance shyly. "You haven't known me long, Rutledge, but I'd be very glad to have you count me in among those friends for any aid I can give."

Jim's heart warmed to the friendliness of the man. "I don't know anyone I'd turn to quicker," he said, with an eager, boyish smile. "And there's one thing you can do for me, if you don't mind. Miss Lawson wants to see me or one of my friends about something. Would you mind looking her up and finding out what for? You might tell her that I'll probably be out tomorrow."

"I'd be delighted," Sackville said.

He was pleased at the commission given him. Not for a long time had he met a man he liked as well as this slim, brown Texan. Jim Rutledge had in him a force that permitted nobody to consider him negligible. It made him friends, and it made him enemies. There were few who did not look at him twice.

Passing down the corridor, Sackville found another visitor waiting in the jailer's room to see Rutledge. The man was a bowlegged puncher. He sat in a rocking chair smoking a cigarette.

"Hell's bells!" protested Hank. "This boy's in jail, Jerry. He ain't runnin' for Congress. You'd think by the way you fellows act that he was entitled to one of these here gold medals for stickin' a knife in Joe Shear. I've a doggone good mind not to let you see him."

Jerry Denver grinned. "What's eatin' you, old-timer? It don't do any harm for us to see him, does it? You'd ought to be much obliged to him for making yore old calaboose so popular."

121

"You can have ten minutes with him. No more."

The cowboy removed his dusty boots from the table. "'S enough," he said, rising. "Lead me to him."

"I drapped in to report progress," Jerry told the prisoner as soon as they were alone. "First off, about that ace of spades. The old man told me to go look at it. The sheriff has got it in his office. It came from a blue deck."

Jim nodded, his eyes gleaming. "Good! That clears up one point."

"Dad gum my hide if I can see what it clears up," Jerry said, looking at Jim for information. He always liked to know the inside details. As his employer had once suggested, he had missed his vocation. He should have been a reporter.

"You mull it over in yore mind," Jim suggested. "Any other news?"

"There's no doubt Shear an' old man Moss had a row after Joe had his set-to in the restaurant with Sam an' Pete. Tucumcari Bill was present when Joe blew in an' started the shindig. Seems Buck Roe kinda got drawn in. It was about you consid'rable. Joe stood up for you. I dunno why. You know old Devil Dave Moss — or maybe you don't. He sat hunched up there like a spider an' let Buck do the talkin' for him. Devil Dave is the slickest proposition on this reservation, if you're askin' Jerry Denver for info. It got kinda hot, an' Shear gave Buck the choice of drawing steel or eatin' crow. Buck ate his humble pie, Tucumcari Bill says. He hated like Sam Hill to do it, but with that killin' machine's

122

eyes blazin' at him Buck allowed he wouldn't call for a showdown. Do you blame him?"

"What was the row about?"

"Kinda mixed up. You know Shear. He had to be major-domo of any roundup he was in, or else he wouldn't play. 'Far as I can make out, he was sore because he thought old Devil Dave was using him to draw the chestnuts outa the fire for him. An' he had a personal an' special grievance at Sam Moss. For those that like his kind, Sam is a good-lookin' guy. The story is that he'd been shinin' up to Mamie Dugan — an' Mamie was a very particular friend of Joe Shear."

"Any evidence of that?"

"Only what folks are saying. It's being whispered, as you might say." The cowboy lit a cigarette before he continued. "Tucumcari allowed that old man Moss tried to shush-shush Joe an' the marshal didn't get down to brass tacks about the details of his complaint against the old devil. Seemed he thought Moss was double-crossin' him somehow. Likely he was, too. That's the best thing Dave Moss does. Far as I'm concerned, an' I reckon you'll go fifty-fifty with me in that, I wouldn't of been unconsolable if Shear had bumped off old Dave an' Buck Roe before he cashed in. But that pious wish don't go if either of 'em hears of it."

"Shear saved my life from a pair of Moss killers. Maybe that was the trouble between him and the old man," Jim said.

"Might of been part of it. You have to do a lot of moling to find out the whyfors of that old Satan's actions. Referrin' to Moss, not Shear. Funny how good a fellow's hindsight is. I can see now that Joe wouldn't have a dead man's chance against Moss if he ever let the old man get to talking. His one real good bet would of been to empty his six-shooter into Dave an' any other Moss guys around an' walk out of the powwow."

"You think Dave had him killed?" Jim asked.

"Y'betcha! I dunno whose hand held the knife that did the job, but it's a plug of tobacco to a herd of longhorns Dave's brain guided the hand. They patched up their difficulty in a way, the old man an' Shear. Maybe that peace talk went for Joe, but it didn't for Devil Dave. He figured Shear was too headstrong an' too dangerous a guy to be walkin' around sore at him. So he said thumbs down."

"Maybe so. Shear had a lot of other enemies."

"The job's branded with a Moss running-iron. 'Course he had luck. Yore fool cowboys helped him out, but if it hadn't been that way it would have been another."

"We don't want to shut our eyes just because the Moss gang are my enemies. Anyone may have done this. For instance, that gambler Black. I'd like to know more about him. Could you go to Newton and make inquiries? Find out whether he and Shear ever had a run-in, and if so, details."

"Sure," the cowboy agreed. "I'll go today."

CHAPTER
FIFTEEN

Ellen Gets Four Proposals

Pete Moss grinned malevolently at Ellen. "Dad wants to know why you didn't come when he sent for you," he said.

Ellen did not let the flutter stirring in her bosom reach the brown eyes. "What does he want with me?" she asked.

"He didn't tell me. You're a good guesser yore own self. Figure it out."

He was jubilant. She could see that, and it was a weight on her heart. Whatever it was old Dave and his sons wanted would be something hateful to her. No need to tell her that. She knew it already, just as she knew by some bell of warning within her that it had to do with Jim Rutledge. For her happiness was involved in his safety, and the surest way to disturb one was to strike at the other. That was her shameful secret, that she was in love with a man who had never given her two thoughts except when her presence had forced her on his attention. She blushed at her abandon, flogged herself with her own scorn, and rejoiced brazenly at the floods of emotion that engulfed her. It was unmaidenly. All the maxims of her upbringing told her as much. But she would not have had it any other way, for never before had such exquisite tides of life flowed through her.

"All right. I'll come," she said quietly.

"He wants you right away."

"Tell him right away."

"You can tell him yoreself that you *have* come. I'm going with you."

"I don't need yore company, Pete Moss," she told him with resentful dignity. "I know the way to his house."

"You might get lost," he said impudently. "You might stray off into some place where it isn't fitten for a lady to go. You might meet that Texas coyote an' get insulted by him again."

"If you mean Mr. Rutledge, he has never insulted me. He saved me from being insulted once."

"Much obliged, missie. I'll remember that one. You've got so you don't know when you *are* insulted. What you need is a guardeen, an' I aim to be him, permanent. When a fellow goes to stick a bowie in another guy an' uses a girl for a screen, I'd call that 'most an insult."

"He never did that," she flared. "He didn't kill Joe Shear."

"So *you* say." A spurt of rage boiled up in him. "What call you got to carry on with a scalawag who shot yore brother?"

"I'm not carrying on with him just because I want fair play for an innocent man, an' if I were it's none of yore business, Pete Moss," she cried. His charge had whipped the color into her cheeks and her eyes were starry with anger.

"I'll show you about that. Get yore bonnet, girl."

She faced him, the fingernails biting into the pink palms of her hands. A sense of outrage rode stormily through her veins. He talked as though she were his woman, and she was sure she would die before that day ever came.

"I'll get it when I'm good an' ready," she said.

"You'll get it now."

The passion died within her. Why fight with him about this trifle when she ought to be saving her strength for the ordeal before her? She would need all she had to stand up to Devil Dave.

"I think you're the most hateful man," she burst out, and turned on her heel.

Three minutes later they were walking side by side down Front Street. Presently they turned up the hill toward the residence section, following a dirt road not flanked by sidewalks. The houses were of frame, unpretentious and unpainted. At one of these they stopped.

Pete moved aside, with mocking politeness, to let Ellen go in first.

"Room to the right," he said.

She knocked on the door. A husky voice said, "Come in."

Inside were two men. One of them was Sam Moss. The other was his father. Sam lounged in a rocker reading a newspaper.

Jerry Denver's figure of speech had been an apt one. Dave Moss, hunched up before the table, his head sunk down into the broad rounded shoulders, clawlike fingers at the end of the long arms, more than suggested a spider waiting patiently for the victim fly. He turned his eyes slowly and looked at the girl. She shuddered. It seemed to her the look of a creature about to devour her. He did not say anything. He just sat there with his opaque eyes on her. They had as much life in them as obsidian.

"You sent for me," Ellen said. She could hardly keep her voice from trembling.

"Why didn't you come before?"

"I — I was busy."

"Oh, you were busy." The husky voice was honeyed with sarcasm.

"But I was just ready to come when Pete got to the house," she added.

"That was thoughtful of you — to come and see a poor old man, my dear. I am glad you have come. I've been thinking about you — quite a lot." He chuckled, deep in his throat, making almost a rumble of his mirth. "Of yore happiness, my dear. You need a protector, someone to love and cherish you. I'm selfish. I want to keep you under my own eye. Can you blame me for wanting a daughter, since I have none of my own?"

128

To her there was something dreadful about it. The purring voice, the expressionless eyes that told her nothing, the long claws tapping on the table; they seemed to belong to a creature less than human.

"I — don't want to marry Pete, please." She heard another girl, not herself, speaking. So it seemed to her.

"Indeed! Pete has the bad luck not to please you? Too bad for Pete. But it can't be helped. I have other sons. Here is Sam, a likely boy. I've been hearing he is a favorite with the ladies." Again his husky mirth rolled forth. He was perhaps thinking of Mamie Dugan. "How would Sam suit you, my dear? He's gentle, kind, warranted to pull in double harness. I can recommend Sam."

"I don't want to marry anyone," she burst out.

"Sho! Girls must marry, my dear," he chided. "Male and female created He them. Shall we say Sam, my dear, since poor Pete is out of favor?"

Pete took a step forward to protest, but his father stopped him with a look.

"I — please, I — I'd rather not marry," the girl cried.

"Nonsense! Just maidenly modesty, my dear. Sam, put down that newspaper. How can you expect young ladies to be interested in you if you don't pay any attention to them?"

Sam lowered the paper he had been reading and grinned. His gaze traveled over the girl coolly and went back to the old man.

"How would you like to have Ellen for a wife, Sam?" old Dave asked.

Again the young man looked her over. "She's quite a hellcat, I hear. But anything you say, Father."

"I'm not going to be his wife. I wouldn't marry him if he was the only man in the world," Ellen said passionately.

"Clay then," suggested Dave Moss. "He is a li'l mite rough, Clay is. But a heart of gold, dearie."

"No."

"That leaves only little Dave, my Benjamin. He's young, but time will cure that. I'll send for Dave and we'll have the ceremony tomorrow. No use keeping loving hearts apart."

"I won't have anything to do with it. I told you I didn't want to marry. Why do you pester me?"

"For yore own good, my dear. I consider myself in a sense yore guardian, and I can't have you falling under the influence of an evil man like this young Rutledge. Better to have you settled, so I think we'll just say Pete."

"What do you mean falling under his influence? I barely know him. I've only seen him twice."

"Twice is enough. We must protect you from him, though I hope to see the hangman do that."

He gloated, his big shapeless body shaking with unholy mirth.

"Why do you say that when he didn't do it?" she said indignantly. "I know he didn't kill Joe Shear, for I was dancing with him just a moment before. He couldn't have done it."

Moss shook his head mournfully. "Shows what a hardened villian he must be. Of course he did it. Buck

130

saw him shoot the light out. So did Pete. It was a trap. His lawless cowboys came in to support him. All arranged beforehand. Nobody else could have done it."

"Buck Roe could have done it," she challenged. "Or anyone — anyone in the room."

"Maybe Shear did it himself," Dave murmured ironically. "He likely stepped over and borrowed yore friend's knife and gouged himself by accident."

Ellen's throat grew hot. She felt herself on the verge of tears, and she fought to choke down the lump that was gathering. This man wanted to frighten her in order to bend her to his will. Whatever he said she must not let him know she was afraid.

"Steve says that Buck had quarreled with Mr. Shear. They were sitting next to each other. Maybe —"

"Yore brother talks too much. We'll find a way to stop that." The man's oily voice had grown cold and hard. "Listen, girl, I've put up with enough from you and from him, too. Get it into yore heads that what I say goes. You are going to marry Pete tomorrow. He's going to stand there and smile and like it. Steve, I mean. What's more, he's to talk when I say so and keep his tongue padlocked when I give the sign. Understand?"

She controlled the fear fluttering in her breast. "Why should you talk thataway to us? We're not yore slaves. We're living in a free land. You can't act like — like you're the Czar of Russia and send us to Siberia — or somewhere."

"Can't I?" His black eyes gleamed malicious triumph. "That's where you're wrong, my dear. I can send him to the pen whenever I say the word."

The bottom dropped out of her courage. "You wouldn't do that," she begged. "You and yore boys have made him what he is. If he did something — broke the law — it was because you led him to do it."

"That's a nice way to talk," he told her virtuously, "and every one of us trying to keep him straight."

"Steve is good, if he is wild and reckless. You know he is," she protested.

"I've protected that boy, but I expect I'll have to stand aside and let him pay for what he's done. Neither he nor you are grateful."

"Is it about — about that money he was playing poker with?" she begged.

"You seem to know all about it," he said, rubbing his chin with the palm of a hand and watching her as a cat does its mouse.

"I knew something was wrong. That's why I went to try to stop him from gambling. I don't know what's come into Steve. He doesn't tell me anything any more," she wailed.

"He's in a tight sure enough, missie. The bills he was playing with were marked. They were stolen from the Ellsworth stage."

"Oh!" she cried out. "Do you mean he — helped to hold up the stage?"

"How would I know where he got them?" old Dave asked, lifting his hands in deprecation of such a question. "Point is, he had 'em, and possession is nine points of going to jail."

She knew that Dave Moss had somehow contrived to bring it about. That was like him, to arrange a trap in order to get somebody into his power. He was a creature full of impudent and menacing slyness.

"Do the officers — does Mr. Manders know he had the bills?" Ellen asked despairingly.

Old Dave shook his head gloomily. "Don't know. They can't have much evidence except the bills themselves. It wouldn't be easy to prove they were the ones Steve had — unless Buck or Pete happened to have noticed them. We can get the boy off slick as a whistle, if you and he will behave yoreselves."

"What must I do?" The girl's heart was heavy with dread.

"Be reasonable. Do like I tell you to do. Stay away from that fellow Rutledge and have nothing to do with him. Quit standing up for him like you've been doing. Think I don't know how you went to Pendleton with a message for him?"

"He stood up for me. He showed the sheriff how I couldn't have killed Joe Shear."

"Nothing to that. It was plain you didn't do it. What he was playing for was to get you to alibi him. And you fell right in with his scheme. Now listen, Ellen. He killed Shear. We're aiming to prove that and to have him hanged. You've got to do yore share by telling the facts." His stormy eyes looked at the girl unblinkingly.

"I have. I've told everything."

"No, you haven't. The fact is that you saw him shoot out the light and then he slipped away from you in the dark. That's all I ask of you. Just stick to that."

"But I can't. It's not true."

His shallow cruel eyes, his thin lip smile, held her fascinated. Her soul cried out in horror at the evil in him.

"Sure it's true. Now you be a good girl and do like I tell you and there won't any harm come to Steve. I'm that boy's friend. I'll look after him and see he makes the grade. Tomorrow you and Pete will be married nice and comfy, and you'll be as happy as a pair of turtle doves."

"I can't, Mr. Moss. I don't love him. Don't make me marry Pete," she pleaded.

"You'll like him fine once you're married, my dear. It's for yore own good. And for Steve's. Don't forget that."

Ellen wrung her hands. "Why haven't I a father? Why do I have to be bullied into this? You can't be so heartless, Mr. Moss. I'm just a girl. I'd rather die. I would. Believe me."

"Now — now — now. Don't be plumb foolish, child. We can't all do every li'l thing we want. Things ain't fixed that way for us. I wouldn't say a word if it wasn't for yore own best good. I allow to be a father to you and Steve. Now, you and Pete have been keeping company for quite a while. We don't want folks talking scandal, do we?"

134

"I haven't kept company with him. I've always told him I wouldn't marry him. If you won't make me do this I'll do anything else. And I'll see Steve behaves — does what you want him to."

"Meaning that you and Steve will see it my way what took place at the Longhorn?"

"Oh, Mr. Moss, anything but that — anything else. We can't lie a man's life away. You wouldn't ask it. Surely you wouldn't."

"She means she'll do anything if it's what she happens to want to do," Sam jeered.

Pete thumped his fist on the table, palpably annoyed. "When she's mine I'll promise to take that foolishness out of her, Dad. I sure will, or bust a tug tryin'. I never did see a girl so bullheaded. She'll be hell to live with till she's broke."

Old Dave chuckled huskily. "Well, we'll see if you can make good, boy. She'll be yore woman — tomorrow afternoon."

"No," Ellen cried.

"That, or Steve will be arrested. Take yore choice, my dear."

"If you'd listen to me —"

"I've listened a-plenty. This gabfest is over, girl. You tell that woman where you're staying, the widow Glen, to buy what dofunnies you need to fix you up for a wedding and to charge it to me. Get the stuff at Wright's. Say she's got to have everything ready by three o'clock tomorrow. And you'd better see she does — if you are fond of Steve. That'll be all now — Want to see me, Buck?"

Roe had come into the room and stood watching the girl with amusement. "Fixin' up a little love nest, eh?" he asked her.

Ellen left the room without answering him. Her eyes were blind with tears. Hope was dead in her heart. She would have to do as Devil Dave said. How could she stand against him alone? She must marry Pete. There was no other way to save Steve. But she would never, never tell any lies that would hurt Jim Rutledge.

CHAPTER
SIXTEEN

"Everybody Holds Back Something."

Sheriff Manders sat in the cell of his star prisoner, smoking an after-breakfast cigar. He had offered one to Jim, but that young man preferred to roll a cigarette. The officer was taking it easy, to use his own words. He occupied the only chair, and his feet were crossed and rested on the bed. Through a screen of smoke he observed his well-worn boots lazily.

"I got to get me a new pair of boots," he mentioned casually. "These are all run down at the heel. I hate to break in a new pair. Funny how a fellow gets attached to his old clothes, like they were friends."

"That's so," Jim agreed, looking at the boots indifferently.

"Well, that's got nothing to do with the price of longhorns, as the old saying is. I reckon I'm here to third-degree you. But what would it get me? You'll tell me what you want to tell and no more. Probably you're holding out on me right now."

He had hit a bull's-eye. Jim was holding out a good deal. No more definite reason urged him to keep his own counsel than the desire not to broadcast suspicions that might reach the unknown guilty party. If the killer knew the line along which he was moving, results could be checkmated.

"Why should I hold back on you?" the young trail driver asked, smiling at him. "I'm more interested in finding who killed Shear than you are."

"In a case like this everybody holds back something," Manders complained. "If they didn't the trail would lead right to the man we want. Maybe it's something that puts them in bad, or points a finger at a friend; or maybe it's something that might help an enemy. Then the public hollers because the officers don't get the guilty guy."

"Do you really think that is true, Sheriff? That everybody holds back something, I mean." Jim was interested in the sheriff's querulous contention. It was a point of view that had not occurred to him.

"Sure. Take your friend Miss Ellen." Manders turned his cold gaze on the prisoner as he continued: "Her evidence wouldn't be worth a last year's almanac if she knew anything against you."

Jim flushed, and was annoyed because he did. "That's plumb foolish, Sheriff. She's seen me only twice."

"No value a-tall. She's as sweet and nice a girl as I've seen for quite some time, but in that case I wouldn't give a plugged nickel for her testimony. So there you are."

"I don't think she's holding back anything, but it's certain some others are. For instance, Pete Moss and

Buck Roe claim I fired the last shot. They are lying. Maybe they know who did. They sat one on each side of Shear. Their legs and their elbows must have been touching his, they were that close. Looks reasonable to me they must know something about who killed him."

"Is that any more reasonable than that you ought to know who took your knife — if anybody?" Manders asked, eyes stabbing into his.

"It looks so to me, but I'm an interested party. How do you pry information out of a witness who doesn't want to tell it?"

The sheriff laughed sourly. "If I knew that, fellow, I would have had this killer in jail before now — that is, if I haven't got him here in this cell."

"I don't reckon you have, Sheriff," Jim replied. "That is, speakin' for myself. I didn't do it. Did you?"

For a moment Jim regretted his pleasantry. The bulbous eyes of the sheriff lost their friendliness. They bored into those of the prisoner. The young man grinned. Manders relaxed slowly. He too smiled.

"Thought you meant it at first," he said. "Better be careful what you say about this thing even when you're joking. Words are like sticks of dynamite, liable to explode anywhere."

"That's so," agreed Jim. "A fellow can be too plumb careless of them."

He spoke lightly, but his mind had picked up and was turning over a curious bit of food for speculation. Manders had stated a general proposition. Was it true of him, too? Had he also something to conceal?

"You Texans sure stick together," the sheriff said, reverting to the object of his call. "Looks like every trail driver in town has been at me to turn you loose. Not one of 'em has a vote here, but Dave Moss and his friends have. Politically it won't do me any good to free you."

"Nor any harm," Jim added. "You won't get the votes of the Moss faction anyhow. So what's the diff?"

The shrewd eyes of Manders observed the young man. "You're nobody's fool," he remarked. "Well, you and your friends win — for the present. Personally, I think you're safer right here in my calaboose than any other place. Don't blame me if Dave Moss has you bumped off."

"I wouldn't be here to blame you," Jim commented. "I've got to take my fighting chance of that."

"Hmp! It wouldn't be a fighting chance if they strike at you. What kind of a chance did Shear have?"

Their eyes met. So that was Manders's opinion. Naturally it would be, Jim reflected. A man is not a logical thinking machine. His thoughts are affected by his hopes and by his interests. The sheriff would prefer to think that this crime had been committed by his foes rather than by his friends. He would look to the Moss crowd as its author rather than to the Brown brothers.

CHAPTER
SEVENTEEN

Footprints

Dr. Aubrey drew back a cloth that covered the table. Seven or eight rough plaster casts were exhibited to view.

"I don't know what good they will do you, Jim, but there they are," he said.

"You certainly did a good job," young Rutledge approved. "I notice you've even got 'em labeled."

The doctor was a heavy-set middle-aged man with a fine head of silvery hair. He had a precise, rather oracular, manner of speech. Before he spoke he had a way of settling himself on his feet and clearing his throat, as though giving the matter due deliberation.

"I thought I might as well be thorough," he replied. "There are here casts of three sets of footprints. I should say partial prints in some cases. Unfortunately numbers five, six, and seven are defective. Another foot blotted out a portion of the track."

"Three sets," Jim repeated eagerly.

"Without doubt three. Examine number one. A large boot made it, one comparatively new, with long pointed heel set well forward."

Jim nodded. "Yes, sir. A cowboy's boot sure enough made that track. I'd guess he was a big man."

"Take the one I've labeled *2*." The doctor set his feet and his shoulders before he proceeded. "Made by a short, broad boot with a heel not so long or so pointed."

Pendleton added a contribution. "Not a range rider's or a trail herder's boot. An' notice how the outer edge of the heel is wore clean away."

"I'm noticin' that," Jim said slowly. His mind was puzzling to recall where he had recently seen a heel run over like that.

Dr. Aubrey went on with his little lecture. "Exhibit three. A long, narrow footprint squared off at the toes. It doesn't in any way resemble either of the other two. I should judge this may have been stamped by a custom-made boot."

"May or may not be that. Anyhow, it's one that leaves an entirely different track from the other two," the big cattleman said.

"Correct," assented Jim. "No doubt at all that three men made these footprints."

"Two of these casts were made from prints left by men moving toward the window of the alcove room at the Longhorn, the third by someone going from it," the doctor explained.

"Lemme do a little guessing, Doctor," Jim said. "I'd say that exhibits one and two are the brands of the fellows headin' toward the window, an' this square-toed one of a guy awful busy leaving the neighborhood. Do I win?"

"You win," boomed the cattleman. "How come you to know so much, boy?"

"Mostly a guess," Jim admitted. "Throw me out if I interrupt again, Doctor."

"Here is another cast, not very clear," Aubrey explained, picking up the one labeled 4. "The ground was too hard to leave a deep impression."

Young Rutledge took one look at it and turned to number five.

The hand of the doctor ranged over the remaining three. "The rest are all defective and probably quite useless for whatever purpose you may have in mind. As I said before, all of them have been defaced by other prints stamped above them."

"Gee!" Jim exclaimed. "Gee, we're lucky. We sure got a good break that time."

"I decided to take casts of them even though they were spoiled. I think I mentioned that my training tends to make me more thorough than is sometimes necessary. The medical method in diagnosis is to consider all possibilities and to eliminate gradually the obviously incorrect ones."

"I'm certainly glad you did, Doctor. Yore way of diagnosis suits me fine. Unless I'm 'way off, these plasters you call useless are gonna be a big help to us."

"S'pose you come clean, boy. What's on yore mind?" Pendleton inquired.

Jim did not answer immediately. He had picked up a button from the table. It had been lying on a card, upon which was written, in Dr. Aubrey's fine neat chirography: *Exhibit 8*. It was a cloth-covered button, and one edge of it showed a streak of white.

"Meanin' what, Doctor?" Rutledge asked.

"I don't know. Mr. Pendleton found it just beneath the window."

"Brought it along for you to play with," the cattleman blared with friendly derision. "If you're going to be a detective, you've got to have all the clues, haven't you?"

Jim's eyes lit up. He put the button down very carefully on the card. "Looks like I can hardly help being one with all the sign you gentlemen have cut for me. I'm sure glad to see that button. How high is the window sill from the ground outside?"

"About five feet, more or less," Pendleton said. "You got a mind like a flea, boy. It hops all over Kansas. Quit being so mysterious an' talk United States to us."

"It's a kinda long story, but I'll tell what I've been thinkin' and see how it looks to you gentlemen," Jim said. "It goes back to Blackbeard and the moment when the light in the card room was shot out. I'm satisfied that the fellow who fired the gun was standing outside the window. I'd say there were twelve or fifteen people in the card room. Nobody remembers seeing anybody else fire the shot."

"Buck Roe an' Pete Moss claim they saw someone do it," the big cattleman said with a grin.

"So they do, but they are lying to try and convict me. What they say has no weight with us. It looks reasonable to me that since nobody saw the shot fired or noticed a gun being drawn we can come pretty near saying nobody in the room did it. I'm positive nobody in the main hall did it, for I was facing that way at the time. That leaves as a possibility some fellow standing outside at the window. It wasn't square toes, so it must have been either the big cowboy or broadfoot."

"How do you know it wasn't square toes?" the doctor asked.

"Because he wasn't standing at the window. Square toes, or Blackbeard if you'd rather call him that, was in the room when the light went out, but he wasn't there when the candles came. For some reason he went outa that window like a scared rabbit. He lit a-runnin', and he didn't quit till he was quite a ways from the Longhorn."

"You are deducing that, Jim," the doctor cut in. "You may be right or you may be wrong."

"I'm reasoning from known facts to unknown ones that logically follow, the way anyone does who is trailing man or beast. Blackbeard was in the room when the light went out. The eye patch proves that. He wasn't there when the bartender brought the candles. There wasn't time for him to get out by the doors before they were closed. So he went out by the window of the card room, which would have been the easiest way anyhow, with all that mob millin' in the big room. You've proved by the footprints that one person at least got out of the window. Where else could he have come from, since he left no tracks leading to the window?"

"I reckon the boy is right," Pendleton said. "Blackbeard and the square-toed gent are one and the same."

"Probably," Dr. Aubrey assented. "But when you say he was in a hurry, pursued by fear —"

"Why did he leave the way he did, Doctor?" Jim inquired. "The reason jumps right at us. He was scared to stay and be found there because he knew what had happened to Shear. So he went, and he went like a streak of cat with a brindle pup after it."

"Yes, you're right," the doctor agreed. "He had a very urgent reason for departure."

"It wouldn't have been healthy for Mart Brown if he'd been found there rigged up in a disguise and a knife in his enemy's heart," the cattleman said. "Prove he was Blackbeard and we don't need to look any farther for the killer."

"It looks black for him, but I wouldn't say the case was proved against him," Jim differed. "It looked black for me at first. Before we fasten this on Blackbeard we've got to find out about two other men, the ones outside the window. One of the two shot out the light. Why? Was he a friend of Blackbeard? We don't know. Was it the big cowboy or the gent with the short, broad feet?"

"Anyone can ask questions till the cows come home," Pendleton snorted. "I've got a little kid can shoot 'em at me all day."

"You've got to ask them before you can answer them," Jim said mildly.

"He's right again," Aubrey admitted. "We've got to know what those fellows were doing there before this is cleared up."

146

"That's why these defective prints, as Dr. Aubrey calls them, interest me as much as the others," Jim explained, examining one of the casts. "They ought to help us piece out the story. We know one of the men was outside when the shot was fired. Were they both there at the time?"

Pendleton shook his head. "No way of showing that by the footprints. They may not have been together, but we know they had both been there before Blackbeard jumped out of the window. Doc's exhibits five and six prove that. See? In number five here he blotted out all the heel of the broad-footed gent's track. In six his foot landed squarely inside the hole left by the cowboy in the mud."

"They may have been waiting for him," Jim hazarded. "Perhaps they were pals of his ready to help out if necessary."

"Can't we find that out later?" Pendleton asked impatiently. "This Blackbeard did the actual killing. We know that much. If he had friends in it with him we'll get them later."

Jim looked at his huge friend, a quizzical smile on his face. "I've got a proposition to submit for consideration. If one man can go out of a window, what's to prevent another man from going in?"

Pendleton frowned at him, puzzled at the question. "I don't get yore drift, boy. What you mean, go in? Who wanted to go in?" Then, as he stared at young Rutledge, the eyes of the cattleman came to life. "Great Jehosophat, you mean — ?"

"You're on a hot trail, Mr. Pendleton," Jim murmured. "Stay with it."

"— that maybe someone slipped in by the window and killed Shear."

"An' then slipped out by it again before the lights came. Why not?"

"If someone else did it, Blackbeard must have known. He wouldn't have run otherwise," the doctor said.

"He knew," Jim replied. "That's sure."

"An' if he wasn't a party to it, how did he know?" the cattleman asked. "I don't reckon he can see in the dark."

"Likely he did it himself or knows who did. All I'm suggesting is that other parties have to be considered, too. Were there a lot of these footprints in the mud, Doctor?"

"None but the ones I made models of. The ground was hard except where water from the roof softened the soil."

"Our luck sure stood up fine," Jim cried. "You've done yore part, Doctor. If we don't solve this thing now we're woodenheads."

"You're widening the field, Jim, to show it might have been anybody in town did it," Pendleton said. He added, with obvious sarcasm, "Practically every man in town an' on the trail wears boots. All we got to do now is invite 'em to send in their boots for inspection."

"That's all," the doctor agreed with a laugh.

"By jinks, you're a helluva detective, young fellow my lad. All you do is say, 'Don't you reckon this fellow did it?' an' then give us the laugh."

"We've got to look at the facts, Mr. Pendleton."

"Hmp! You're lookin' at a-plenty. Maybe Doc Aubrey here did it. I'm about the only fellow with an alibi. I claim I couldn't of got through that window."

"Glad we've got someone we know didn't do it." Jim grinned. "*If* we know about you. I'd like to take measurements first."

"Me, personally, Harrison Pendleton, by jinks, I don't take any stock in yore notion that someone went in through the window. You've done proved to my satisfaction that a fellow dressed up as a pirate, probably Mart Brown, stuck that knife in Joe Shear. Quit when you've gone far enough, I say. Don't run a good thing into the ground, boy."

"Yet, Mr. Pendleton, you're the one who brought in evidence that somebody did go in through the window," Jim retorted, his eyes twinkling with mischief.

"I did not," exploded the big man. "I don't have any such fool idea. No, sir. What evidence did I bring?"

"I don't recall how the Longhorn looks outside," Jim said. "Has it been whitewashed lately?"

"There goes yore mind hoppin' around again," Pendleton accused.

"As a matter of fact, it was whitewashed early this spring," the doctor replied.

Jim once more picked up the button and handed it to the cattleman. "Handle with care, Mr. Pendleton," he said. "This give you any information?"

"Sure. Some fellow lost a button."

"How?"

"You tell us how," the cattleman challenged.

"I'll do some more guessing. A fellow jumped up to get into an open window at the Longhorn. This button caught on the sharp edge of the sill as he drew himself in. It was torn off. This white smudge on the cloth is from where it scraped on the whitewash."

Pendleton stared at the young man, mouth open. "By golly," he said at last. "You've sure enough got a head on you, boy."

The doctor set his feet and shoulders. "More deductions, Jim. That button may have been there weeks before the murder," he said.

"That's what we've got to find out. I can see a busy week ahead of me."

"What's your next move, boy?" the doctor asked.

"I aim to do a little burglary," Rutledge said gaily.

"Burglary!" Pendleton stared at him.

Jim explained what he had in mind.

CHAPTER
EIGHTEEN

A Warning —
or a Threat

Jim walked down Front Street with eyes in the back of his head. They moved about twenty feet behind him, and they belonged to Sim Hart and Jack Barton respectively. Rutledge knew he was a marked man. Word had reached him by the underground railroad along which all rumors travel that Dave Moss meant to destroy him. Just now the plan of his enemy was to convict him of the murder of Shear. This would be a two-edged revenge. It would score off both him and his father; moreover, it would bruise the pride of Chandler Rutledge beyond recovery. But Jim did not put over-much faith in Dave's sly molishness. It was quite possible that Sam Moss and Buck Roe might become too impatient to await the consummation of the old man's scheme. It was certain that they would strike at once if they felt Jim's investigations would incriminate them. Therefore it was as well they knew that he did not go unguarded.

Sackville came out of a store and saw him. The Englishman stopped for a word. "I saw Miss Lawson," he said. "She asked me to tell you to look out, that your enemies meant harm to you."

"Not news to me," Jim answered, with a grim smile. "But please tell her I'm much obliged."

Hart and Barton moved closer. "Look who's here," Sim warned in a low voice.

Buck Roe and Pete Moss came down the street, their spurred boots jingling. At sight of Rutledge they stopped.

"He's out," Roe cried with an oath. "Talked Manders into turnin' him loose. Didn't I tell you that cockeyed sheriff would throw in with him?"

"Yep," Pete jeered. "I wonder if he's bought another knife yet. May be our turn next, Buck."

Roe laughed, savagely. "Or his."

The friends of the young trail driver waited. It was his business, not theirs, to make such answer as he chose. And it seemed that he chose to make none, unless that hard-eyed scornful look, which gave no more weight to their offensive swaggering than one gives a snarling dog, could be regarded as an answer.

"Or his," Pete amended. "A fellow can go just so far. This town has made up its mind about him. This town knows who killed Joe Shear. It ain't fooled any by grandstand plays. Not none."

The voices of both men were heavy, overbearing. They were ready to bring to issue now their quarrel with this man.

But Jim was not ready. He had to clear his name. He had to discredit them if he could, completely and finally, for his father's sake as well as his own.

152

"Got his helpers with him, the guys that shot out the lights before he did his dirty work," Roe went on, taking up his share of the duologue.

"Come to town to terrorize decent citizens, I shouldn't doubt," Pete came back. "An' folks are so dumb an' got so little guts they sit down an' let themselves be stomped on."

Sim Hart spoke. "Howdy, Buck?" he said with a grin. "Bring on them decent citizens an' lemme terrorize 'em, like yore young friend says. Sho! fellows, what's eatin' you? Can't we walk peaceable down the street without gettin' picked on?"

"Who's pickin' on you? Do you claim we are?" Pete demanded fiercely.

"Quit stompin' on the boys, Sim, an' both of 'em so tender and innocent," Jack Barton drawled, sarcasm lurking in his voice.

The sheriff could be seen crossing the street. He did not appear to be hurrying exactly, but he was letting no grass grow beneath his feet. He could not hear what was being said, but he knew the group gathered there had inflammable potentialities.

"Morning, gentlemen. Kinda blocking traffic, aren't you?" he said with brisk assurance.

"Meanin' anyone in particular, Allison?" Buck Roe drawled.

"Meaning everyone in general, Buck, including you," the sheriff retorted promptly. "In a busy town like this folks have to keep moving to prevent a jam."

"You don't say. An' you're marshal as well as sheriff now, I reckon?" Roe asked, the light eyes in his leathery face solicitously sarcastic.

"Don't worry about that, Buck. I'll try not to exceed my authority."

Buck murmured his thoughts aloud, apparently to himself. "Funny how it goes to a man's head. I can remember this guy when he was human, before they elected him czar of Rooshia."

"He's not elected for life anyhow. That'll do to think about, Buck," cut in Pete spitefully.

"That's so, Pete. Seems to me I've heard his term's out soon. Well, we'll mosey along." Roe turned to Rutledge, meaningly. "See you later, fellow."

The two rustlers went jingling down the street. They were characteristic products of the frontier country, which found in this roaring town its hours of wild effervescence after months of toil and hardship. Yet though they were a natural part of the life, such men were a very small minority. Among the hardy pioneers who were winning the plains for civilization vicious parasites like these were in a ratio of less than one to a hundred. They survived for a brief day; then were swept away, excrescences not to be tolerated by society.

"A nice pair to draw to," Jack Barton commented.

The sheriff looked at him. "You one of the Circle R trail herders, young man?"

"You win first crack outa the box, Sheriff," Jack said lightly.

"You're likely one of the fellows that went into the Longhorn and played hell there the night Shear was killed," Manders said coldly.

"Me?" Jack's face was a map of surprised and injured distress. "Why, my dad is a preacher down in Lampasas."

"Maybe so. I've heard of these preachers' sons. What I've got to say is that you boys of the Circle R outfit had better stay out at your camp and start for Texas soon as you can. I don't want trouble here, and I won't be answerable for your safety if you stick around. That goes for you, too, Rutledge. Finish your business and get out."

"I aim to do that very thing," Jim told him.

"'Far as I can find out you've been in trouble ever since you started this drive. Course when I say get out, Rutledge, 'far as you're concerned, I mean if you're cleared in this Shear business. Not till then."

"I understand you thataway, Sheriff. An' I expect to be cleared soon."

"Interesting, if true," Manders replied dryly. His hard gaze fastened to the face of the young man. "I've been hearing about you setting up for a detective. Found the guilty man yet?"

"Not yet," Jim admitted.

"Let me tell you something, young fellow. The rumors that come to me come to others too. If you tread on a wolf's tail, he'll bite, I wouldn't wonder. Keep out of this business. I'm paid to attend to it."

"I'll consider that advice, Mr. Manders," the Texan said.

"It's more than advice. It's a warning."

Jim regarded intently the cold lights in the bulbous eyes of the officer. A warning! Did Manders know more than he was telling? Was it the Moss crowd he had in mind? If not, from what source might the danger be expected?

"I'll mull it over, Sheriff. That may be good medicine."

"It is." The voice of the sheriff was curt, almost harsh. "Folks live longer in this country who mind their own business."

He turned and moved away. Jim's gaze followed him, a thickset man of weight who walked with a strong firm tread. He was hard as steel, tough as a hickory withe, one not to be chosen lightly as a foe. Rutledge knew no harm of him. His reputation —

The young man's eyes came to sudden life. They were resting on the boots of the sheriff. The soles were notably wide, and at the outer edge *each heel was worn down almost to the counter.*

Jack Barton turned to his trail boss gaily. "You know the old sayin' about threatened folks livin' long. 'Far as this Moss trash goes, while they're sure enough dangerous — Why, what's the matter, Jim? You seen a ghost?"

Jim brought his attention back to his friends. "Not a ghost, Jack, but something right interesting."

"Let us in on it," the cowboy said.

Rutledge shook his head. "Not yet. I reckon I'm getting too much imagination. What I think I saw ain't so. It can't be."

156

"You're sure enough turnin' into a mysterious guy. Let's go somewheres an' have a drink — anywhere but the Longhorn. I'd as lief not go there."

"Suits me." Jim did not want a drink and he did not intend to take one, but while the others were drinking he could abstract his mind from the business in hand and consider the amazing possibility that had occurred to him.

Sackville excused himself and departed.

While the others were taking their drink Jim's brain worked. He knew now where he had seen a boot very like one of those which had left a print outside the Longhorn window. He could not be sure this was the same boot, but it was that or its twin brother. Outwardly he was quite cool, but excitement sent the blood drumming through his veins. Was it possible that Manders could be responsible for the murder of Shear or be in any way connected with it?

The two had not been friends. Ever since Shear had come to town they had been antagonistic. The faction politically opposed to Manders had been grooming the marshal as a candidate for sheriff. Jim put himself in the place of Manders. Probably Shear would be defeated, and at once he would become an implacable enemy of the one who had beaten him. He was the kind of man with whom an issue must be personal. If he lost, he would find a cause of quarrel. So Manders would reason, and his reasoning would be sound. The safest way out of the difficulty, short of refusing to run for the office — a solution not acceptable to Mander's

157

stiff-necked pride — would be to destroy Shear before he became dangerous.

Jim did not want to believe Manders guilty. He did not want to think him the kind of man who could murder in cold blood. But he could not let his feelings obscure the facts. Whatever these were, they must be dragged to the light.

Outside again presently, Jim saw Pendleton headed down the sidewalk toward him.

" 'Lo, you Circle R waddies, where are you plottin' to start trouble now?" the cattleman shouted.

"We been jumped on," Sim Hart complained. "First off, Buck Roe an' his young friend got heavy. Then Manders acted like he thought we were the guys huntin' trouble. An' I've got to say we're the most peaceable outfit ever come up the trail."

"I s'pose someone roped you boys an' dragged you-all into the Longhorn that time you shot the lights out," Pendleton said. "What was Manders kickin' about?"

"Wanted me to keep my hands off this investigation," Jim explained. "Figured I might live longer if I 'tended to my own business."

"Ho! Ho!" the cattleman boomed. "That's Al all over. Doesn't want any mistake made about who is sheriff of this county."

"Do you reckon that's it?" Jim asked, relieved.

"Sure that's it. He's thataway. Jealous of what you-all might call his prerogatives. Joe Shear and he were always watchin' each other to see neither stepped over. If this town hadn't had two such renowned peace

158

officers I reckon they never could have kept from trouble," he laughed.

"They never actually quarreled, did they?"

"Not likely. I never heard if they did. I expect they were special polite to each other. I'd have hated to have Joe as polite to me as he probably was to Al Manders sometimes."

Jim filed that away in his mind for reference. Pendleton's view was a reflection of public opinion, that the day had not been distant when these two men would be bound to clash. Along with it he filed also a fact and an impression. The fact had to do with a pair of run-down-at-the-heel boots, the impression with the look in the eyes of the sheriff when he had given him the warning that sounded more like a threat.

Pendleton drew Jim to one side. "I got a message for you, boy," he said, with his most knowing smile.

"I'm listenin', sir," Jim said warily.

"From that young lady you hardly know — the one you've only seen twice."

"Yes?"

"The redheaded young lady."

"I know who you mean," Jim told him. His voice was cool, his manner unperturbed. He did not intend to be joshed into either impatience or embarrassment.

"She's got to see you — right away — on most important business."

"All right. I'll see her."

"You act like a wooden Indian in front of a cigar store. Haven't you got any red blood in yore doggone veins?" Pendleton asked.

"Some, I reckon. Where will she be?"

"Waitin' for you at the Trail's End. Come up to my room."

"I'll be there in ten minutes."

CHAPTER
NINETEEN

"He Means to Hang You If He Can."

Ellen Lawson was born to the heritage of a warm heart. By nature she was trusting. From her childhood she retained a certain innocence, a certain eagerness. Her response to friendliness was instinctive. To Rutledge she had seemed spring rather than summer. In her eyes was still the dream, the look of misty wonder that contact with life must soon drive away.

Today she was troubled. She drooped. All the youth in her was quenched.

She had been sitting, but she rose instantly when Jim came into the room. Another woman was present, a plump motherly person of middle age. Pendleton stood by the window. The older woman was introduced as Mrs. Glen.

Ellen broke into speech. "I've come to warn you, Mr. Rutledge. Mrs. Glen offered to come. But I had to tell you myself. I had to be sure you understood."

"Old man Moss sent for her this morning," the cattleman explained. "He made threats against you, Jim."

"He's going to prove you killed Joe Shear. He means to — to hang you if he can," she cried.

He smiled, to allay the alarm in her eyes. "I'm not worryin' about that, Miss Ellen. It was right good of you to come, though. Did he tell you how he meant to prove it?"

"Pete and Buck Roe are ready to swear anything. He wants Steve and me to tell lies about it."

"Does Steve feel the way you do about it?" the young man asked.

"I don't know how he feels." There came to the girl a passionate urge to unburden herself. "He's a terrible man — Dave Moss. He'll make Steve do as he wants. Maybe he'll make me, too. I don't know."

"How can he make Steve come through for him if he don't want to?" Jim asked. "Steve's a grown man. He's a game fellow. I happen to know that. How can Devil Dave make him do what's wrong?"

"He can. It doesn't matter why. There's something — Never mind about that," she cried wildly.

Jim looked at her. "You don't mean Moss can prove Steve killed Shear?"

"No — no — no. How can you say that? Steve had no more to do with it than you."

"I felt sure of that. But there's something he's got on the boy. That's the way of it, I reckon."

"Never mind what it is. I'm warning you. Don't depend on Steve."

"Or on you? Didn't you say he might make you back up what he rigs up against me?"

"I told him I wouldn't — and I won't. But —"

She broke off, a sob of despair in her throat. Gently, Jim helped her out.

"But he'll turn the screws on Steve if you don't. Is that the way of it?"

"I don't want to talk about that. I just want to tell you that — that he's plotting against you. He'll get you if he can. First thing you know he'll —"

Ellen looked at this brown-faced Texan youth whose smile reflected a spirit undisturbed. He was so quietly master of himself that his serenity distressed her. Why did he not give more weight to the enmity of Devil Dave? One could not go laughing through deadfalls like a god whom hate and malice could not touch. That gallant head she loved would be in the dust before he could lift a hand to save himself. A wave of terror shuddered through her.

"I'll look out for myself," Jim promised. "Don't you worry about me, Miss Ellen. This fellow is nothing but a bad *hombre*. I've got friends, on account of my father. More than Moss has."

"By jacks, that's right," Pendleton cried in his deep voice. "I can gather twenty Texas drivers in this town quicker'n scat, all of 'em his friends."

"The question isn't about me, but about you an' yore brother," Jim told the girl. "If you're in a jam, we're here to help you. But we can't do a thing till we know what the trouble is. Devil Dave has got something on Steve. Can't you tell us what it is?"

"No, I can't. It's not my secret."

"You trust us, don't you?"

"Oh, yes — yes."

163

"Don't you think you'd better tell the gentlemen?" Mrs. Glen suggested in a low voice. "I do, my dear. Tell them everything." ¨

"No." Ellen shook her red head despairingly. "They can't help. It's — it's got to be the way Dave Moss says — about me, I mean."

Young Rutledge's lean jaw squared. What was it Devil Dave had decided about her? Why did all the life die out of her face when she spoke of it? He would find out. He would show her that the Moss gang did not have the say-so about everything. "That's where you're wrong," he said. "It doesn't have to be his way. Just let us know the facts, so that we can stand up to him."

There came a knock on the door. Pendleton opened it. Steve Lawson was standing outside.

"Come in, boy," the cattleman said, and turned to Jim. "I sent for him."

"Good!" agreed Rutledge. "Let's get at the bottom of this."

Steve came into the room a step or two. He looked at his sister and the two Texans, a sulky suspicion on his face. "What you want with me? What's she doing here?" he asked Pendleton, nodding toward his sister.

Jim offered his hand. "First off, let's get bygone grudges outa the way. Sorry I shot you. But you'll admit it was foolish to reach for yore pistol. I had to act quick to save my own bacon."

"That's all right," Steve said grudgingly. He took the other young man's hand with no heartiness. Of late he had been an unhappy youth, driven by fear and dread. He was being crowded into a corner, and within him a

164

sick despair rode his soul. Like all hunted men, he felt
that he stood alone against a hostile world.

Pendleton came to the point with bluff frankness.
"Boy, I sent for you because I want you to line up with
us an' not with Devil Dave's outfit. We're all in a jam
more or less, looks like. Jim here is. I've a notion you
are, an' maybe yore sister is, too. What I want to say is
that we're ready to be yore friends. Can you say that
much for Moss and his crowd? Trail with them an'
you'll head straight for trouble. You know that well as I
do. They're a bad outfit, every last one of 'em."

"I ain't in any jam," Steve denied sullenly. "Who told
you any such a thing?" He looked at his sister
resentfully.

"Do you take us for dad gum fools, boy?" the
cattleman asked impatiently. "What did Miss Ellen go
to the Longhorn for if she didn't figure you was in
trouble. She hasn't told us a thing, except that Moss is
aimin' to railroad this boy here to the gallows. But we
can use our heads. He has served notice on her that
both of you are to lie to back up the story he has got
fixed up. She's scared. Why? Because he has got
something on her or something on you. Well, there ain't
anyone got anything on her. She's too nice a girl. But
you — you're an ornery young waddy an' you've helled
around consid'rable, I reckon. Looks to me like he's got
you where the wool is short."

"All right. Say for argument he has. Do I look like a
fellow who would squeal on his pals?"

"You look to me like a trifling, no-'count scalawag
whose whole big body is not worth as much as your

165

sister's little finger," Mrs. Glen said, speaking up suddenly with strident emphasis. "Don't talk to me about squealing on your pals. What kind of pals are they that tell her she's got to marry a young scoundrel whether she wants to or not, or else see you get into mighty serious trouble? Always thinking of yourself, you are. A selfish pup not worth the powder to blow you up, by my way of it." The lady stopped and glared at him, her eyes snapping.

"You promised not to tell, Mrs. Glen," wailed Ellen.

"Got to marry who?" demanded Steve.

"Pete Moss, of course."

"What you mean got to marry him? She hasn't got to marry him if she don't want to, does she?"

"Old man Moss says she has."

"You said you wouldn't say anything about it," the girl protested.

"Why has she got to marry Pete?" Steve burst out excitedly. "She hasn't got to do any such thing."

"So *you* say. Dave Moss tells it different."

"Don't keep Dave Moss-ing me," young Lawson cried. "How can he lay the law down to Ellen?"

"You tell us how," Mrs. Glen replied. "*She* won't."

The boy stared at his sister, eyes dilating. In that look which passed between them a question was asked and answered. Steve gave a cry of rage.

"I'll not stand for it. Let him do his worst," he said desperately.

"What is his worst?" Jim asked.

Steve looked at him. "That's my business," he said.

"Seems to be Miss Ellen's business, too," Jim drawled.

"Does that make it yours?" young Lawson flung back quickly.

Jim flushed. "She saved my life out at yore homestead. She came through with the truth when Buck Roe tried to hang the Shear killing on me. Now she has taken the trouble to warn me of what Dave Moss is planning. Do you reckon I ought to walk off an' let that old devil ruin her life, me never liftin' a hand to help her?"

"If you want to know what I think, you're one of these smart alecks who interfere in other folks' affairs. Ellen an' I can look after ourselves. We're not askin' any help from you. Understand?"

"You can speak for yoreself, but not for her," Rutledge replied. "I'll go the limit for her. That's how much claim she has got on me. I don't aim to let her be sacrificed for any of yore foolishness."

The two lads confronted each other, the one filled with boyish fury, the other quietly determined. Watching them anxiously, Ellen knew there was more strength in the Texan's cold resolution than in her brother's hot flurry of anger. Her heart was lifted at Jim's strong support.

"I just finished tellin' you she don't have to do as Dave Moss says," Steve blurted. "What's eatin' you, fellow?"

"You've told us, but we're not convinced," Jim answered. "Get this right, Lawson. Mr. Pendleton is

167

with me in this. We don't aim to let her be sacrificed to save you."

"What have you got up yore sleeve? Why do you keep harping on that? Come clean, fellow. Who says I'm in trouble?"

"Any blockhead could see that," Mrs. Glen snapped. "Why else has she got to marry Pete Moss tomorrow?"

"Tomorrow!" Jim echoed.

"Those are the orders," Mrs. Glen said. "We're to fix up clothes today."

A hot tide of blood swept through Jim Rutledge and moved him to a rash decision and an even more rash declaration. "It won't be tomorrow or any other day," he cried.

CHAPTER
TWENTY

Ellen Thanks
Mr. Rutledge

"Why won't it?" demanded Steve. "Ellen will marry Pete Moss or any other man for all the say you've got in it."

"I'm tellin' you she won't," the Texan denied.

"Far as Pete goes, he ain't such a bad fellow. She might do a whole lot worse. Anyway, you can't butt in. I never saw such a nerve," Lawson fumed.

Ellen's heart beat fast. What did this Texas man mean? She understood the resentment of her brother. It was no concern of Jim Rutledge if she married Pete. What right had he to say flatly she could or could not marry him? But she felt as yet no anger at Jim. Her emotion was of a wholly different nature.

"What has Moss got hung on you, boy?" Pendleton asked impatiently. "We can't do a thing till we know that."

"I'll 'tend to that myself," Steve tossed at him.

"Cattle rustling, horse stealing, or what?"

"Not a one of them."

"He won't lift a hand for his sister," Jim said to the cattleman. "We got to move without him."

"Move how?" Steve jeered.

"Make it impossible. Fix it so she can't."

Ellen spoke. Her quiet voice denied the racing blood in her veins, but it held a tremulous note that made the denial ineffective. "Don't you think you'd better quit quarreling over me an' let me decide it myself?" she asked.

"We're not quarreling. I'm telling him," Jim explained.

"But —"

"I'll put a spoke in old man Moss's wheel an' marry you myself."

There was a moment of amazed silence. Mrs. Glen broke it. "I think that's the most sensible thing I've heard yet," she said, and her face was lit by an expansive smile.

Ellen stared at Jim, a tide of color flowing into her cheeks to the roots of her red hair.

"Bully for you, boy," Pendleton boomed. "The Lone Star State forever. Take it all back, what I said about you no-account young Texans."

Steve let out a bark of angry sarcastic laughter. "I reckon not. My sister ain't marryin' any man accused of murder. I won't stand for it."

"I'm much obliged to you-all for fixin' it up for me," Ellen said, her eyes flashing stormily. "First off, I want to thank Mr. Rutledge for takin' pity on a poor girl."

"I meant I'd marry you if you'd have me, an' I ain't takin' pity on you," Jim said, embarrassed.

170

"I wouldn't take advantage of yore kind heart," she said bitterly. "I'm aimin' to marry Pete Moss tomorrow."

"No," Jim protested.

"An' it's awf'ly nice of the rest of you to fix it up who I'm to marry without asking me," she went on with still ironic politeness. "It's very thoughtful of you-all, but I won't trouble you any more now it's all settled."

Jim knew nothing about girls, but it was plain to him that he had made a technical mistake. He had been intent on saving her and had forgotten all about her feelings. His excuse was that he had been absorbed in finding the surest way out of her difficulty and it had not occurred to him that she would be outraged at his blunt assurance. They were allies, working together to defeat Dave Moss. Naturally she would co-operate with him.

But he had grievously offended her pride. Helplessly he looked to Mrs. Glen for aid. She deserted him without hesitation. "Ellen is quite right," she said decisively. "We've all been talking as though it were our business more than hers. An' come to think of it I never did hear a more impudent proposal — if that's what you call it, tellin' a young lady you aim to marry her without a by-your-leave."

Words and voice reproved Jim, but it seemed to him that Mrs. Glen's eyes were trying to carry to him a message of a different kind. What it was he could not guess.

"I'm right sorry," he said humbly. "I didn't mean to act any ways impudent or biggity. My idea was to block

Devil Dave's game. I kinda forgot Miss Ellen might not like me." Jim looked down at the hat crushed in his hands and shifted his weight from one high-heeled boot to the other. At that moment he could have been bought for a nickel.

"Like I said, one of those smart alecks that butt in on other folks' affairs," Steve commented virtuously.

Without another word Ellen walked out of the room, her straight back and stiff neck eloquent of indignation. Mrs. Glen followed her. Steve filed in behind them.

Jim leaned against the table and looked down gloomily at the floor. "Well, I sure put my foot in it that time," he said. "I don't reckon she'll ever speak to me again. Beats all what a plumb fool a man can make of himself when you give him rope enough."

"You was a little mite sudden, don't you reckon?" Pendleton said helpfully.

"I was a doggoned idiot. Trouble is, my mind was all filled up with how to save her from that Moss crowd. Well, she sure put me in my place good an' proper. I know where I'm at now."

"I like that little girl, an' I hate to have her marry a Moss," the cattleman ruminated aloud. "Pete may be the best of the outfit for all I know, but he's tarred with the same brush as the old man. She's walking right straight into trouble. No two ways about that."

"An' now we can't do a thing for her," Jim mourned. "I don't s'pose any fellow trying to help a girl ever was so dumb about it before. She *had* to get mad at me if she had any spunk at all."

"You got to make over a girl some before you pop the question," the big cattleman told him. "An' then you got to ask her. You can't just tell her. When a fellow is courting a girl he's got to study her till he knows her like a cowman does cattle. No, sir, I can't give you a thing on the way you pulled that off."

"Worst of it is I've driven her to Pete Moss. She'll marry him now out of cussedness, just to show me where I get off."

"She's a redhead an' naturally spunky. Well, anyhow, we did our best. Don't you worry, boy. Maybe Steve is right an' Pete ain't so bad. We'll hope so," Pendleton concluded cheerfully.

Jim did not find his friend's optimism catching. He could not understand the depression that rode his spirits. The thought of Ellen married to Pete Moss distressed him greatly. He did not like to think of her buoyant vitality crushed by sorrow. But his regret held an emotion more poignant, more personal than pity. There was in it the stab of a wound wholly his own. He did not want Pete or any other man to marry her. He wanted her for himself.

That conclusion came to him as an astounding surprise. It took hold of him with a force he could not comprehend. He wanted the girl. He wanted her for his own. It was imperative that he win her. To think of her in the arms of Pete Moss was intolerable. It filled him with a jealous rage.

Moreover, interwoven with the suddenly awakened possessive desire of a lover was an emotion more generous. He loved the fine brave youth in her, the

173

innocence with which she lifted dewy eyes to the stars and asked that dreams come true. He had not until now realized it, but he knew now it would have been a joy beyond expression to walk beside her and help to make them true.

CHAPTER
TWENTY-ONE

Jim Reads Two Letters

Jim rode out to the Circle R camp on the edge of town. As a convenience to Sackville his riders were still holding the trail herds, though they had been checked, delivered, and paid for by the Englishman. The Wyoming cowboys who were to take the steers to the Indian agency had not yet reached town, though they were due to arrive within a few hours.

The trail herder's mind was absorbed by more important matters while Sim Hart made his garrulous report of progress.

"Most every homesteader in five miles came an' offered free pasturage — wanted we should camp on his quarter section. I says to myself, says I, some guys have fixed up to josh us, an' I promised every last one to camp at his place. Well, by jings, the welcome committees sure enough meant business. These yere Kansas nesters wanted the cattle chips for winter fuel. I told 'em to come down an' live in God's country."

"Yes," Jim said absently. "You keepin' the boys out of town?"

"Much as I can. 'Course they're hell bent on gettin' in to blow their wages."

"Tell 'em they're liable to get in trouble. If Manders can prove who shot the lights out at the Longhorn they'll go to jail sure."

"It don't do any good to tell a cowboy anything," Sim complained indignantly. "I recollect onct when we were drivin' a herd up the Pecos Valley —"

Jim's heels touched the side of his bronco and the animal moved out of verbal range. Just now the young man was not in the humor to listen to reminiscences. Sim was never annoyed when anyone deserted him in the midst of one of his stories. He was used to it.

Young Rutledge drew up in a draw not far from camp. He swung from the saddle and dropped the reins to the ground.

In a pocket over his heart was an oilskin package given him by his father with instructions to open if he got into a jam with the Moss gang. He was certainly in a jam with them now. They were intent on framing him for murder. They were forcing the girl he loved to marry one of them against her will. It was time he got all the help he could.

Jim ripped the oilcloth that covered the package. Wrapped in a piece of cloth were four or five papers. One was a copy of an affidavit signed by the express messenger who had been left dying after the hold-up of the S. & G. train nine years before this time. The man who had shot him had removed his mask and the messenger's description of the bandit fitted Buck Roe to a T. Another of the papers was a two-column clipping from a newspaper telling the story of the robbery. The other two were letters, one a copy of one written apparently by Robert Jelks to Chandler Rutledge, the other from Jim's father to him, penned the day before the trail herds had started from the ranch.

It appeared from the context of the first letter that Robert Jelks had served with Chandler Rutledge in the Confederate Army and that he had slipped through the lines to visit his sick mother at Lawrence, Kansas. He was in that town when the infamous Quantrell raid occurred. The letter had been written a few days after the massacre. It described the affair vividly. One paragraph had been underscored, probably by Chandler Rutledge:

I sneaked through the gully into the field, carrying my mother in my arms. We hid in a thick blackberry tangle at the corner of a stake and rider fence. Someone came running straight for us, three fellows on horseback after him. They were firing at him as he ran. I could see the devils laughing at him when he dodged. He was a boy, and he was scared white. He reached the fence, and tried to scramble over it. A bullet dropped him. They rode up, those grayback devils, and laughed at him while he begged hard for his life. One of them came up closer and shot the boy in the head. The one that did it was Dave Moss, who deserted from our company the day before we moved into Arkansas. He stood there within ten feet of me. I could swear to him on a stack of Bibles.

At the foot of the letter was a notation in the handwriting of Chandler Rutledge:

Bob Jelks was killed in a skirmish with Federals at Bee Gum, March 23, 1864.

Jim turned to the letter from his father. It plunged directly into the subject matter:

I hate to write this letter, son. We Rutledges come of good stock since long before the first of the family came over to this country. Never was a black sheep among us far as I know — until this generation.

My brother Joe was twelve years younger than I was, a kind of a Benjamin born to my parents in their old age. They started right in spoiling him. After my father died he ran hog wild. My mother couldn't control him at all. Long and short of it is he went bad. I blame Dave Moss for it some. He led the boy and influenced him for the worse. I had moved farther west and did not see much of him till he was grown.

Then I was elected sheriff and began to have difficulties with Dave Moss and his crowd. Finally they robbed the S. & G. fast train. My brother Joe was in it. He had changed his name after killing a man in Austin and was known as Joe Shear. You may meet him at the trail's end this trip. I hope not.

Jim stopped reading, taken completely by surprise. Joe Shear had been his uncle, his father's brother. That was why he had turned on Buck Roe and Sam Moss and old Devil Dave, at least it was one of the reasons. That was why he had saved Jim's life in the restaurant. Bad man though he was, the call of blood ties had

178

stirred in him at last. He had refused to let his nephew be sacrificed to the revenge of his associates. There had been other causes of difference between him and the Moss family. For instance, there was Mamie Dugan, who lived down by the railroad tracks, and was a particular friend of Joe Shear and also a friend of Sam Moss. Jim meant to have a talk with her as soon as possible. But the fact remained that at last the marshal had remembered he was a Rutledge and served notice on the Moss crowd to keep hands off his kin. That might be the deciding factor which had caused Devil Dave to have him killed.

Jim resumed his reading.

The evidence was circumstantial in the S. & G. robbery. It was not proved that the Moss gang did it, not so they could have been convicted in a court. But in my own mind I was satisfied. Dave Moss sent me word to lay off. He gave me two reasons. The first was that I would get killed if I did not quit hunting for evidence. The other was that my brother was in it deep as anyone else. Dave and I met. He drew on me, and I wounded him. After that it was war between us. I got too hot on the trail, and Dave moved out of Texas with all his outfit. My brother became notorious as a killer. I have never seen him in late years. Ever since then Moss has tried to do me dirt. Last year when his ruffians tried to stampede our remuda on the trail you know we killed accidentally his nephew Slim Gorham. Whatever you do, boy, keep out of that man's power. He will get you if he can.

That was all, except the signature of Chandler Rutledge.

The information given by his father did not help Jim much. Robert Jelks was dead, and his letter would have no weight in a court of law. The death of Shear removed the possibility of getting at any evidence from the inside. But, as his father had said, Jim at least knew more clearly where he stood.

CHAPTER
TWENTY-TWO

Jim Tries Again

Jim did not stay long at the camp. He had ridden out as a matter of duty to see that all was well, but he had before him a busy day and night. He had to see and placate one girl. He had to meet and get into the good graces of another. Petit larceny was on his program for the next twenty-four hours, also the burglary of a house. Most important of all, he must become engaged and attend his wedding. As a preliminary to the last two it was necessary to change the mind of a redheaded young woman who was probably employed just now in persuading herself that she hated him.

The illegal part of his schedule did not disturb Jim as much as that side of it which had to do with human contacts. He had no confidence in himself as a masterful lover nor did he know how to approach Mamie Dugan with any prospect of success.

It is possible that his humility was an asset rather than a drawback with Ellen Lawson, though it would have surprised Jim to know it. His feet carried him reluctantly to the Glen cottage. His knock on the door was timid.

Mrs. Glen answered it. At sight of him her eyes lit, but her greeting was noncommittal. "Something I can do for you, Mr. Rutledge?" she asked.

"I — want to see Miss Lawson, if you please," he said sheepishly.

The response of the widow held its edge of malice.

"She's busy getting ready for her wedding tomorrow. I don't know as she can see callers."

"I've got something to explain," he said.

"I can believe that," she said tartly. "But does Ellen want to hear you?"

"I don't *know*. I've got to see her, Mrs. Glen. It's — mighty important."

"Have you come to let her know who she is to marry now?"

He winced. "Don't *you*, Mrs. Glen. Let's agree I'm a lunkhead, but — help me out."

Swiftly she came over to his side. "What can I do?" she asked in a low voice, glancing over her shoulder into the house.

"I've got to get her to change her mind. I — I can't stand to have her marry that Pete Moss. He'll make her unhappy sure."

"Do you know anyone would make her happy?"

He blushed to the roots of his hair. "I know someone would try."

Mrs. Glen beamed. "You're showing signs of gumption at last. If I let you see her, will you tell her how pretty she is and that you love her instead of big talk about marrying her to save her from Dave Moss?"

182

He met her gaze directly, though his face retained its crimson hue. *Love* was a word he shied from as a young colt does from a newspaper fluttering in the wind. "I reckon," he promised.

She shook her head dubiously. "Lord help you, you big sumph! And remember to keep telling her you're daft about her. Come in."

Three minutes later Ellen walked into the sitting-room. "You!" she cried, staring at him.

She had been crying. The storm had left its mark on her cheeks.

"I — I had to see you, Ellen," he said.

"Mrs. Glen told me somebody had a message for me." Her heart was behaving queerly. She wanted to run to her room and hide, but the pride he had humbled so cruelly would not let her go.

"I've been a dumb fool," he told her bitterly. "I don't blame you if you give me the gate, but —"

She waited, still uncertain what he meant.

"I think an awful lot of you, Ellen," he gulped out. "I don't want you to marry Pete Moss or anyone but me."

Her affronted eyes met his. "I heard you say that this morning, Mr. Rutledge," she reminded him.

"Yes, but — it's different now, Ellen."

"I wouldn't think of taking advantage of yore pity even if I needed it."

He flung his hat toward a chair and stepped forward, holding out his hands. "If you marry Pete Moss I'll be wastin' all my pity on myself," he cried. "I want you, girl. I need you." He spoke in a low voice, rough with emotion.

"That's not the way you talked before," Ellen told him.

"I was a fool. I didn't understand. Do you reckon you could — care for me?"

Pride still struggled with the love that warmed and irradiated her. "If you're being kind to me —"

"I'm being kind to myself. I — love you." He had got the words out at last.

Her heart jumped with joy. "You — mean that?" she murmured.

"I never meant anything so much in my life."

His arms went around her warm and slender body. With a shy quick animal grace she nestled close and made her naive confession.

"I've loved you since the first day I met you."

Presently they came to a practical consideration of the situation. They must be married at once, as quietly as possible, since it would be better to confront Dave Moss with a fact accomplished rather than a plan proposed.

Jim went to make the arrangements. He dropped in at the Trail's End to see Harrison Pendleton.

The cattleman took the news with a whoop. At one feature of the arrangements he demurred.

"No wedding with two-three witnesses. I'll sashay around an' bring every big cattleman in town. The idea is to let Dave Moss know we're all with you, that he's got a tough combination to buck. The boys will keep it under their hats till after you're hitched up, then it don't matter how quick the news spreads. You gonna have her brother Steve there?"

"Yes. Ellen wants it thataway. She's mighty fond of the boy. She thinks she can talk him into coming."

"All right. Light out, son, an' make yore arrangements. I'll have Texas real well represented."

At the county clerk's office, where Jim got his marriage license, the clerk opened his eyes wide. He started to make a jocose remark about the law against bigamy, but after another look at the Texan he changed his mind.

"I don't aim to be buttin' in or anything, Mr. Rutledge, but there's already been a license taken out today for this young lady, or one of the same name, to be married to another man," he said.

Jim leaned across the counter and murmured in his ear. "If I was in yore place an' didn't want to get into trouble I'd forget about both licenses for a few hours. I knew an old donker once who lived to be more'n a hundred mindin' his own business."

The clerk was pigeon-chested and pimply. He wore slicked-down hair plastered across his forehead according to the prevailing barber shop mode. The last thing he wanted was to have any difficulty with either the Moss family or this upstanding Texan.

"I'll bet that's a good idea," he said with a knowing grin.

Jim called on a preacher, then visited a dry-goods store and bought a new suit. After which he had a haircut and a shave.

CHAPTER
TWENTY-THREE

Meet Miss Dugan

So they were married. Jim kissed his bride good-by and went to make the acquaintance of another lady, a popular actress at a local theater.

Mamie Dugan looked at him curiously, her dark slant eyes bubbling with provocative laughter.

"So you're Jim Rutledge," she said. "You have a nerve, young man, coming here to see me. Oh, yes, indeed!"

"Why?" he asked disarmingly.

"I'm s'posed to be a friend of those who're not friends of yours. What would you do if Sam Moss showed up now?"

"I'd tell him he was coming to see a mighty pretty girl," Jim said, smiling at her.

He had not overstated the fact. She was a dusky beauty of lithe and sinuous grace. Indeed, she was so dark that Jim suspected Mexican blood mingled with the Irish. Her speech and accent confirmed this.

She laughed. Bubbles were always coming to the surface of those orbs so languorous in repose. It was perhaps this inheritance from two races, Irish esprit superimposed upon Latin banked fire, that gave the girl her extraordinary fascination.

"If you tell me pretty things like that I'll be sorry when you're hanged," she told him.

"The rope isn't woven yet that will hang me," he replied cheerfully.

"No? The señor speaks with confidence." Her tinkling mirth mocked him. "But I have noticed that Dave Moss usually gets what he wants, one way or another. I have heard a story, oh, so romantic, about a little friend of yours upon whom your eyes have rested with much kindness, and alas! tomorrow she is to marry. It is a pity. Not so?"

"Yore dates are mixed," Jim informed the young woman. "She was married an hour ago, or perhaps a little less."

Miss Dugan sat up. "Married? To Pete Moss?"

He took her surprise coolly. "No. To a better man. It seems that Pete was a laggard in love. He waited too long."

"You make fun with me because I am young and trusting," she accused.

"Part of that is so," he admitted. "You're young. I don't know how trusting you are. But I am giving you straight goods."

"And who is the happy man?"

He bowed. "Congratulate me."

There was admiration in the long look she gave him. "You do not — what is it they say? — let the grass grow beneath your foots." She spoke English quite well, but at times her tongue became tangled in its intricacies. In general she used it quaintly.

"I'm a regular young Lochinvar," he assured her.

"I do not think I know the gentleman. But one thing I do know, though it is not my affair, no, not at all. If I was Mr. Jim Rutledge, the so happy groom, I would fly far and fast *muy pronto.*"

"This is a right good climate," he demurred.

"Yesterday for my health I took a walk," she mused aloud. "Past Boot Hill. So many at rest there, all once so strong and so sure, then pouf! one little moment, and no more. It is sad. You think so?"

"I'm much obliged for yore interest."

"Ah! but inside you laugh and say, 'I am not afraid.' So did the others." She leaned forward eagerly. "Listen. You have spoiled the plan so carefully arrange' by Dave Moss. Do I not know? From someone I hear everything. His witnesses are lost to him now. What will he do? Ask yourself. Will he not think some quicker way will have to do instead of hanging? You have brought danger, oh, so close to you."

"It has been close for some considerable time," he told her. "I'm on my guard, but I can't leave now. Got to clear my good name. About the killing of Joe Shear — I've got to find the truth."

He could see the instant change in her, the starch of wariness stiffen her figure.

"Ah!" she murmured. "So you come to me, my friend. I ask myself why."

188

He had not intended to be so direct, but he had found her quite different from what he had expected, franker, more friendly, less hard on the surface.

"You knew Shear well. He was yore friend. Perhaps you might help me find his assassin."

"Did I see Joe Shear killed? Was I at the Longhorn?"

"I don't expect you to tell me who killed him, but you might help me to a motive."

"You think so?"

"Where do you stand? Do you want the killer caught? Or don't you?" Jim asked bluntly, brutally.

Her slant eyes mocked him. "That would depend. It is so romantic that you marry and then come to spend your honeymoon with me that I would be sad if *you* are the guilty man and are caught. Oh, ver-ry sad!"

"And if it was Sam Moss?" His steady gaze held her. "What then?"

A flare of reminiscent resentment lit her face. "I will whisper a secret, Mr. Bridegroom," she told him recklessly. "If it was Sam I would say how too bad it was, but I would save my tears. I would not weep in my heart at least. He is too — too much like Joe Shear. I am to do this. I am not to do that. But I — I will do what I like."

"You know they quarreled about you — Shear and Sam Moss?"

"And why?" she demanded. "Am I a horse, a cow with a brand? *Por Dios*, no!"

"I reckon they were both arrogant," he prompted. "Acted like they owned you, probably."

"When I marry I will not be a peon for my man to trample on. He must be a nice man and must make money while I sit in the parlor and play the organ," she explained.

"Have you picked him out yet?" he asked.

Mirth overflowed in her mocking eyes. "Alas! they are all married, these perfect men. I meet them too late."

He ignored any personal application there might be in her remark. "No, I don't reckon either Joe Shear or Sam Moss would grade up a hundred percent as husbands. Too bossy. Both of 'em. No wonder they were sore at each other about you."

"Ah! If I wanted to talk. But no — I am a little jug corked all tight."

He nodded sagely. "Yes, I figure you would be scared to talk."

"Scared," she cried, the Irish in her flaming out. "Me? Scared of Sam Moss." She snapped her fingers. "Pouf! I laugh at him."

"But you stay a little jug corked all tight," he drawled.

"And why not? He is my friend. Must I tell all I know to please you? For what reason?"

"I reckon yore talkin' wouldn't help much, anyhow," he said lightly, with a glance provocatively skeptical. "If Sam had anything to keep quiet he wouldn't be tellin' it around to his lady friends."

"I know what I know," she flung back. "But I am not one to chatter."

"No?"

190

"And now, Mr. Bridegroom, it is nice that you have come to see me. Ver-ry — what you call — flattering, is it not? But we must not forget there is another lady waiting at a window for her new and handsome husband. And on your so rapid way back to her I advise, out of my kind heart, that you pass Boot Hill and count the graves — one, five, ten, and so many more."

"You're so thoughtful, Miss Dugan."

"And then for a honeymoon a swift ride to Texas."

He knew she would tell him no more. With a smile he offered a brown hand in farewell.

"*Adios*. I've enjoyed meeting you. An' if you ever want to take the cork out of that little jug — well, I'm a right good listener," he said.

She accepted his hand gaily. "You are a good sport, Mr. Bridegroom. I ask myself, why are they all already married?"

Jim found no ambiguity in her meaning. "Maybe they're not all," he suggested hopefully. "I'll bet he's waiting round the corner somewhere."

That she knew something Jim was sure, but he was certain she was not going to tell it at present. As for her warning, he had given the subject consideration before meeting her. His marriage had been a direct challenge to the Moss tribe. More than that, it had been an extinguisher of their hope of convicting him of the Shear murder. Old Devil Dave would get into action without delay and probably without further finesse.

CHAPTER
TWENTY-FOUR

Harrison Pendleton, Spokesman

Jim had never found anything easier than burglary. All you had to do was to open a window, go through it, find what you wanted, and go out through the same window, closing it behind you. He was very careful not to leave any burned matches on the floor, for he did not want it known that anybody had been in the room. But, easy though it had been, Jim breathed freer when he had left the house and was back on Front Street. There was something hair-raising in moving about a house filled with darkness when one had no right to be there.

Technically Jim might not qualify as a full-fledged burglar. He was not sure about that, since he had taken nothing from the house except information. This he carried to Harrison Pendleton at the Trail's End.

"I've found out who Blackbeard is," he told his friend. "Broke into Mart Brown's house. His wife is out of town right now, so there was nobody at home. The pirate's costume was on the floor of a closet in the bedroom."

"You didn't bring it with you?"

192

"No, sir. That wouldn't have brought us a thing. Someone less interested than I am has to find that suit."

"I'll see it's found within an hour by several good witnesses," Pendleton said.

"There's a pair of square-toed boots at the foot of the bed I'd bring along, too," Jim suggested. "Who are you going to take for witnesses? I'd say fairly prominent folks."

"Roundtree and Garrick. They've been drivin' herds to this town for years. They're respected here by the merchants. Their word will be held good."

Jim nodded assent. "Better go round Red Top hill so as not to be seen. It's the little house right up against the bluff. The window on the south side is unlatched. You'd better go without me, don't you reckon?"

"Yes. We'll keep it under our hats that you went to the house first. Might raise a question of you having cached the stuff. Just let it ride as my idea and not yours."

"Good! I'd like to go along when you see Manders afterward."

"That's all right. We'll drift back this way an' pick you up."

"If you see any loose decks of cards lying around you might bring them. One of 'em might be shy an ace of spades. Not likely, but you never can tell."

"By jacks, you're whistling, boy! We'll keep our eyes open."

The trail drivers were back within the promised hour. They brought with them a pair of square-toed boots, a pirate's costume, a mask, and two used decks of cards. An examination of the cards showed that the ace of spades was missing from neither deck.

None the less Pendleton was jubilant. "Doesn't prove a thing. He's no fool, Mart Brown, an' anyone with a lick of sense would have destroyed the deck. But we've got him by the short wool just the same. He'll have to do a right smart of explaining to talk away that Blackbeard business. I expect we'd better move over to the sheriff's office now."

"How about stopping at Dr. Aubrey's to see if these boots fit any of the plaster casts he made?" Jim asked.

"Sure. An' I'll bet a dozen four-year-olds they do," Pendleton cried.

They found the doctor at his house. He slipped into a street coat, adjusted his tie, combed his hair, and was ready for the street.

"Did you make the other set of casts, Doctor?" Jim asked in a low voice.

"Yes. I don't know what you want with them, but I did it."

"Much obliged. I know it was a lot of trouble, but I can see where we may need them. You haven't told anybody about making the second set, have you?"

"No, nor the first, for that matter."

The doctor unlocked the bookcase containing the casts. The square-toed boots fitted exactly the cast labeled 3. Even the design on the toe cap showed its markings.

"Got him. Got him cinched," Pendleton shouted exultantly.

Jim was not so sure. "We've proved he is Blackbeard, but we have not proved he killed Joe Shear," he said.

"How much proof you want?" the big cattleman asked impatiently. "I never did see such a fellow. Doc, can we have that valise there to tote these casts over to Manders in?"

They found the sheriff in his office. He sat with his feet on the desk smoking a cigar. His jade eyes passed from one to another of them.

"Quite a delegation of important citizens," Manders said dryly. "Find chairs, gentlemen, and get comfortable. We're having a spell of real hot weather. The farmers are beginning to complain again."

"We've got some evidence about the Shear killing, Sheriff," Pendleton said bluntly.

"Evidence or opinions?" the officer asked ironically. "This town is filled with high grade amateur detectives all set to solve this mystery. They offer me everything but facts."

"For a change we'll submit a fact or two," boomed the big cattleman. "Enough to prove who knifed Shear."

Having seated his visitors, Manders sat down again and replaced his boots on the desk. "Have you brought him with you?" he asked, and he let his gaze rest on young Rutledge.

Pendleton opened the carpetbag and removed from it a pair of boots, a scarlet sash, a pair of blue pantaloons, and a black beard.

"Going to a masquerade ball, Pendleton?" the sheriff inquired. He had seen that costume before, under a not very favorable light, but he did not betray either interest or surprise at sight of it.

"These pants an' boots won't fit me," Pendleton boomed back at him. "They were made for a smaller man — for the one who killed Joe Shear."

"Interesting, but probably not true," Manders differed. "I don't doubt you think so. I'm ready to listen to reason."

"Let's get down to brass tacks. First off, who in this town had the most pressing reason to bump off Shear?" the big driver asked.

"You tell me," the sheriff jeered. "If I was guessing, I might not get the right answer to your puzzle. I might name any one of a dozen innocent and pure-minded pilgrims such as your young friend here, or his new brother-in-law Steve Lawson, or Pete or Sam Moss, or Buck Roe, or that tinhorn Black, not to mention that good Christian old Devil Dave."

"Not a one of 'em would be right," Pendleton said confidently. "Go on, Sheriff. You'll hit on the right fellow by an' by. I'll give you a clue. Who was the last man Shear killed?"

"Doc Brown. You don't think Doc came to life and did it, do you? Or was it his ghost?"

"Who did Shear serve notice on to get out of town in a week? Who had to get out or be killed, or else kill Joe?"

Manders looked at the big Texan, a sneer almost impudent on his leathery face. "Opinions so far. Now for the facts, Pendleton."

"We're Johnny-on-the-spot with plenty. The night of the killing a fellow in this pirate's costume was at the Longhorn. He was present in the alcove room when the lights went out. He wasn't there when the candles were brought. Why did he light out so sudden? What was burnin' him up to get away in such a doggone hurry?"

The sheriff waved a hand toward the others. "Someone else take a guess. Chances don't cost a cent. You have a shot at it, Rutledge. You'd ought to know the answer, since you rigged up the whole thing. What's the idea in being so modest and sitting back there with your tongue in your cheek?"

Jim shook his head. "Mr. Pendleton is doing the talking. He's major-domo of this outfit."

"Opinions are all right, Manders, when you back 'em up with facts enough," the big man went on. "Here's one for instance. We'll say someone wanted to get right close to Shear without being recognized. Say it would have been practical suicide to walk right up to him except in a disguise. This masked ball at the Green Parrot would give him an excuse to rig up so he wouldn't be known. We'll say the guy wore a big beard to cover his face and a patch over one eye. He could stand three feet from Joe an' pump lead into him without anybody guessing who he was till it was all over."

"So he could," the sheriff admitted. He turned to Dr. Aubrey. "Did you overlook some bullet-holes, Doc? Was that how Shear was killed? Kinda funny none of us noticed it before."

"I'm sayin' he could have done it. Maybe he meant to do just that, but when the lights went out he changed his mind. Saw a chance to do the job without anyone knowing who did it. When it was done he lit outa the window on the jump."

"Fine work, Pendleton," the sheriff said, his voice heavy with sarcasm. "And while you're guessing, how'll this do for a shot in the dark? We'll make your young friend Rutledge the hero of this one. Someone has threatened his life. He sees how he can kill his enemy in the dark and nobody be any the wiser. He moves up close and drives his knife into the fellow. When the candles come he finds he has made a mistake. Natural enough in the darkness and in all the jostling crowd. He'd killed Shear instead of the man sitting next to him — Buck Roe."

Jim looked into the opaque, expressionless eyes of the officer. It was clear that Manders was trying to sidetrack their investigation, but that was to have been expected. No doubt he knew by now who Blackbeard was, and the Browns were close political allies of his. What struck Jim was that he must revise his estimate of the sheriff. He had known the man to be both shrewd and audacious, but he had not given him credit for subtlety. The hypothesis he suggested was not only plausible but possible. Shear might have been killed by someone striking at Roe. Jim had not thought of that before. By one stroke Manders had brought him back into the list of most probable suspects. What had been lacking in the case of Jim was a real motive. The sheriff had supplied an urgent one.

Why? What was the motive of Manders? Did he advance this new theory seriously? Or was it a veiled threat, a warning to Jim to keep his hands off?

"I never thought of that, Manders," spoke up Roundtree. "At that you may be right. There was consid'rable millin' around and Shear may have been killed in the dark by mistake for someone else. Not by Jim, of course, but by some of Roe's enemies. I judge he had plenty."

"Almost as many as Shear," the sheriff said promptly. "I don't say your young friend did it. I say he had both motive and opportunity, and the knife was his."

"Possible but not probable that the killer was trying to get Roe," Jim said with quiet force. "Whoever did this pretended he was jostled against Shear. He let his free hand drop to the long ringlets and made sure of his man. He had to locate his victim's body accurately to drive home the knife."

"That's right," Garrick agreed. "He would know for sure that it was Shear."

"Your point can wait, Sheriff," Jim went on. "We've brought evidence in to you. Let's consider that."

Manders looked steadily at him. "Still doing my work for me?"

"Still trying to clear my name," Jim differed, "an' meaning not to quit until I do it."

"You're one of those fools rush in and won't take advice. All right. Go ahead, I'm listening."

The sheriff eyed him as a bulldog does a rival.

CHAPTER
TWENTY-FIVE

The One Essential Clue

Pendleton took the floor again. "No sense in gettin' sore, Manders. We're here, like you are, to find out who murdered Joe Shear. I should think you'd welcome any information."

"I told you I was listening," the sheriff snapped out.

"That's all I ask, for you to listen with an open mind," the cattleman retorted. "We're here to show you who did this — and how — and why."

"When you've quit talking, all I'll have to do will be to hang the fellow you've picked on," Manders said tartly. "What's the need of so much powwow? Why not come right out and tell me the Browns killed Shear? That's what you're driving at."

"Yes, sir, that's what we aim to prove. We found this outfit of clothes at Mart Brown's house half an hour ago."

"Who found it?" demanded the sheriff.

"Garrick and Roundtree and I. Fact is, I suspicioned Mart Brown all the time. It all fitted in too neat. He arranges for a costume ball at the Green Parrot so as to give him a chance to disguise himself. He goes to the Longhorn. He's in the card room when the lights go

200

out. He's not there when the bartender brings the candles. It *had* to be one of the Browns. No other way to it. That's why he went out the window. If Mart killed Joe Shear he had to get away, for when he was found in the room disguised everyone would know who did it. If he did not kill Joe, there wouldn't be any reason for him to leave so sudden. So we burglarized his house an' found these dofunnies."

"Probably planted there to throw suspicion on him," the sheriff said casually. "That's an old dodge. Come to that, how do you know this Blackbeard was in the card room at all, let alone when the killing was done?"

The big cattleman developed the evidence of the green eye patch.

"Got witnesses to prove Blackbeard was wearing it?"

"Two. Jim here and Miss Ellen."

"The chief suspect and his wife," the officer said derisively. "That ought to go a long way."

"We'll find others," Roundtree chipped in stoutly.

"Maybe so. Then all you've proved is that Blackbeard was among those present. Like I said, these clothes were probably planted by the real killer to convict Mart. You don't know they are his or that he wore them."

"I know the boots are his," Pendleton said. "There's not another pair like 'em in town. Forty men will swear to having seen them on him."

"Will these forty men swear this Blackbeard had them on that night at the Longhorn?" The sheriff swung on Rutledge and flung a pointed finger at him.

"Come clean, young fellow. Could you swear that yourself?"

"No," admitted Jim. "But it's not necessary. That's covered by other evidence."

"What d'you mean?"

Dr. Aubrey took his plaster casts from the carpetbag and put them in order on the table. He cleared his throat, set his feet, and shifted his shoulders in the seersucker coat.

"When we discovered that somebody had left the cardroom by the window, Mr. Manders, we thought it as well to make a permanent record of any footprints there might be outside. You will recollect that it had been raining during the early part of the day and in places the ground was muddy. We decided —"

The sheriff waved his explanation aside impatiently. "I know all about it, Doctor. I'm not sitting here like a bump on a log. Word reached me of what you'd been doing. Some more amateur detective stuff. Why didn't you come to me instead of pulling off that mysterious soft-footing around?"

"We've come to you now, sir, just as soon as we have something tangible to offer. I have brought with me the casts of the footprints we found outside the window. You will observe that this boot exactly fits the depression made by one of the parties outside."

"Ah! You found footprints left by more than one person. That what you mean?"

"Yes, sir. To be exact, of three different persons."

"How do you know that the track left by that boot was not made earlier in the day? How do you know it wasn't one of the others that was worn by this Blackbeard?"

"I will take your questions categorically, Sheriff," Dr. Aubrey replied, in the precise way characteristic of him. "The answer to your first is that I have other tracks here showing the prints of the second and third men trampled out by one made by this boot. Please examine for yourself exhibits labeled 5, 6, and 7, to bear out my statement. The answer to your second inquiry is that this exhibit 3, the footprint made by the boot found tonight, so I have been told, at the home of Mr. Brown, was the only one pointing from the window. This must be an impression of the track made at the point where his foot struck the ground when he jumped from the window."

"More theory," Manders jeered. "You claim there were no footprints of the other two fellows that pointed from the window. Why not? Were the guys still waiting there when you sleuths arrived?"

Dr. Aubrey flushed. He was a man of dignity and he did not care to be mocked.

"The reason is quite clear, sir," he answered stiffly. "The muddy spot was only a small area made by water draining from the roof. When the other men stepped back from it they left no footprints that could be deciphered."

"I see." The face of Manders was hard and expressionless as a block of wood. "What's your idea, gentlemen — that I should arrest Mart Brown and charge him with this murder?"

203

"Why not send for him and see what explanation he has to offer?" suggested Roundtree.

"All right. I'll do that. Now."

The sheriff stepped to the door and called a colored boy who was passing.

"Yessah?" the boy asked.

"Take a message for me to Mr. Mart Brown at the Green Parrot. Ask him to come and see me right away." Manders tossed the lad a quarter.

"Yessah. I'll shorely do that, mistah," the boy promised.

The sheriff came back into the room. "What about the other fellows outside, gentlemen? You're not going to tell me you don't know who they are, are you?" he scoffed. "Not going to admit there is anything you haven't found out about this case?"

Jim looked amiably at the sheriff. "We're only amateur detectives, Mr. Manders. You've had more experience than we have. Maybe you can help us out. Maybe you can tell us who one of the other men is, or both of 'em."

"Maybe I can, and maybe I won't." Hard-eyed, the officer looked at him with sullen annoyance. "It's just possible I've got a line or two on this thing that you haven't."

"I'll bet you have," Jim agreed. For one flitting instant the young man's glance swept over the boots of the sheriff and observed anew an interesting detail concerning them. "I'll bet you could give us spades. You don't get us right. Speaking for myself, I don't aim to butt in on yore business. Point is, I won't lie down with a charge of cold-blooded murder against me. I aim to see my name is cleared, as I told you before. Prove we're wrong about Mart Brown, an' it'll suit me fine. I'm human. It won't hurt my feelings if you can tie the Shear murder on my enemies. You know who they are well as I do."

"But you can't keep out of it. You've got to horn in and try to hang it on someone else. Listen to me, young fellow. The Browns didn't do this. I don't care what evidence you work up. But you're smart. Nobody can fool you. So you overlook the only clue worth a damn in this whole business." The sheriff spoke with a cold but savage anger.

"And what's that?"

"The ace of spades. Everything hangs on that. It's the one essential clue the killer left. There's always one if you can find it — and only one."

"Are you sure the ace of spades is that clue? Someone standing outside shot out the light. How do you know that's not the real clue?" Jim asked.

The sheriff flashed a swift look at him. "Where do you get that — about someone outside shooting out the light?"

"I knew it from the first, because nobody inside could have done it without being seen. But Steve Lawson saw an arm and a flash. He started to tell you so the night of the killing, but Buck Roe gave him a look an' he stopped. Later he told his sister."

"What does that prove?" Manders asked.

"That some fellow standing out there was in cahoots at least with the killer, if he didn't do the job himself."

"And Buck Roe didn't want young Lawson to tell what he'd seen?"

"That may have been because he wanted to hook it on me."

"Or it may have been because he knew who was out there. Fits in exactly with what I claim. Young fellow, find out why that ace of spades was pinned to Shear's body and you'll know why he was killed."

"I judge you know more about that than you are telling," Jim said.

"I'll tell you two things. The first is that the old road brand of Dave Moss is an ace of spades. He doesn't use it now, but he was using it in the old days. The second is that the show at the Elkhorn is right interesting this week."

Pendleton slapped his great thigh with a hand like a ham. "By jinks, the ace of spades was sure enough Dave's road brand in the old days. I'd plumb let that slip my mind."

"'Course that may not cut any ice here, Harrison," Garrick spoke up. "Prob'ly a coincidence, wouldn't you say?"

The sheriff pushed his point aggressively. "Say it was more than a brand. Say it was a sign the members of the gang used with each other. What if old Dave figured Shear was breaking away from him and knew too much? Wouldn't he maybe hit two birds with one stone — kill Shear and leave the ace of spades as a warning to some other fellow in the gang who might be figuring on cutting loose from him?"

"Something to that," admitted Roundtree after a moment's consideration. "It's the sort of trick old Devil Dave would pull to scare some weak-kneed pilgrim he'd tricked into joining the gang."

"If we could find that wobbly pilgrim," Jim suggested. "Who runs with his crowd, except the boys an' Buck Roe?"

"There's a lad called Slim Rogers and another named Tim Henry," the officer said. "Off and on they are with the Moss crowd. So are other riders. It's a loose organization. Likely enough some of the lads have done nothing worse than some brand-blotting."

"Dave is a wily old wolf full of mystery," Pendleton said, frowning at the table in absent-minded thought. "They'll know only what he wants 'em to know."

Jim said nothing, but his eyes sparked with light. Manders might be right in saying that the ace of spades was the essential clue. But there was no apparent certainty that it pointed to the Moss gang. It might be a gesture of old Dave, a warning to subordinates of what they might expect if they did not come to heel when he whistled. That Joe Shear, the most notorious killer in the West, had been used as the victim to point the moral would make it particularly impressive.

On the other hand the ace of spades might have been used solely to divert suspicion from the real murderer to the Moss outfit. Jim had once ridden for a week with a band of Texas rangers following some horse thieves heading for the Cherokee Strip. On three separate occasions the outlaws had left false trails to deceive the pursuers. Was the ace of spades a red herring drawn across the track? Or was it a true clue left defiantly by the killer for a private reason of his own?

"What do you mean about the show at the Elkhorn being interesting? What's that got to do with what occurred at the Longhorn, Manders?" asked Roundtree.

The sheriff's answer gave no information. "A ticket to the show costs eight bits," he said.

A light footstep sounded outside. The door of the office opened and a man entered. He was slender of build and he moved gracefully. His gray eyes were restless. They had a way of stabbing with keen thrusts at first one and then another of those present.

"Take a chair, Mart," the sheriff said. "Know all these gentlemen?"

Brown nodded a casual greeting to the four older men. When his gaze returned to Jim it remained with him. "I think I haven't met this gentleman," he said.

"Meet Mr. James Rutledge. He's a great detective. When he's around I don't have to do a thing but loaf," Manders said.

"I've met Mr. Brown before," Jim said pleasantly.

"So? Don't remember when," the gambler returned carelessly. "You sent for me, Al?"

"Yes. These gentlemen want I should hang you."

"Now?"

"Not right away. After a while."

CHAPTER
TWENTY-SIX

Mr. Brown Suggests a Hypothesis

Brown was a cool customer. His manner lost none of its jaunty insouciance. He laughed heartily.

"Interesting," he said. "A new experience. I've been shot and gouged and more or less drowned, but I've never been hanged yet. By the way, any particular reason? Or just on general principles?"

"For killing Joe Shear."

"Oh, did I kill him? I should think they'd want to vote me a gold medal for it — if I did. No accounting for tastes, as old man Pruitt said when his brother Coe took a skunk for a pet." Brown selected a cigar from several he had in a case and offered the others to anyone who might like to smoke. He bit off the end and lit up. "All point of view, I reckon. If I'd killed Shear I would have been proud of it, for he was the most cold-blooded gunman I ever knew. He had it coming, if ever a man did."

Pendleton's big voice boomed. "We'd like you to explain one or two things, Mr. Brown."

The keeper of the dance hall smiled at the cattleman with a raffish insolence. "Been elected county attorney recently, I take it, Mr. Pendleton?" he asked.

The color deepened beneath the bronzed tan in the face of the Texas driver. "Suit yoreself," he said curtly. "You don't have to tell us a thing."

"But if I don't?" Brown suggested lightly.

"Everyone in this town will know *muy pronto* what we know."

"And just what do you know?" the gambler asked, blowing fat smoke wreaths into the air.

The big cowman told him. "We're not askin' you to say anything that will incriminate yoreself," he added. "But if you claim you're innocent we're ready to listen to anything you want to say. It's up to you entirely."

"I see. A gun at my head, but I'm to please myself. Shoot your questions, Mr. Pendleton. Maybe I'll answer them." He sat against the table, one foot on the ground and the other swinging.

"Do you deny you were at the Longhorn dressed as a pirate the night Joe Shear was killed?"

"Do I deny it? Let me see." Brown turned to Jim as though confidentially. "What do you advise? Shall I say 'yes' or 'no'?"

"I haven't any advice to offer, Mr. Brown, unless it is to say I'd treat this seriously. We know you were there."

"How do you know it?"

"Mr. Pendleton omitted one point." Jim nodded his head toward the boots on the table. "You own those, don't you?"

210

"I thought I did. I paid for them, but you gentlemen make so free with my property that I'm beginning to have doubts."

Jim fitted the sole of the boot into the plaster cast labeled *Exhibit 3*. "This track was left outside the window of the card room at the Longhorn," he explained. "Blackbeard was in the room when the light was shot out. He wasn't there when the bartender brought candles. This is the footprint he left when he went out of the window."

The proprietor of the dance hall was nonplussed, though he covered it with a laugh. "Blood and thunder, fellow, if I were Blackbeard I'd certainly have you walk the plank," he said easily.

Jim admired the cool audacity of the man. He was not denying, except technically perhaps for purposes of legal defense, that he was Blackbeard. His quotation of the words he had used to Rutledge the night of the murder was a defiant admission of the fact.

"Shiver my timbers, Teach, I'd sink you forty fathoms deep first," he flung back.

"Got nothing to tell us, then, Mr. Brown?" Pendleton demanded impatiently.

"I'm particular about my neck," the gambler laughed. "I wouldn't care to be hanged. So I'm going a little slow, if you don't mind. Say for argument's sake that I was in the card room when the lights in the Longhorn were shot out. It doesn't follow that I killed Shear because I left in a hurry."

"Then why did you leave?" Pendleton asked bluntly.

"Speaking always in a hypothetical way, if you'll excuse the long words, Dr. Aubrey, I might have left because I discovered Shear had been killed and knew who would get the blame for it."

"How did you know he had been killed? How could you know it? Nobody else did — except the murderer."

"I might have been standing beside the man who did it — so close that I was brushing up against him. There was quite a gather of people in the room, I've been told."

"Could you describe the man?" Jim asked, his eyes shining. "I reckon even a hypothetical man could be described."

Brown looked coldly at him. "I could not. It would be impossible for me to describe any man who had killed Shear and did not want it known he did it."

"Did you know he was going to kill the marshal?"

The man looked at Jim with eyes as expressionless as a stone wall. "No. Did you?"

"Sure the killer wasn't this young fellow here?" Manders asked sourly.

"No. Might have been. I don't want to swear it was, though. If he killed Shear he stands ace high with me. Saved me the trouble of doing it."

"Didn't you go to the Longhorn that night to kill him?" Pendleton flung out at the gambler.

"I don't seem able to remember whether I was at the Longhorn that night," Brown replied with a thin ironical smile. "But if I had been there and found a chance to kill Shear, you can bet your last cow I wouldn't have overlooked the opportunity."

212

"I think you killed him," the big Texan said flatly.

"That's your privilege. It's a free country. If it wasn't that I hate a braggart I'd come out and claim the honor whether I did or not."

"You can't talk away the evidence against you." Pendleton swung around on the sheriff. "I demand you arrest this man."

Manders looked at him with dogged anger. "Still running my business. You're about as bad as that young pup who is egging you on. But since you want arrests so bad I'll make you a proposition. I figure there's a lot more evidence against your smart young friend Rutledge than against Mart. But I'll be a sport if you insist. I'll arrest 'em both."

Jim grinned. It was a good come-back.

"I don't insist on arrests if Mr. Pendleton doesn't," he said.

Pendleton grumbled, but gave up the point.

"Anything more, gentlemen?" Manders asked ironically.

"Not just now," the big cattleman said.

As the Texans and Dr. Aubrey walked downtown they discussed the affair from various angles. Jim alone said nothing.

Roundtree asked him at last why he was so quiet.

"I've been wondering how many shoemakers there are in town," he answered.

"Shoemakers? What's that got to do with the price of yearlings?" Garrick wanted to know.

"Well, I notice the sheriff has had a new pair of heels put on his boots. It kinda interests me."

"You get interested in the darnedest things, Jim," growled Pendleton. "If you'd keep yore mind on important matters! But I reckon you got to be a kid half the time an' a man the other half."

Jim accepted the rebuke meekly.

"It says in the Good Book that when you become a man you've got to put away childish things," the big man roared genially at him.

"That's sure enough so," Jim agreed. "I'll begin to act grown-up tomorrow morning. I reckon I'll be a kid tonight an' go see a show that's been recommended to me." He looked at his watch in the moonlight. "I'm in time to see the last half of it, anyhow."

"You'll do no such a thing," the big Texan told him brusquely. "I never did see such a fellow. Have you forgot you were married today? You go right back to that little girl an' don't go hellin' around to any the-ay-ters. The night air of this town is poison for you, an' first thing you'll get bumped off an' Ellen will be a widow. If you had a lick of sense you'd know that. *I'll* take in that show at the Elkhorn an' find out what Manders meant."

"Yes," Jim assented.

He said good night and moved up the street.

Five minutes later he was at the ticket window at the Elkhorn Theater exchanging a dollar for an admission slip.

214

CHAPTER
TWENTY-SEVEN

An Ambuscade

The last act of a wild melodrama of the old-fashioned type was drawing to a close at the Elkhorn Theater when Jim slipped into his seat. It was apparently a stage play. Mamie Dugan, costumed as a dancing girl to represent the ace of spades, sat in her dressing-room presumably after the performance. The door opened and a man walked in. He wore a cloak over evening dress and was clearly the villain. Stroking his imperial, he gloated over her.

"Have you made up your mind?" he asked in deep chest tones.

She clasped her hands in agony and looked up at him. "Spare me if you have a heart," she moaned.

He had none. From an inner pocket of his coat Lord Winton drew a paper. "You shall be mine tonight," he hissed, "or —"

Despair flooded her soul as she gazed at the parchment. "The mortgage," she cried.

"The mortgage," he echoed. "Your mother and five fatherless children will be flung into the street tomorrow to perish, unless —"

"Is there a God in heaven?" she begged.

Winton laughed, such a laugh as only a fiend in human form could utter.

Once more the door had opened to let in a man. "There is," he said in a clear, ringing voice. "And He has heard your cry."

The beautiful chorus girl flung herself into his arms. "Back from California!" she said with a sob of joy.

"With uncounted gold," the young man answered.

"'Sdeath!" the villain ground out between his teeth. "I will not be foiled."

He drew a dagger and leaped at the hero. There was a struggle. Winton gave a cry, the shriek of a lost soul, and fell to the floor, clutching at his side.

"I have killed him," the stalwart youth murmured. "So be it. I shall be charged with murder, but —"

"Not so. I have seen all." From behind a screen stepped the dwarf whom the virtuous dancing girl had always befriended. "You struck in self-defense."

"My hero!" cried the girl, and she flung herself into the arms of her lover once more.

As the curtain fell the girl looked up adoringly into the eyes of one of nature's noblemen.

Jim passed out of the building with the crowd. His eyes were open for enemies, but he saw none among the hundreds of men present. As fast as he could he disengaged himself and moved down the street toward Mrs. Glen's house. A girl was waiting anxiously for him. He had done enough for one night. Just now he wanted to escape from an atmosphere of intrigue and danger to one where he could let down and not be on his guard. He walked fast as he left Front Street and started to climb the hill.

Scudding clouds raced across the sky and hid the moon. There was a promise of rain in the air.

Jim heard someone moving up the street behind him. The man called "Look out, boys."

It was a signal. From the shadow of a house the roar of a gun shattered the quiet. It was the first of a fusillade. Flashes of light flung out momentary beacons, warning Jim of the positions of his enemies. He dived across the street to a lumber pile, dragging out a .45 as he ran.

An excited voice raised a question, "Did we get him?"

Rutledge blazed at the spot from which it had come. He heard a cry that was a screaming oath. More shots followed. As ragged clouds chased heavier ones across the face of the moon, Jim made out figures dimly. He guessed they were circling around to surround him and cut off escape.

Twice he fired, then ran back of the lumber pile, came to a fence, and vaulted it. Without warning, he found himself hurled to the ground. He had collided with another running figure. For an instant they lay breathless. As Jim scrambled to his feet he could see the other man rising and could hear a cry lifted for help. The fellow closed with him.

Rutledge had no time to lose. He knew that in a few seconds they would be on him. The slap of running feet sounded louder. He wrenched his right arm free and struck his opponent's forehead with the barrel of the revolver as it swung down. The blow staggered the man. He stumbled back drunkenly.

Into the darkness Jim plunged, running low and fast. The crash of a shot told him that a wild bullet had been flung into the night after him. He footed it for his life.

A hundred yards farther up the hill he caught sight of another figure. "Jim," a voice of terror cried.

It was Ellen, driven from the house into the street by her fear for him.

His arm swept around her waist. "Come," he cried, hurrying her down the walk toward the house. He slammed the door behind them and bolted it.

"Back door locked?" he asked.

"I — think so."

"Make sure."

Without another word he walked into the parlor where Mrs. Glen stood, white-faced and anxious. He strode across the room to the table and blew out the lamp, then pulled the window shade.

Mrs. Glen was trembling. "Who is it?"

"Don't know for sure. They tried to get me — a crowd of 'em."

Ellen had come into the room. "The back door is bolted — and the kitchen windows. Did they — hurt you?"

"No. I got one. Hit him, at least. Go upstairs, you an' Mrs. Glen both, an' lie down on the floor till I come up."

"What will they do?" Mrs. Glen asked.

"Don't know. Not a thing, I reckon. They won't attack the house. But we don't want to run any risk. If

218

they're drunk they might fire a shot or two this way. We'll find out soon. Don't be scared. Do as I say, an' it'll be all right."

"What are you going to do?" Ellen asked breathlessly.

"Going round the house to make sure it's all locked up. Then I'm coming up. I'll kinda do some sentry duty at the windows to make sure they're not stickin' around."

He watched for an hour, but there was no sign of the attackers. They had retreated. Their ambuscade had failed, and they had no mind to try to storm a house from which they could be picked off at leisure by a wary foe.

Ellen sat beside him, her hand in his. He told her the story of the past few hours, from the burglary of the gambler's house to the attack after the play.

"Mr. Manders must have meant that perhaps Sam Moss killed Mr. Shear on account of Mamie Dugan. That's why he sent you to the play," she suggested.

"Yes. And that the killing in the play gave Sam the notion. His point was that the ace of spades led to the Moss gang, whether Sam did it on account of the girl or the old man had it done. What he says is true enough — unless the killer used the ace of spades for a blind to throw suspicion on the Moss crowd."

"Yes, but — I think it was Dave Moss back of it, just as he was back of this awful attack on you tonight."

"Even that last isn't proved, honey." He gulped out the word of endearment awkwardly. "I'm crowdin' the Browns an' maybe Manders, too. They might have thought it best to bump me off before I got any busier.

I'd hate to believe it of Manders, but he may have mighty good reason for keeping in his own hands the investigation of Shear's death. He acts thataway. I may know more about that tomorrow."

"Why tomorrow?"

"Just a chance I may. I aim to drop in an' see the town cobbler."

"What for?"

Jim told her.

Her fingers tightened on his, almost convulsively. "I wish you'd quit this — this detective work. It's dangerous. Someone will — hurt you. I know they will. Let's get away from here to yore home in Texas."

He smiled, grimly. "I will, sweetheart, soon as I've hung this murder on the fellow that did it. Got to clear my good name."

Jim was surprised to discover that the word "sweetheart" had come easier than the word "honey." He was getting used to the idea. As he watched her, sitting beside him in the moonlight with her big eyes turned lovingly up to his, there swept through him an emotion almost unnerving. She was his, this soft innocent young creature moving toward life with such eager and impassioned love. Her happiness was in his care. It came to him with more than a touch of awe that this was a life job he had entered upon so lightly. He could add to all that joy and zest, or he could destroy it utterly.

CHAPTER
TWENTY-EIGHT

A Boot Heel
Tells a Story

While the newlyweds were eating breakfast Mrs. Glen brought the morning *Globe* into the house from the yard.

"Here's something about last night's doings, but they've got it all wrong," she cried excitedly, handing the newspaper to Jim.

A headline on the front page stared at him: Texas Desperadoes Fatally Wound Sam Moss.

The heart of the young man sank, but he read the story aloud:

While the honest citizens of this town were preparing for well-earned slumber last evening a band of Texas ruffians roamed the streets with murder in their hearts. They shot down and desperately wounded Sam Moss. They attacked and knocked senseless Buck Roe, who says he thinks his life was saved by the chance arrival of passers-by.

Though he is desperately wounded with a bullet in his side, Sam Moss states that he recognized the leader of the miscreants as one James Rutledge, recently arrested for the murder of Joe Shear and afterward released by the sheriff. Roe also recognized Rutledge. These assaults, which occurred at different times and places, were entirely unprovoked. Both of the wounded men were witnesses against Rutledge in the Shear case, and it is believed that this was a cold-blooded attempt to put them out of the way.

Law-abiding cattlemen are welcome in this city, but it is time for the desperadoes who enlist as cowboys to learn they cannot run this town for their criminal purposes.

The *Globe* urges a searching investigation and swift punishment. Sheriff Manders, do your duty.

"That Walt Hickman who runs the *Globe* is hand an' glove with old man Moss," Mrs. Glen sputtered indignantly. "Everybody knows that."

"But it's so unjust," Ellen protested, the angry color in her cheeks. "I never heard of such a thing. To try to kill you an' then to say you attacked them with a lot of desperadoes."

"It's kinda nervy," Jim agreed, grinning ruefully, "but no more than I'd expect. Old man Moss is some fox. He started right out to get the jump on me with his story."

"What will Mr. Manders do?" inquired Mrs. Glen.

"I wonder," Jim said dryly. "It wouldn't surprise me if he put me in the calaboose again."

"Why should he?" demanded the plump matron. "He knows that Moss outfit an' he don't love 'em any."

"Sometimes I think he doesn't love me, either," the young man answered. "Probably it's six of one an' half a dozen of the other."

He finished a cup of coffee and excused himself. "I'll be runnin' along," he said. "Sorry, honey, but I got to check up one or two things."

"I'm going with you," Ellen said.

"I don't reckon you better," he replied. "Best for you not to get mixed into this business."

Mrs. Glen had left the room, and he took occasion to tell her in the wordless ways of a lover that she was the only woman in the world.

"But I've got to be mixed in everything that concerns you now," she argued. "It would be perfectly safe for me to go with you. I — I want to go very much."

"You win," he told her gaily. "Sure it will be safe. The Moss tribe have shot their wad — until dark. Get yore bonnet on, honey, an' we'll start right off."

Walking down the street, she mentioned what was in her mind. "I hope you didn't — that Sam will get well. He deserves what he got. You weren't to blame at all. But —"

"I hope so, too," he answered quietly.

"His father will be crazy mad, and he's a terrible man."

"I reckon."

But his thoughts were of her, not of his danger. She was his wife, this lissome, light-stepping young thing about whom still clung the rapture of dreams not yet blown away. His wife! A bugle of joy sounded in his breast. His partner for life, and it had not been a week

223

since he had walked into the kitchen where she was making pies and seen her for the first time.

There was only one cobbler in town. He had a little shop sandwiched between a drugstore and a saloon.

"Like to have these heels built up while I wait," Jim said, showing his boots. "Can you do it for me? Or are you rushed?"

"I'm always busy," the little man said. "But I can do it." He bustled about and found a chair for Ellen.

Jim took off one of his boots and sat down on a spare bench.

The old man was garrulous, and it was easy to start him on a tide of reminiscence. He had mended a pair of boots once for General Phil Sheridan, and once had made firm a loose sole for Senator Ingalls. The best people in town came to him.

"More folks come for half-soling than for new heels, I reckon," Jim suggested.

"Yes, that's so, but they come for heels too. Why Sheriff Manders was in only yesterday and had his boots reheeled. Some men's boots run over more'n others. Depends on the way they walk."

"So Sheriff Manders is one of yore customers?"

"I've fixed Al's boots for years."

"What do you do with all the old soles and heels?"

"Fling 'em in that pile, and every once in a while burn the whole caboodle."

"Probably you notice peculiarities in different men's boots," Ellen said. "I wouldn't be surprised if you could pick out of all that pile the heels you took from the sheriff's boots."

"Right you are, ma'am," the cobbler nodded proudly. He leaned forward, selected a pair of run-down heels, and handed them to her. "Those are the very ones I took off'n his boots yesterday."

Jim showed astonishment. "Well, that's surprising. Every man to his trade. I'll bet you could even swear to these."

"Sure enough I could. You can't fool me after I've handled a fellow's footwear. I'd know them heels a year from now."

A swift glance passed between husband and wife. The cobbler rose from his bench to get a piece of leather he needed. For a moment he turned his back. The dusty heels were dropped into Jim's coat pocket. They were there when the Rutledges left the shop ten minutes later.

"Let's go to Dr. Aubrey's office," Jim said.

The doctor was in. He greeted them in his punctilious fashion, bowing to Ellen from the hips. After which he shifted his shoulders in the seersucker coat and looked at Jim significantly.

"When a man takes in holy matrimony a beautiful young woman he owes it to himself and to her to give her a nice honeymoon trip. It would be not quite fitting for you to stay in town at this auspicious time. I recommend St. Louis or Kansas City or Denver," the doctor said.

"In fact, anywhere but here," Jim said, laughing. "We understand, Doctor. An' I'm much obliged for the hint. Soon as I can get away I'm going."

"He means we're going, Doctor," Ellen corrected, smilingly.

Jim blushed. "That's what I mean."

Aubrey shifted his weight. "A honeymoon can't wait. It must be taken at once — or never."

The emphasis on the last word did not escape Jim. "That's right," he said carelessly. "If it ain't taken right away it won't be a honeymoon, will it? Say, Doctor, like to look at yore exhibits again if you don't mind."

Dr. Aubrey unlocked and brought out his second set of plaster casts. Jim selected the one labeled *Exhibit 2*. From his pocket he drew the heels obtained at the cobbler's shop. One of these he fitted into the heel of the cast. It was a perfect fit.

"You have discovered the identity of one of the parties outside the window at the Longhorn," Aubrey said, his eyes gleaming with excitement.

"Looks thataway," Jim agreed.

"Who is he?"

"You can come along with me while I tell the sheriff what I know, if you've got the time," Jim said.

"Can't. I have a call to make immediately."

Jim murmured a name.

The doctor stared at him. "You mean that his foot made this imprint?" the doctor asked, astonished.

"That's what I mean, but keep it under yore hat, please. Well, if you can't go with me I'll get Mr. Pendleton. Got to have moral support. I'll ask you to lock up that heel mighty carefully. I'll take the other one along, and the button, too, if you don't mind."

226

Half an hour later the big Texas trail driver and Rutledge dropped into the office of the sheriff. Ellen had reluctantly gone home.

Manders was at his desk, writing. He grinned at sight of them. "Brought your young friend around to surrender, have you, Pendleton?" he asked. "Good! Saves me the trouble of going after him."

"That story in the *Globe* is nothing but a doggone lie from start to finish," Pendleton burst out with his customary roar.

"Not the way Dave Moss tells it. He's been after me mighty hard to arrest Rutledge, and you know how reliable Dave is. Wouldn't say anything that wasn't so, would he?"

"They jumped him while he was going home from the Elkhorn The-ay-ter. He was alone. There was several of them. If Jim wounded Sam Moss and knocked out Buck Roe he did it in self-defense. More power to him, I say."

"You seem to know quite a lot about it, Pendleton," the sheriff said dryly. "Weren't among those present, were you?"

"No, but Jim was."

"So old man Moss has been telling me right earnestly. I judge he thinks boiling in oil is about what the boy deserves. Both Sam and Buck were moseying along figuring out what church they would attend tomorrow when this young hellion and his gang started the fireworks. It's an outrage and an atrocity, Dave claims, and he isn't going to stand for it. And what's the law for anyhow if it's not to protect innocent citizens?"

In four sentences Jim gave an account of the attack on him. Manders did not for a moment doubt his story, but he did not choose to say so.

"Funny that all the damage was done to them if they are the ones that attacked," the officer drawled. "Right negligent on their part, I'd call that."

"I was lucky," Jim admitted.

The cold, protuberant eyes of the sheriff rested on him. Nobody would have guessed that behind that stony stare lay admiration. "I've noticed you're lucky, fellow. I'm wondering how long that luck will stand up."

"It would have been his own fault if the Moss gang had drilled him full of holes," roared Pendleton. "I told the dad-gummed young idiot to go home an' leave me to 'tend that show, which I was aimin' to do tonight. But he had to go waltzin' to the Elkhorn alone. An' of course, like I said, they bushwhacked him on the way home."

"So your friend Rutledge says. No witnesses to prove his story, I reckon?"

"Are you going to take the word of any one or all of that durned Moss outfit against his?"

"I'm taking nobody's word for anything these days," Manders replied. "I'll believe anything if it's proved to me good and plenty."

"If you feel like believing it," Pendleton amended.

"Referring to that little matter of Mart Brown, I presume. A thing that's not so can't be proved, and

228

since Mart didn't kill Joe Shear, what evidence you produced didn't get anywhere with me. Fact is, I knew it all before you told me."

"You knew more than that, Sheriff," Jim cut in. "You knew who one of the men outside the window of the Longhorn that night was."

Manders turned cold, fishy eyes on the young Texan. Not a flicker of expression crossed his face.

"Did I?" he asked evenly.

"You knew — and I suspected," Jim retorted.

"The young detective getting in his work again," the officer murmured sarcastically.

"Yes, I only suspected then. Now I, too, know."

"Going to find another man for me that stabbed Shear, are you?" Manders jeered.

"I don't know. I hope not."

The eyes of the two men met and held.

"Who is it this time?"

"This time it's Sheriff Manders."

"So I killed Shear, eh?"

"I haven't said so."

"Spill it, young fellow — whatever's on your mind."

"Understand, I'm making no charges, Sheriff," Jim said. "I'm mentioning a few facts and citing what your friend Mr. Brown calls a hypothetical case."

"I don't give a billy-be-damn about your hypothetical case. Let's hear your facts."

"Let's go back for a motive first," Jim said, his steel-ribbed eyes hard as agates. "You had a real one. If you beat Shear for sheriff — an' it looks to me like you would have — it was only a question of time until he killed you, *unless you killed him first*."

"So I stuck a knife in him in the dark to save my own bacon," the sheriff said harshly.

Jim disregarded the interruption. "To go against Shear in the open would have been just plain suicide. They tell me he could let any other man get his pistol out before he drew and still beat him to the shot. A man might figure it would be fair to get rid of Shear before the marshal deviled him into being murdered."

"He might, if he had no guts," Manders agreed. "I'm not interested in your guesses but your facts. Unload them."

"All right. Someone standing outside the window fired the shot that blew out the light in the card room at the Longhorn. You were at the window. Can you prove to me you didn't fire that gun?"

"How do you know I was at the window?" the sheriff demanded.

"You had yore boots reheeled yesterday, Mr. Manders," Jim said quietly. "I wondered why, so I went round to the cobbler's and got the old heels."

"Smart as a whip," the officer commented with savage irony.

From his pocket Jim took one of the worn-out heels. "Here's one of them. Would you mind letting me see if this fits the impression in the plaster labeled *Exhibit 2?*"

The sheriff did not bat an eye. "Too bad. I was careless about those casts and left them in a corner of the room on the floor. The black boy who does the janitor work swept them out."

Jim was as cool as Manders. Not so Pendleton. The big cattleman let out a roar of anger.

"And accidentally they got smashed, I suppose," Jim said, smiling grimly.

"Just what happened. How did you guess it? Of course I read the riot act to the boy, though that didn't do any good."

"I'll bet you did," Jim acquiesced.

He took the news cheerfully.

It was Pendleton who slammed a hamlike fist on the table in excitement. "I don't want any more proof, Manders. You're guilty as the devil. Either you're standing in with Mart Brown, or —"

"Or?" suggested the sheriff, eyes opaque and hard as stones.

"You can't bully me, Manders. I say what I think."

"And you think?"

"I think you smashed those casts because you were scared of what they would prove."

"Go slow, Texas man," Manders warned. "I mentioned an accident, though I'll admit personal negligence on my part."

"Don't blame yoreself too much, Sheriff," Jim said casually. "The damage is not beyond repair." He could do a little in irony himself.

"I reckon your exhibits are pretty completely smashed," the officer said, with mock regret.

"You'll be glad to know we've got another set of the prints."

"What!" roared Pendleton, staring at Jim.

Manders could not wholly conceal his disturbance. "Did you say another set of plaster casts?"

"That's what I said," Jim drawled. "Funny, but I figured something might happen to the first ones."

The sheriff did not lift his hard gaze from the insouciant youth. "Go on," he ordered. "Put your cards on the table."

Jim looked down at the heel in his hand. "I reckon this one wouldn't fit the impression we have, but the mate of it would. And did — like a hand fits a glove."

"You're slick, young fellow," Manders said. "How do I know you're not lying? How do I know you've got duplicate casts?"

"You don't," Jim came back. "But I reckon you'll take my word for it. I'm not a plumb fool, Sheriff. I'll say that I've been noticing the heels of yore boots for se-ve-real days. Do you think it likely we'd put in yore hands evidence like this until we were sure of you?"

"And you claim the mate to this heel fits one of the tracks you've taken?"

"Fits it to a T. Nobody knows that better than you do. When I saw yore brand-new heels resting on the table here yesterday I decided I'd like to have the old ones for souvenirs. So I went an' got them."

"I knew I ought to keep you locked up," the sheriff said by way of comment. "You're the world's champion busybody. It beats me how you've managed to live so long."

"Well, you didn't keep me locked up. It's too late now."

232

Manders drew toward him the newspaper lying on the desk. "I'm not so sure about that. Hickman and I don't usually agree, but he may be right this time. *Sheriff Manders, do your duty,* he says, meaning for me to bear down hard on Mr. James Rutledge. I've got a notion to do it."

"And you've got a better notion not to," Jim answered, his boyish grin working. "You put yore cards on the table, too, Sheriff, unless they're marked ones you daren't show. First off, I take it for granted you claim you're innocent of killing Shear."

"I didn't kill him, but as Mart Brown says, I'd subscribe to a gold medal for the fellow who did — if I knew who he was."

"And Brown didn't kill him, by yore way of it?"

"No, nor Brown either."

"If that's the case, what are you worrying about? Come clean with what evidence you've got and work with us."

"Get this right, young fellow," Manders corrected hardily. "I'm not worrying."

"If you killed Shear or helped do it, my evidence is poison to you. If not, we'll dig in and find out who did. It's up to you, Sheriff."

Manders looked steadily at him. "I'll go you. We'll send for Mart and make it a showdown," he said.

CHAPTER
TWENTY-NINE

Three Suspects Table Their Cards

The Sheriff and Mart Brown had a long whispering conference before they joined Rutledge and Pendleton.

"We've got very little new to tell you," Manders began. "This young sleuth here worked the whole thing out pretty straight. Mart has told you his story. Fact is, he was making for Shear himself in the dark when he bumped up against the fellow who beat him to it."

"I was leaning against him when the fellow drove the knife into Shear's heart," Brown added. "I want to tell you I never was so surprised in my life. It gave me a jolt, and it didn't take me long to see that it was my job to make a quick getaway. I must have followed the fellow right out of the window."

"It was too dark to recognize the man, I expect," Jim suggested.

Brown waved his hand with a debonair flip of the fingers. "Not interested in recognizing him," he said. "Probably he wouldn't care for my thanks anyhow."

"What makes you think he went out of the window?"

"Maybe he stayed right there. Perhaps you can correct me on that point."

Jim smiled. "As it happens, I can't. Was he a big man?"

"I couldn't swear to that," Brown said.

"I savvy. Anything more to tell us?"

"Nothing except that just as I reached the street I saw the sheriff just ahead of me."

"Going the same way as you?"

"Going right out of the alley between the buildings, four or five feet ahead of me."

"Did you speak to him?"

"I said, 'Drift into the Longhorn. Maybe you'll be surprised.' "

"What did he answer?"

"Said he knew some fellows had been shooting up the place. I told him he'd better go in and learn some good news."

"Was that all either of you said?"

"Yes. He went in the front door of the Longhorn, and I lit out for the Green Parrot. I stayed there maybe half an hour, then went home and got out of my Blackbeard costume."

"Did you think then that the sheriff had killed Shear?"

"No. I thought some fellow who had been in the room all the time had done it. But afterward I wasn't so sure. Someone from the alley shot out the lamp. After I talked with Al I knew he hadn't done it."

"Why?"

"He told me he hadn't."

"You think he would tell the truth about it if he had?"

"He'd tell *me* the truth," the gambler amended. "Why not? It would be safe, and he knew it would. When you told me about the footprints of a third man outside the window I knew he was the fellow that shot out the light and might be the one who had knifed Shear."

"But you don't know who he is?"

"Not the least idea. I'd like to know, too, for my own satisfaction."

"Must have been some mighty close connections," Jim said. "How did it happen this third party and the sheriff didn't meet?"

"Did the third party tell you we didn't meet?" Manders asked with obvious sarcasm.

Jim's eyes were shining. "You mean you did meet him?"

"He brushed by me as he was making his getaway."

"You'd know him again?"

"No, I wouldn't. I was coming up between the buildings from the back alley when he went by me. It was dark."

"You didn't try to stop him?"

"Why should I try to stop him? I knew there had been some shooting, but I didn't know he had anything to do with it."

"When did you find out what it was?"

"As I stood a moment at the window I heard someone inside say some cowboys had shot out the lights. I didn't wait, but passed right on to Front Street.

Thought I'd better get inside and see what had happened."

Jim flung a sharp question at him. "How did you happen to come up along the side of the Longhorn?"

The officer smiled blandly. "Mrs. Rutledge was responsible for my being there."

"My wife," Jim said blankly.

"Not your wife then. She'd met me a few minutes before and told me her brother Steve was losing a lot of money to Shear and Buck Roe at poker. She'd begged me to go in and get the boy out so she could talk to him. I saw she was worried, but I couldn't do a thing. A man has to stand on his own feet in this town. But I was kind of curious, too. I passed down the street and then along the alley back of the Longhorn. At first I thought I'd go in the back door. But I didn't want to seem to be watching the party. So I thought I would pass the card-room window and take a look in. I couldn't have got in anyhow by the back door. Folks were crowding out to get away from the Circle R hurrah boys shooting up the place."

Jim nodded. It was a plausible enough story and might be true.

"Are you trying to find out who the fellow was that brushed by you?" Pendleton asked bluntly.

"I'm sheriff, Pendleton," the officer returned curtly. "It's my business to find him. And if he turned out to be one of the Moss outfit I'd be right glad to put cuffs on him."

"You think he was one of them?" Jim asked.

"I think old man Moss or one of his gang did this job, and I'd certainly like to hang it on him."

"You don't mean you think old Dave did it personally?"

"Probably not. More likely had it done. If you asked me to put a name to the killer, my first choice would be Buck Roe. It had to be someone with guts, someone cold-blooded and nervy. He was nearer Shear than anyone else."

"That wouldn't matter — unless the boy detective here was near him too," Brown said, with a sly smile. "It all comes back to Rutledge. His knife did the job. Question is, who had a chance to get the knife? When you are talking about me or Roe or Sam Moss or young Pete or you, Al, as suspects you have to remember that the guilty party had to find Rutledge's hog-sticker in the dark and then find Shear. That's asking a good deal. The point is that the boy detective didn't have one of these difficulties to contend with. The knife was already found. Maybe he slipped up on the other one at that and did not kill the man he was after. Roe had threatened his life. Pete Moss was after his girl. He might have been trying to get either one or the other and in the darkness made a mistake."

The gambler grinned cheerfully at Jim. The smile meant, *How do you like that, young fellow?*

"Fact is, we're all three still under suspicion and each claims he didn't do it," Jim summed up. "My opinion is that none of us did, in spite of the evidence. Do you agree with that, gentlemen? Let's come clean."

238

"I've seen men hanged on less evidence than there is against you, Rutledge," the sheriff said bluntly. "But I don't think you killed Shear. Same goes as to Mart. I know I didn't."

"Why did you have yore boots reheeled, then?" asked Pendleton brusquely.

"Because your young friend was getting warm and I didn't care to have any questions raised that would confuse the issue."

"How about you, Mr. Brown?" Jim asked.

"I can't claim the honor myself," Brown admitted lightly. "Sorry, but I can't tell a lie. Someone else did in Shear. I don't think Al did it. As to you, young fellow, suspicion certainly points a finger straight at you. But I'm an accommodating cuss. Like to oblige a friend. I'll vote not guilty, with the privilege of changing my mind if I find it necessary later. Will that do?"

"That'll do," Rutledge said. "I'm reserving that privilege myself about Blackbeard. My idea is that we should pool our efforts from this time and concentrate on the Moss outfit as suspects. In the bottom of our hearts we all think some of them did it. What say?"

"It's a deal," Brown flung out instantly.

"Still trying to be sheriff, Rutledge," the officer grumbled. "There's no way of heading you off. All right. I'm with you. It's understood any one of us can draw out if he serves notice."

From a pocket Jim drew an envelope. It contained a cloth button, one edge of which was marked with a white streak. The button was on a cardboard, and underneath it was written neatly: *Exhibit 8*.

"Mr. Pendleton and Dr. Aubrey found this button on the ground outside the card-room window of the Longhorn. It lay in one of the footprints, so it must have fallen there after the track was made."

"In which track?" Manders asked quickly.

"In the one of the unidentified man."

Brown whistled softly. He was thinking that the button lying on the table might hang a murderer.

"The button didn't come from the pirate costume," Jim said. "It was torn from someone's coat as he jumped up to get in the window. Caught on the ledge and rubbed the whitewash off where it caught. You're wearing the same clothes you were the night of the killing, Mr. Manders, and the buttons on yore coat are bone not covered by cloth. That proves you're not the man."

The brown eyes of the owner of the Green Parrot were alive with interest. "Begad, you've struck a lead sure enough this time, young fellow. I give you good on that. You've proved the button came from the coat of the unknown man outside and that it was probably dragged off as he climbed in the window. By the way, the Longhorn is whitewashed, I reckon?"

"Yes," Pendleton told him.

"What was this fellow doing in the room? Why did he leave before the candles came? He was killing Shear. That's what he was doing. Find the fellow wearing the coat this button came from and you've got the man you are looking for, Al." A quick excitement had come into the voice and manner of the gambler.

240

"Suppose the man missed the button and had a new set put on his coat," the sheriff suggested.

"Not likely. He wouldn't know where he had lost it. Very good chance he knew it was loose before that night and was not surprised when he found it missing. Button, button, who's lost the button?" Brown misquoted gaily. "It'll be my favorite game from today for a while."

As Jim walked downtown with Pendleton the cattleman offered an opinion: "I still think Mart Brown killed Shear. Take his story to pieces. Is it likely two men were in the card room trying to kill Joe in the dark at the same time? We've got to believe that before we accept his story. He practically admits he had moved back of the marshal intending to get him."

"It's improbable," Jim agreed. "But this whole thing is full of improbabilities. One of them is that in this age a man would be walking the streets who had killed twenty-four men. He had enemies everywhere. Shear, I mean. The chances are that this was the first time he had ever let himself be caught in a dark room filled with men."

Pendleton grunted, a grunt incredulous.

CHAPTER
THIRTY

Jerry Denver Returns

Jim let Mrs. Glen answer the knock on the door. These days he was being very watchful about such things. It would be easy for someone to stand back in the porch shadows and pump lead into his body as he stood in the light of the hall.

"Jim Rutledge in?" a voice asked.

At once Jim recognized the speaker. "Come right in, Jerry," he called. "When d'you get back?"

Jerry Denver followed him into the sitting-room. He clumped in in high-heeled boots, but otherwise he was in "store clothes" except for his wide hat.

"On the evening train. I had a man's work to do with a steak smothered in onions, but after that I came right up. Hear you've done gone and ruined a young lady's life."

Ellen came smiling into the room and hoped it wasn't true. She was, she said, bearing up very well so far.

"What's the good word from Newton?" Jim asked.

"No luck, far as that tinhorn Black goes. If he an' Joe Shear ever had a run-in, the fact's not known in Newton."

242

"About what I expected," Jim admitted. "Have to cross him off our list of suspects, I reckon."

"But I bumped into something that's maybe right important. Young fellow called Slim Rogers roomed where I did. The place was crowded, so the landlady put us together. He's one of the Moss crowd, an' I kinda played around with him. The boy was some oneasy in his mind. I could see that. One night he got all corned up an' spilled the beans. He was scared of old Devil Dave, an' was laying holed up at Newton."

"What was he afraid of?" Jim asked, much interested.

Jerry looked at Ellen hesitantly.

"I'll leave if you like," she said quickly.

Jim put his brown hand on hers with a swift pressure. "You can say anything you like before my wife," he told the cowboy.

"It cost me about a pint of tanglefoot to find out," Jerry went on. "He's scared because he knows too much."

"About the Shear business?"

Denver nodded. "He happened to go to the Moss house that night to ask when young Dave was coming to town. Seems he always has walked right in without knocking. Someone was talkin' in the back room where some of the boys sleep. Slim opened the door an' saw Sam with the old man. There was a basin on the table and a towel. Either Dave or Sam had been washing his hands. Soon as the old man saw Slim he threw the towel over the bowl and covered it. But he was too late. One of the two had been scrubbing blood from his hands."

"What time was this?" Jim asked.

"Slim couldn't give me the time, but he says he was on Front Street inside of five minutes an' heard that Shear had just been killed."

"Why didn't Sam an' the old man hear him coming?"

"He saw a light in the boys' room from outside, an' thinking the boys were in he got some fool notion of surprising them. So he tiptoed in. When he come to think it over afterward he got scared for fear he'd get what Shear had. So he lit out. Seems he'd been trying to break away anyhow an' couldn't quite make the riffle."

"Why not?"

"Search me. Reckon the old man had something on him."

"I'll bet he didn't leave any too soon," Jim said. "Think of him walkin' in on that suspicious old bird right then, and tiptoeing in at that, like he was spying on him. I'd stay holed up if I was Slim. He's certainly a bad insurance risk right now."

"Of course, next mornin' he denied everything he told me. Claimed he had been stringin' me. But me, I know when a man's scared. He jumped whenever a man came into the room onexpected. Figures they'll follow an' bump him off soon as they find out where he's at."

"Is he intending to stay at Newton? Can we find him there when we want him?"

"Don't know about that. He'll hop off like a flea if he gets a notion the old man knows where he's at."

"I'm surely much obliged to you, Jerry. You've done good work. How much do I owe you?"

Jerry mentioned the amount of his expenses and intimated that he would accept no more.

"Glad to do what I can for you," he said. "I never did like the Moss outfit anyhow. The whole caboodle of 'em wouldn't have stood up to Joe Shear in the open. Say what you want to about him, he'd go through from hell to breakfast. But of course he didn't stand a chance against old Devil Dave workin' in the dark. Say, boy, I hear you had a run-in with the bunch while I was away. Cleaned up on 'em, didn't you?"

"They jumped me an' I ran away, if you call that cleaning up on them," Jim answered. "I took a wild shot in the dark and hit Sam. They gave it out that he was badly hurt, but Doc Aubrey says the bullet made a clean shoulder wound."

"An' Buck Roe?"

"Buck bumped into something hard in my hand as I was hightailin' it down the street. He's mad as a bear with a sore paw but otherwise undamaged, they say."

"Well, if there's anything more I can do for you, let me know."

"I can think of one or two things I'd like, but you can't get them for me, Jerry."

"For instance?"

"For instance, the left-foot boots of Sam Moss and his dad. I'd be obliged if you could borrow the loan of them for me."

The cowboy shook his head. "I ain't on borrowing terms with them." He grinned. "You get 'em yore own self, boy. You're on their visitin' list an' go on night frolics with them."

"The only thing they want to loan me is bullets. We're on shooting terms, but otherwise social relations are a little strained, as the old fellow said to the bear that had him treed."

"I'm awf'ly worried," Ellen told the cowboy. "It's all very well for Jim to make jokes about it, but I can't laugh at them when I know old Dave is sitting up in his room thinking up ways to — to trap my husband."

"Take him away from here, ma'am," advised Jerry.

"He won't go."

"I'll go soon as I've proved Dave or Sam Moss killed Shear," promised Jim.

And with that she had to be content.

As Jerry left the house a buggy drew up in front of it. Dr. Aubrey descended from it and walked to the front porch with the precise even gait that marked him. He could have carried water on both shoulders.

"How is yore patient, Doctor?" Ellen asked.

He smiled at her and cleared his throat. "I have more than one," he told her.

"I was thinking of Sam Moss," she said.

"Sam appears to be doing well physically, but like all of the family with whom I come in contact he appears mentally disturbed, consumed by an irritable restlessness. I have observed this in his father and in his younger brother Peter. There is a rumor that Peter has been disappointed in love, but I hardly think that would explain his father's unease."

246

Ellen blushed and laughed. "I don't suppose old Dave ever was in love. He was born superior to such weaknesses. I'm glad Sam is better."

"So am I," agreed Jim. "Any news about that other little matter, Doctor?"

"Negative news," the doctor replied. "But even negative information is sometimes positive. When a physician finds certain symptoms lacking in a case under examination he can eliminate possibilities and concentrate on others."

"Yes," agreed Jim. He would have liked to eliminate verbiage just now, but Dr. Aubrey told a story his own way and could not be hurried.

"I found my opportunity this morning by sending the nurse out of the room for some hot water. My patient was reading the newspaper, though I can't say that he seemed to find much pleasure in it. His boots were at the foot of the bed. I observed that they had large feet with long pointed heels set well forward. From my bag I took the plaster cast labeled *Exhibit 1* and attempted to fit the sole of the boot into the depression. It would not fit at all. The boot is much narrower than the one that made the print outside the Longhorn."

Jim's eyes sparkled with excitement. "Let's Sam out. Old Devil Dave killed Shear himself."

"Yes," breathed Ellen. "But can we prove it?"

"I'll follow his trail till we do," the young man promised. "Things are breaking our way at last. Wonder if the sheriff could arrange to have him come to the office while I was there."

"You let old Dave alone," Ellen said, smiling admonishment at her newly acquired husband. "He's a wolf, an' he'd just eat you up."

"I know I'm a lamb 'side of Devil Dave," Jim admitted. "Still, at that, I'd like to have a talk with him."

He was to have his wish before he was many hours older, under circumstances that were to send a shock of terror through his heart.

CHAPTER
THIRTY-ONE

The Spider's Web

Figures buzzed in the head of Jim Rutledge. They covered sheets of paper that littered the table. They flowed from the end of a pencil in computations of addition, subtraction, and multiplication. For he was making up the accounts of the long trail drive, preparatory to sending his cowboys back to Texas.

A worn notebook with a record of daily expenses supplied the data for his bookkeeping. In it was set down all the money advanced to his riders for tobacco, boots, socks, shirts, medicine, and night-life remittances. The total for medicine was fifty cents, to buy pennyroyal for mosquitoes. The amount turned over to the boys for purposes of diversion ran to many hundred dollars.

He heard a knock on the front door. Ellen had gone with Mrs. Glen to a strawberries-and-cream church festival, leaving Jim alone to wrestle out his financial statement. He had been sitting where no shadow from the lighted lamp would betray his position to any foe outside. Now he moved lightly toward the hall, craned his head forward a few inches, and called, "Who's there?"

It was possible that a crash of bullets might answer his question and he preferred not to be in the line of them.

"Jimmy Bissell," a high boyish voice replied. "Got a note for you, if you're Mr. Rutledge."

"Who from?"

"From Miss Mamie Dugan."

"Anyone with you?"

"No, sir."

"Shove it under the door and wait there till I've read it. If it's all right, I've got a quarter for you," Jim told him.

He tiptoed forward, picked up the note, and retreated noiselessly to the light.

The envelope was pink and scented. Jim ripped it open and read:

Señor Bridegroom, come quick to the cottonwoods south of the track. Do not fail me. I will speak with you, for one little minute, on my way to the Elkhorn tonight. The little jug is corked not so tight now. Me, I am not afraid of old Devil Dave. What can he do to me, who am the darling of the town? But come quick, my friend, oh yes.

Not yet have I found the Prince Around the Corner.

Below, cramped in for lack of space and running around the lower edge of the note, was an injunction:

Bring this letter with you.

The note was not signed. It needed no name to tell the young man who was the sender. The references to the little jug and to the prince around the corner could be known only to Mamie Dugan and himself.

Quietly Jim went his soft-footed way to the door and flung it open. A revolver was in his hand, though it still rested in the scabbard.

The boy was not there. He had not waited for the promised tip. Why? Jim did not like that. A quarter is two bits, and even if Jimmy had been paid at the other end he would be glad to collect again. So would any normal boy.

Jim had wanted to ask the lad a question or two. He would have been interested to know whether Mamie Dugan had given the note to the boy herself and whether it had been seen by anybody else since that time. Now he had to take this for granted.

Young Rutledge went back into the house and re-read the message. Mamie had written it with fear knocking at her heart. That was plain, though she had tried to push the dread of it from her under a mask of gaiety. She had something to tell, something that would incriminate Dave Moss or his son. That was written in the words of her note. But back of them lay a cry for help against forces sinister and threatening, too powerful for her to combat alone. She knew she was in peril, though she tried to laugh it away.

Then, of a sudden, Jim saw, back of the written words on that trivial perfumed paper, something at once curious and dreadful. The lines blurred, became a web. From the depths there seemed to swim up a creature resembling a spider. Before his eyes it changed to a face of a human being, a face leering and distorted and malignant. For one instant he saw it before the illusion vanished.

With swift economy of motion he made his preparations. He looked to his weapons. He wrote a two-line note to Ellen telling her where he was going and pinned it to the back of the sofa.

Out of the back door he slipped, after having scanned closely the immediate vicinity. Dusk had given way to the growing darkness of night. Jim moved swiftly and warily. He crossed Front Street, making a circuit to avoid the better-lit parts of town. The railroad grade came to meet him out of the unrevealed background. It lay behind him now. The cottonwood grove was close, over to the left.

He was conscious of a growing excitement. There were both suspense and dread in the emotion that had set his heart beating fast. Some bell within rang a warning that the fateful hour was about to strike.

The vague shadows of the cottonwoods loomed ahead. His fingers rested on the handle of a revolver as he passed into them. There was no hesitation in his step. Precautions would not serve him now. Every tree was potential cover for an enemy.

Out of the darkness appeared her figure, an indistinct blur of white outlined hazily. Her dress, he thought. He drew a deep breath of relief, and as he strode forward called softly her name.

She did not answer. She did not move toward him. There was a strange stiffness in the way she stood.

252

Again he spoke her name, and as he did so fear caught at his throat. Why did she make no sound, no motion? Through him there shuddered a stark and naked terror.

His staring eyes ratified a moment later that flood of fear. There was a rope around her neck and she was hanging from a cottonwood, the toes of her shoes just scraping the ground.

He stood frozen with horror, his heart drumming against his ribs. For one instant he was motionless before he sprang to action. As he ran forward to raise the body he caught sight of an ace of spades pinned to the bosom. A sound that was neither a cry nor an oath broke from his lips. It was more like a moan of utter despair.

Low laughter mocked his wail. That sinister mirth fell on his ears with shocking impact. It had in it something fiendish and inhuman.

Echoes of that glee ringed him around. He was surrounded, trapped, marked for destruction. If his enemies had been less sure of him they would have bound and disarmed him before they exulted.

Even then, with the certainty that he was doomed strong on him, his senses registered the fact that Mamie Dugan was dead, had been killed before the rope had been put around her neck. The stain on the white dress told him so.

CHAPTER
THIRTY-TWO

Devil Dave Enjoys Himself

"You keep yore appointments prompt, Mr. Rutledge," a low voice jeered.

The voice was one he had never heard before, but as his Scotch mother would have said, it gave him a scunner. A chill ran up and down his spine.

Jim repressed an impulse to reach for his revolver. The least offensive gesture on his part would send bullets crashing into his body. He must play for time, in the hope that some chance circumstance might upset the plan of his enemies.

They came out into the open, four of them, three from behind trees, the other dropping from the branches of a cottonwood. Two he knew, Buck Roe and Pete Moss. The third, a dark sullen man with straight black hair, must be the oldest Moss son, Clay. The last was old Devil Dave himself. Jim had never seen him, but he had no doubt whatever that the great shapeless body and the evil leering face belonged to the villain against whom his father had warned him.

254

"You murdered her," Jim charged, the words vibrant with horror.

"We — executed her," the old man corrected with suave cruelty. "How did you ever guess it?"

Though he spoke in a low tone, exultation leaped out at the young man. They had killed her. They would kill him! Devil Dave counted him already dead or he would never have made such an admission. It was intended that Jim draw this inference, and he did.

"You spawn of hell!" young Rutledge cried.

Dave smiled. He was well contented that this lad should rave at him.

"Free yore mind," he urged with malicious suavity. "Don't mind pore Dave's feelings. Take the lid right off yore can of cuss words."

"Better disarm him, hadn't we?" Clay suggested to his father.

"I reckon, if he'll excuse the liberty."

They took his weapons from him. Then, with a sudden violent oath, Buck Roe brought the barrel of Jim's own .45 crashing down on his head.

"You wiped me with it. See how you like it yore own self," Roe cried savagely.

Jim staggered. He would have fallen except for the hands that steadied him.

Their talk came to him through a mist.

"He's got more than that comin' to him from me," one voice said. "I've a mind, right damn now, to —"

A laugh cut short the threat. "Hold yore horses, Buck. We don't want a dead man on our hands — yet. Not till he's had time to savvy what he's up against.

Me, Devil Dave, I've got a few things to say to him first."

"We'd better finish the job an' get out," one of his sons said. "This is no healthy place for us to camp long."

"We'll finish it when I say so an' not till then," the old man answered, each word dripping rancor. "Don't get in a sweat an' pull yore picket pin, young fellow."

The blood ran down the side of Jim's head and along his cheek. It came to him that he must control both his anger and his horror. He must meet whatever was in store for him with cold disdain. Any display of weakness would be meat and drink to the hate of Dave Moss and his allies.

"You back again with us, Mr. Rutledge?" the old guerrilla asked with revolting silkiness. "None the worse for Buck's love tap? Good! We're having a nice friendly little powwow before you — say good night. I don't hardly know where to begin, we've got so much gossip to swap. Might go back to the days when yore dad did me so many good turns. A fellow had ought to pay his debts. I reckon I'll pay some of mine to Chan tonight. An' while I think of it, have you got any messages for him, *in case you might be delayed seeing him again?*"

Buck Roe laughed, cruelly.

Jim looked at the old man and said nothing. He was chaining up within him the fear and the terror that had for a minute ridden his soul.

"No messages?" old Moss went on. "Suit yoreself. Yes, I owe Chan a lot. He! He! What with one thing an' another, quite a lot." He stopped to chuckle again with hateful glee.

If he expected his prisoner to say anything he was disappointed.

"I don't aim to go all over the score," Moss continued. "He finished off by killing my nephew Slim Gorham last year. Then you started in business. You had a little luck, and you got a notion you was a kind of young Napoleon, I reckon, and could buck up against me. That was certainly bad medicine. You ain't the first, by quite a few. There was Joe Shear for one. Quite a man, Joe! Twenty-four notches on his gun. But he didn't last two days after I made up my mind. Went out like that." The old man snapped his fingers carelessly.

"You didn't even stop at murdering women," Jim said, his voice edged with icy contempt. "Four big men to rob the life from one happy little girl. Boast of that, too, you devil!"

The younger men winced at the thrust, but the old one did not bat an eyelash. His unctuous voice flowed on. "Ah! The little jug is corked tight now. In the regrettably few minutes left you, think of this for a moment. *You* killed her. You must have the cork out of the little jug, and so — alas! — we are forced to drive the cork in permanently."

"You got hold of her note to me somehow," Jim said.

"Do you take me for a fool? That is not a wise mistake to make. When she became dangerous, I had her watched. Naturally I stopped her messenger and added one line to the note. I told you to bring it back with you. You have it? Excuse me if I help myself to it."

Pete retrieved the note and handed it to his father. Dave glanced at it and put the envelope in his pocket.

Young Rutledge looked at the Moss boys, cold contempt in his eyes. He spoke, as though to himself. "I'd have expected it of the old man, for he's a cold blooded murderer, a Comanche at heart. But I didn't think it of them, even if they have Moss blood in their veins."

"I didn't kill her," Pete blurted out. "I wasn't here."

"Nor I," his brother cried.

They hated Jim Rutledge. Within a few minutes they meant to destroy him, but they could not let him go to his death thinking they had killed a woman in cold blood.

"I did it, if you want to know," the old man spoke up, with his terrible inhuman smile. "Man or woman, neither can betray me and get away with it. Knowin' the boys are thin-skinned, I had the little jug corked before they got here. Maybe it will interest you to know that you're going to get the credit for it."

"I?" Jim said.

"You. Reckon you don't know it, but you're going to commit suicide in about five minutes."

"What do you mean?"

"You're going to shoot yoreself through the heart."

"You mean you're going to shoot me."

"Have it yore own way," Devil Dave grinned, "but when they find you the gun will be in yore hand with yore elbow crooked."

Buck Roe explained. "You killed the lady first, an' then got scared an' shot yoreself."

258

"Nobody will believe any such story," Jim said scornfully.

"Now I wonder about that," old Moss murmured. "Most people in this town think you killed Joe Shear. They know how you shot my boy Sam and assaulted Buck here, when they were going peaceable about their business. You've got a nice start for a reputation as a bad man. I've a notion this atrocious murder you've just committed will fit in with the rest of the story. The town is going to hold up its hands in horror at you. Here you are, just married to a real nice girl, and all the time carryin' on an intrigue with another woman you have deceived. You're afraid it's going to get out, so you put the poor girl out of yore way. Seems terrible you're so young an' such a criminal. You'd ought to thank me for helping you to commit suicide, for you'd certainly be lynched by popular indignation."

"If you were sure of that, you'd leave me to be hanged," Jim said.

"Right you are," Dave agreed. "But I've got no real confidence in the citizens of this town. I gave them one chance to do it when Joe Shear was found killed by yore knife. An' they lay down on the job. Fact is, I'd like to hang you myself, but that wouldn't fit in with my plans so well. A man can't hardly hang himself convincingly. So I reckon you've got to blow out what brains you have."

"You're a black-hearted villain," Jim told him. "You can shoot me, but you can't make folks believe I killed that poor girl. They'll know better. Why, I've never seen her but twice."

He spoke with apparent confidence, but his assurance was of manner only. This old fox-wolf would have evidence to back his charges, most of it manufactured for the occasion.

"So you say," Devil Dave tittered. "Shows what a slick young scoundrel you were that you all the time met her under cover. Don't worry. I'll have witnesses. Why, you called on her hardly an hour after yore marriage. Why? To square it with her if you could. You were so crazy about her you went to the show at the Elkhorn Theater that same night an' left yore poor deceived bride at home. A dozen witnesses can swear to that. You sure must be a wicked young hell-hound. I've got here in my pocket a letter written by Mamie Dugan to you, on pink paper, beggin' you not to desert her after she's been to you all she has. She says she hears you're makin' up to another girl but she can't believe it's true, seeing how you swore to love her always when you betrayed her. It's a right touching letter, if I do say it myself. I'm proud of it. Did I mention that it will be found in yore pocket when the body of deceased is discovered?"

"Meaning me?" Jim asked casually. He was afraid, to the marrow, but he did not mean to let this man know it.

"Who else but you?"

"Everyone will know it's a forgery."

"My bets are laid the other way. O' course Chan Rutledge will claim it's forged, but I don't reckon he'll hardly believe it himself. This whole business is liable to be some shock to Chan." The cachinnations of the old man's evil mirth sent a shiver through the blood of his young enemy. There was a note of the abnormal about that glee, such as might have come from one of the creatures of the inferno. "Seems he's raised a viper in his bosom. Te-he! Being so chock full of pride as he is, it'll hurt him consid'rable. Stickin' yore knife in Joe Shear wasn't so bad. He was yore uncle, though maybe you don't know it, and it was all in the family. But sheathing it in popular young ladies is some different."

Pete shifted unhappily on his feet. He was sick at heart over the horrible thing his father had done and he did not want to listen to scurrilous jests. "Time we finished him an' lit out," he said in a low voice.

Once more his father lashed out angrily. "Keep yore trap shut. I'll roll my own hoop."

"I ain't so stuck on this job I want to stay all night on it," Roe cut in. "You didn't tell us about — about the young lady when we started in on it. Me, personal, Buck Roe, I'm aimin' to light out *muy pronto* for somewheres remote. I don't like being mixed up in it."

"Would you want me to sit still and let the girl squawk? That yore notion, Buck?" the old man wanted to know, bleak eyes fixed on the other.

"I ain't sayin' what I'd want to do, Dave. Point is, this town is gonna stand on its head about Mamie Dugan. I hadn't a thing to do with it, so I reckon I'll slide out kinda inconspicuous soon as I can."

"You poor fool, don't you see you've got to stick around an' sit tight? If you run off, you might as well print it in the newspapers that you did it. About the other job — I'll be ready in a minute. Just a word more with Mr. Rutledge before he leaves us." Dave turned to Jim, exuding exultation. "I've studied the young lady's writing. You know she was right flirty and yours wasn't the only affair she had going. My boy Sam was waitin' on her, but his intentions were honorable, not like yours. So, like I say, I've seen some of her notes to him. If she didn't write this letter begging you to be square with her, it's a dead ringer for one she might have written. Wish I had time to show you how the letters are made exactly like she always made them. But the boys are in a hurry, and I can't keep 'em waiting."

Jim looked steadily at him. If the heart had died in his breast he did not mean to give Devil Dave the satisfaction of knowing it. But he played for time, to give himself the benefit of that millionth chance of rescue.

"So you killed Joe Shear, too! I thought it all the time. Do it yoreself?" he asked quietly.

"No harm telling you." Dave laughed. "You'll never spread the story. But we're shy of time to go into particulars. Hang on to his arms, boys. I want this bullet to go just right. Doc Aubrey has got to be satisfied he fired it himself."

"My father will settle with you for this," Jim said quietly.

"Don't fool yoreself, boy," Devil Dave cackled. "I aim to get him, too, right soon."

"What's that?" asked Clay nervously. "Listen."

On the light night breeze there drifted to them a ripple of girlish laughter followed by the deeper notes of a man's mirth. A pair of lovers had come down to the grove to be alone.

"Got to do it quick," Buck said.

Jim lifted his voice in a shout. "Help! Help! They're murdering me."

The barrel of Buck's revolver crashed down on his head and he passed out of the picture. But that cry had for the moment saved the boy's life. It had upset the plan of Devil Dave. Suicide would no longer serve as a tenable theory to account for his death if he were to be shot and left here.

His foes gathered up the supine body and took it with them.

CHAPTER
THIRTY-THREE

Chandler Rutledge Makes a Promise

Ellen and Mrs. Glen came home early from the church strawberry festival. The young wife had been uneasy in her mind ever since she had left Jim. The only reason she had gone to the supper was that he had laughed at her anxiety and made fun of it. She did not want to be fussy, but she was content only when she could see him or, if it was night, only when she could reach her hand out and know he was near. The great love she felt for him sometimes rose and choked her throat, for she was haunted by the constant dread that some time he would go gaily out of the house to his death, that he would be brought back to her laid low by his enemies.

Tonight her footsteps quickened as soon as she saw the house was dark. He had told her he would be at home working over the accounts of the drive. What had taken place to change his plans? Her fingers trembled while she lit the lamp. Swiftly her glance swept the room, in her bosom a dread of what the light might show. Her eyes fastened to the note pinned to the back of the sofa and she flew across the floor to it. She read:

264

I've been called out, sweetheart, by a message from Mamie Dugan. She wants to tell me something. I'm to meet her in the cottonwood grove south of the track. Probably I'll be back before you read this. If I'm not, don't worry. She is afraid of Devil Dave. He must know she knows too much. I think we're near the end of the long crooked trail we've been following, honey. Soon now.

The signature was *Jim*.

"Oh, I wish he hadn't gone," Ellen cried.

"Gone where, dearie?" Mrs. Glen asked, taking off her bonnet.

"To talk with Mamie Dugan. How does he know it's not a trap? How does he know that awful man isn't waiting for him? Why does he do such foolish things?" she wailed.

Mrs. Glen read the note. It made her, too, uneasy, but she did not say so. Her smile was cheerful.

"So he's going to see another girl and you don't like it," she teased. "I don't know as I blame you. There never was anything prettier in this town than Mamie Dugan. An' they say, though she's a play actress an' part Mexican, that she's a good girl. I hope so. Her friends are a queer lot, except your husband, of course."

Ellen waved aside this persiflage. She was not jealous-minded, and just now her spirits were too low to rise to teasing.

"I can't sit here an' wait for him," she fretted. "Why didn't he say when he left here? Maybe he has been gone for hours. Maybe —"

"Maybe you're a little goose," Mrs. Glen finished for her. "Dearie, you'll learn that a wife has to do a lot of waiting for her husband. An' sometimes with a heavy heart. It's part of the price she pays for marrying him."

The bride walked nervously to the end of the room and back. "I don't want to be silly," she confided. "I don't want him to feel that I'm hanging 'round his neck like a stone, an' that he's not free to do what he wants to. But this is such a dreadful business. They tried to kill him the very night we were married. They'll try again. Just as likely tonight —"

She broke off in a wail.

Ellen jumped, staring big-eyed at her friend. Someone had knocked on the door. She ran to open it.

Harrison Pendleton was there, filling the doorway with his huge bulk.

"Come in," she cried eagerly. "I'm so glad you came, because —"

The big cattleman interrupted. "Want you to meet a friend of mine, who has come all the way from Texas to see you," he shouted jovially.

Ellen looked at the stranger, a big bronzed blue-eyed man in the forceful fifties. That he was a cowman she knew instantly, just as she knew he was one to be trusted out of ten thousand. Her heart began to hammer queerly. There was a look about his face that reminded her of Jim.

"Is it — Mr. Rutledge?" she asked in a small voice.

"That's who — Chan Rutledge, yore husband's dad."

266

"I'm — *so* glad." She celebrated her joy by bursting into tears.

Chandler Rutledge moved forward and took her in his arms. "What's the trouble?" he asked, and the very sound of his deep, strong voice was comforting.

"I'm so worried — all the time — about Jim. They want to — to kill him — that old Dave Moss an' his crowd. An' he's so reckless. But now you're here —"

"We'll fix that up now," Chandler promised, and sealed it with a kiss. He held her from him and looked the girl over smilingly. "If I'd been picking a wife for the young rascal myself I couldn't have done half as well. I want to tell him so. Where is he?"

"That's it," she cried. "He's gone out. I left him here an' went with Mrs. Glen to a church supper. He was doing his accounts an' said he wouldn't leave the house. But he went. Come in, please. There's a note."

Chandler read the message Jim had written. He passed it to Pendleton. "What's to worry about this?" he asked. "D'you think this girl is trickin' him?"

"I don't know. Jim says she's all right. But you know Dave Moss."

"I know him," her father-in-law said grimly. "The worst villain that ever went unhung. Well, girl, don't you worry any more. This is in my hands now. Harrison an' I will drift down to the cottonwoods an' see what's what. We'll have that boy back with you before you could shake a cow's tail twice."

He left her immeasurably comforted. This Texan looked so wise and so strong. No harm could come to his boy now, with Chandler Rutledge to look after him.

She even smiled a little to think what a surprise it would be to Jim to see his father.

But Chandler Rutledge was not smiling. As the door closed after him, he said to his friend, "We'll move fast, Harrison."

"Figure it's some of Devil Dave's dirty work?" the big man asked.

"Don't like the looks of it," Rutledge said crisply. "Sooner I get to Jim the better I'll be satisfied."

"I've a notion the girl's straight," Pendleton said. "Folks say so. She's mighty popular in town. An actress. Plays at the Elkhorn The-ay-ter."

"At that Dave may be using her. It's the kind of thing he'd do, the foxy old wolf. Jim has been crowdin' him some, you say?"

"Chan, that boy of yores is a wonder. He's took every trick yet. For a kid he's got the best head I ever did see. By jinks, it's worth the profits on a herd of four-year-olds to see him dive into this Shear murder mystery an' clear it up step by step. Looked to me, to start with, like they had Jim by the short wool. Done with his knife, and he admitted he had it in his belt. The boy never batted an eye, faced the whole hard-boiled bunch like a thoroughbred. First off, he proved Ellen couldn't have done it. There wasn't any way of clearing himself except by showing who did it, and take my word for it you never saw prettier detective work in yore life. He'd look into this an' that, using his brains, finding evidence, sifting it, never satisfied even when it looked like he had a cinch case against Mart Brown, always askin' whyfors an' then answering them.

I would of sworn he had it fastened on Brown, but I'll be dadgummed if he hasn't got it now so it looks like one of the Moss gang killed Joe. You got a license to be proud of that youngster, Chan."

They were striding fast down the hill to Front Street as they talked.

"Reckon we better go up the street a block or two an' then cross the railroad tracks," Chandler said. He was very much pleased at his friend's praise of Jim, but he was not the man to boast about his own. "He's a right satisfactory boy," was all the indorsement he would give the recital of Pendleton.

"Hello! What's going on down there? Looks like there's some unusual excitement," the big man boomed.

"Might as well pass the crowd on our way down," Rutledge said quietly.

He was a man with nerves of steel, but the blood quickened in his arteries. Excited voices were drifting to him. A moment or two ago there had been seven or eight men in the group. Now it half filled the street. There was furious anger in that dull roar of the human pack. As they drew nearer one unrestrained shout lifted to his ears. "Ought to be burned alive, by God." That there had been tragedy of some sort he did not doubt.

"What's the trouble?" asked one of the Texans.

The man to whom he had spoken turned on him, raging at the news he told. "Mamie Dugan! Knife stuck in her heart. Killed by some hellhound."

"By that Rutledge who killed Joe Shear," another cried. "He left an ace of spades again."

"That's a lie." Chandler's voice rang out sharp and clear. "Devil Dave Moss killed Shear. The ace of spades is his road brand. And Devil Dave killed this girl, you'll find."

"Who are you, stranger?"

"Never mind who I am. I know." There was authority in the cowman's manner. "Where is Jim Rutledge? Is he here?"

"No, sir, he ain't. That's just it. He was seen going down into the cottonwoods just before she was killed. He ain't been seen since. What's the answer?"

Chandler could have cried out his despair. The vitals in him seemed to sink as though the bottom had dropped from beneath them. "The answer is that Moss has probably got him, too. The girl was scared of Devil Dave. She was in mortal fear, an' she sent for Jim Rutledge to save her. He got there too late. He was to meet her in the cottonwoods. Has anyone seen Dave Moss? Or any of his boys? Or Buck Roe?"

Nobody had, within the past hour or two.

Manders came swiftly down the street. He had already heard the news. "Who found the body?" he demanded, looking from one to another of the crowd.

A young man and a girl were pushed forward. They told their story. To talk over a certain little matter they had walked down to the grove. A voice calling for help had startled them.

"Man or woman's voice?" snapped the sheriff.

"Man's. He shouted that they were murdering him. Then we heard folks moving away from us. After a while we went to where the cries came from an' we found Mamie Dugan's body lying on the ground. That was the way of it, wasn't it, Lulu?"

The girl confirmed her lover's story. "And then we ran back to town to tell folks," she added.

Her eyes were shining with excitement. It was plain she was shocked at what she had seen, but thrilled at being the center of attraction.

"That Jim Rutledge done it," someone cried with an oath. "Hal Simmons saw him heading for the grove."

"Wrong guess," the sheriff said curtly. "Where is the boy? Anyone seen him lately?"

Chandler spoke. "She sent him a message asking for help, Al. Told him to meet her at the cottonwoods south of the track. He's not been seen since. Afraid the Moss gang have got him too."

"'Lo, Chan! Didn't know you were in town. You may be right. We'll get lanterns and go down to the grove. There may be evidence there. I'll want you, Chan, and Pendleton. And the two that found the body. Nobody else."

"There's about fifty people down there right now," a woman said.

Manders threw up his hands. "Might have known it. No use going there now. They've tramped down whatever evidence there may have been. Where's the body?"

"Al has got to go through all the motions of lookin' for evidence," Rutledge said to Pendleton. "To save my boy we've got to move faster than that. We know Devil Dave is at the bottom of this. Our business is to find him. I'm going straight to his house. Rustle up some of our friends an' come there soon as you can."

"You're not going alone?"

"I'm going alone. This is a hurry-up job. Does he live where he did last year?"

"Yes." Pendleton did not attempt to argue with his friend. There would be no use of that. "Go kinda careful, Chan," he urged, hesitantly, not sure whether he ought to obey orders or insist on accompanying Rutledge.

Jim's father did not walk. He ran. Every moment counted now — unless he was already too late.

The house was dark. He tried, very softly, the doors. They were locked. He went to a window and with the butt of his Colt's broke the glass. Putting his head through the ragged opening, he turned the catch and raised the frame. In another moment he was in a dark room. From a pocket he drew a box of matches. One flared, and he lit a lamp on the table.

Chandler did not attempt to move softly. Anyone in the house must have heard him. He passed from the room into a hall. This led to the kitchen. Nobody in it. Another door opened to a bedroom. Clothes had been tossed here and there. Someone had been lying in the bed, for it was still warm. The Texan went up the creaking stairway. The second floor was as deserted as the lower one.

Harrison Pendleton's great voice shouted at him from outside. "You in there, Chan?"

Rutledge opened the door. "They've lit out. The house is empty," he said.

Four men were with the big cattleman. Two of them he recognized, Garrick and Roundtree. Jerry Denver was one of them.

"Where d'you reckon they've gone?" asked Garrick.

"Hit the trail, likely. Where do they keep their horses?"

The fifth man of the party spoke up. "At the K.C. Corral. Shall I find out if they've gone?"

Chandler looked at him. He was a redheaded, boyish cowboy. "Who are you?" he asked sharply.

"I'm Ellen's brother, Steve Lawson."

"All right. Find out, an' report right away at the Trail's End Hotel. If you're ridin' with us, bring a horse and yore own weapons." Rutledge turned to the others. "They've taken Jim with them. Gentlemen, meet me at the hotel soon as you can, ready to ride. I'm waiting for nobody; soon as I can cut sign telling me which way to go I'm in the saddle."

"If the house is empty they must have stopped for Sam. Likely they brought their mounts here, seeing as he wouldn't be fit to walk." This was Jerry Denver's suggestion.

They examined the ground. There was evidence that six or seven horses had been here very recently. They had headed westward.

"We'll start from here," Rutledge announced. "Move fast, gentlemen. We're following a hot trail."

Within fifteen minutes they were riding out of town. Once more Steve Lawson spoke to Rutledge.

"Looks to me, sir, as though they're heading for our claim. They keep supplies in a cache near there."

"How do you know?"

The boy flushed. "I usta be right friendly with them."

"Not now?" Rutledge flung the question harshly at him.

"Not now, sir."

The Texan's keen gaze sized up the youngster. "All right," he said curtly. "You guide the party."

Steve deflected from the road and cut across country. The others followed.

CHAPTER
THIRTY-FOUR

Devil Dave Dictates a Farewell Message

Returning to painful consciousness, it took Jim a little time to orient himself. He was propped up against a fence. Someone sat beside him, and when he stirred, a revolver was poked against his ribs.

"Listen, fellow," a heavy voice admonished, "if you let out a squawk, I'll drill you."

Young Rutledge was acutely aware of a head that throbbed as though hammers pounded in it. To get information he lifted a hand to the side of it.

"Keep still," he was ordered.

Jim looked at his moist fingers. "Blood," he said, surprised.

Then the situation came clear. He had been trapped, assaulted, and brought here by his enemies. With a shudder he recalled the awful thing Devil Dave had done to Mamie Dugan. It was to be his turn next.

Where had they brought him? He was in the yard of a house lighted both upstairs and down. He could hear men moving to and fro, running up and down. What were they doing?

Presently he heard the sounds of horses coming down the road. A man dismounted and tied them to a hitch-rack.

"That you, Clay?" someone called from the house.

"Yep. All ready?"

"All ready."

The lamps in the house were blown out. The front door was locked. Jim was jerked roughly to his feet and lifted to a saddle. His ankles were tied together by a short rope passed beneath the belly of the horse.

Sam Moss pulled himself to a saddle and rode close to the prisoner. "How you feelin', fellow?" he jeered.

Jim did not answer. He looked at the man, then looked away.

Young Moss, furious at his contempt, flung out an answer to the question he had asked. "I'll tell you how you're feelin', fellow. You're scared — scared stiff. Think I don't know? Yore heart is dead inside you, even if you are throwin' a bluff an' trying to keep yore chin up. Before we're through with you, fellow, you'll beg like a yellow hound dog."

The horses began to move. Buck Roe ranged himself on one side of Rutledge, Clay Moss on the other.

Buck explained a point or two to their intended victim. "You're on the slowest horse in the bunch. It's dead on its feet. No use trying to run. It won't get you anything."

They traveled toward the west, hour after hour. He did not understand this. Had Dave Moss pulled up, bag and baggage? Was he leaving for the Red River country, where he had a ranch and a shebang hidden in the hills? If so, if the old man saw the handwriting on the wall and was running for cover, why not finish the prisoner out of hand without delay?

The cavalcade drew up before a cabin familiar to Jim. He had not long ago dodged into it to save himself from this same Moss outfit. That had been his hour. This was theirs.

The prisoner was dragged from the saddle and hauled into the house. Old Dave sat beside the table in the sitting-room. Jim stood across the table from him. He was not invited to take a chair. They had brought him there for sentence, not for trial.

For the first time Jim got a close look at Devil Dave. He had observed that in spite of his shapeless bulk the man moved with a surprisingly swift energy. Now he saw him beside a lamp, its light turned on the old fellow, on the bald head sunk into the huge rounded shoulders, on the beady black eyes fixed upon those of the boy.

To understand mental reactions is not always possible. Jim stood in the shadow of death. He should have been absorbed in his own immediate future, to the exclusion of everything else. Probably he was. But during the long ride he had schooled his nerves. He must not get panicky. He must make his brains serve him. So now his mind was sending out little tentacles of thought. One of these had to do with the slovenly old man's coat. It had cloth buttons, *and one of them was missing*. He had found the third man who had been standing outside the window of the card room at the Longhorn the night of the Shear murder.

Shrewdly Jim spoke first. Every minute of time he gained was so much. He played coolly to postpone the pronouncement of the sentence against him.

"When you say you killed Joe Shear do you mean you had him killed?" he asked.

"What's it to you, fellow?" Buck Roe answered savagely.

Old Devil Dave offered mock reproof suavely. "You wouldn't speak rough to our guest, would you, Buck? Me, I'm willing to answer all reasonable questions — now. We're in a kinda hurry, but we ain't in too big a hurry to be polite. I'll put my cards on the table, Mr. Rutledge. You can guess why. You're close-mouthed, you are. I ain't scared you'll talk. Te-he!" He leaned forward, showing his teeth in a cruel and malevolent grin. "There's an old proverb which tells about one kind of men who don't talk."

Jim understood. This fiend counted him already dead and was mocking him. The young man resolved grimly that he would get no change out of that.

"I've heard it," Rutledge said.

"Good enough. We understand each other. I'll tell you all about it. I killed Joe Shear my own self with yore little knife. You'll have to excuse me for not doing a thorough job an' bumpin' you off, too. I just didn't have the time."

Moss was boasting, swimming on a sea of self-satisfaction. His voice purred like that of a great cat which has been at the cream.

"But how could you have killed him when you weren't in the room?" Jim asked, a frown of bewilderment on his face.

"You'd never guess," Dave gloated. "I came in by the window an' went out by it."

"In the dark," Jim said admiringly.

"In the dark."

"An' of course nobody recognized you."

"That's where you're wrong, fellow," Pete cut in. "I knew it was Dad all the time."

Jim remembered now the white-faced excitement with which Pete Moss had leaped to his feet, pointed a trembling finger at the dead man, and cried, "Cripes! It's Joe Shear."

"I had to lean right over Pete's shoulder an' I kinda wheeze some when I'm winded. So Pete knew who I was an' Buck 'most knew. If there's nothing more I can do for you, Mr. Rutledge, why, time's slippin' along an' we'll get to business."

"The sooner the quicker," Buck said with a hard laugh.

"I reckon that's what you thought when you shot down Abbott, the express messenger on the S. & G. flyer."

"You've done talked yoreself to death already, Rutledge. No need to say any more," Buck cried angrily.

"Why, yes, there's been talk enough," Dave assented. "Business now."

"Yes, business," Jim jeered. "The kind you're good at — killing when the other fellow has no chance. Even when you were a boy you were busy at it, after you deserted from the Confederate Army. I don't reckon you've forgotten Lawrence, Kansas, though it was years before I was born."

Devil Dave looked at him in astonishment. "What do you know about Lawrence? You claimin' I was with Quantrell there?"

"You were seen there. Don't you remember the boy you killed at the corner of a field? How he tried to climb the fence an' you shot him down, then killed him while he lay on the ground begging for mercy?"

Old Moss was startled. After all these years it was not possible that the law could reach him for what he had done in his guerrilla days. What astounded him was that this boy could know a secret buried so long ago in his nefarious past.

"Who loaded you with that lie?" he asked.

"You know it's the truth. A man lay in the blackberry bushes at that fence corner and saw you."

"What man?"

"Bob Jelks, a fellow in yore company before you deserted."

"Bob Jelks!" Jim could see the man's memory was groping for and dragging back a recollection of Jelks. "I ain't seen him since the war. Where's he at now?"

"My father knows. Let me tell you something, Dave Moss." Jim leaned forward, eyes undaunted, challenging the old villain. "You've got me, but if you go through with what you're plannin' you'll never get away with it. Better figure you're near the end of yore rope — you an' yore whole gang — for Chan Rutledge will

280

sleep on yore trail till he gets you. You'll never escape him — never. He'll get you sure."

"Or I'll get him. You can't talk us out of this, fellow." For a moment unleashed passion leaped from the eyes of the old guerrilla. "You've stood in my way long enough, you an' him both. You poor fool! Thinkin' you could hunt me down an' make it. Ever hear of a lamb huntin' down a wolf?"

For one despairing moment Jim's mind flashed back to Ellen — Ellen whom he would never see again. She too had used this simile.

"Chan tried it, you tried it, an' yore uncle made his brags." Dave ticked them off on his prehensile fingers. "First Joe, then you, then Chan, an' if there's any more of yore family feel biggity, why, I'll get them, too."

Beneath all the talk he had made, another thought had been running in Jim's mind. What forlorn hope of escape was there? He kept it hidden, did not let it reach either words or gestures. If they knew what he was thinking they would eliminate the chance. But what chance? Clay stood at the door. Sam sat on a chair by the window. The others were grouped around the table.

Pete broke out angrily. "I've got something to say my own self, fellow. You stole my girl from me, after you made a fool of me in this very house. You got her to marry you. All right. Listen to me. In about five minutes she's gonna be a widow. I'll give her a fittin' time to mourn. Say six weeks. Then she'll be my wife."

"That's so," Dave agreed. "Bring a chair forward, Pete. Sit down, Mr. Rutledge."

Jim sat.

The old man supplied paper and the stub of a pencil. "Now write," he ordered. "What I tell you to put down. Ready?"

The prisoner, warily intent, waited to hear what the leader of his enemies would say.

Moss dictated. " 'I got to the end of my rope. Tonight I killed Mamie Dugan. She wouldn't keep still about what I'd done to her and about how I stabbed Joe Shear.' . . . Got that?"

Jim's fingers had been traveling slowly over the paper. Pete stood behind him, looking over his shoulder.

"He's written it," young Moss said.

Jim put down the pencil. "I get yore notion," he said. "Where do I get off at? I confess I killed my uncle an' Mamie Dugan, then I commit suicide. That it?"

"You guessed it," the old man jibed. "Pick that pencil up an' go on."

"I reckon not," Jim differed.

"Light a fire in the kitchen stove," the old ruffian ordered Clay. "You'll find a runnin'-iron on the wall outside. Heat it."

If Jim was daunted, he did not show it. "The Comanche croppin' out again," he said aloud.

Craftily, his mind was busy with the situation. It would take some minutes to light the fire and heat the iron. But he must not wait until Clay's return. Already he could hear him lifting the stove lids. The young man had not lit another lamp. Sufficient light for his purpose came in through the open door. One of them out of the room — Buck Roe leaning against the wall back of the old man, his hands thrust deep into the trouser pockets beneath the chaps — Sam still sitting by the window — Pete between him and the door. They had him safe. That was fixed in the minds of all of them. He was one unarmed man surrounded by five armed ones.

Jim heard the fire crackling. He spoke, apparently driven by his fears. "What more you want me to write?" he asked shakily.

Devil Dave grinned. "Thought you'd see reason. You Rutledges won't go through. Write, 'Clay Moss caught me before I got a chance to get away. I grabbed his horse and lit out. But they are on my tail. Got me surrounded. I'm killing myself.' . . . Written that?"

An oath slipped from Pete's lips, an excited cry of rage. "That's not what he's written, Dad. He says we've got him, an' that you killed both —"

He did not finish the sentence. Jim's arm swept across the table and sent the lamp flying into the face of Dave Moss. Almost simultaneously he rose, flinging the table over the old man and ducking across the dark room to the wall.

CHAPTER
THIRTY-FIVE

Jim Makes a Break

Devil Dave gave a yelp of consternation as the lamp leaped at his face. He scrambled back from the table and jumped to his feet. The room had been plunged in darkness complete and Stygian.

Within the four walls urgent and violent force manifested itself. The impulse of five minds was toward furious action. Oaths, cries, the shuffling of feet, the overturning of chairs filled the place explosively. Somebody stumbled over the fallen table and went down with a crash. Sinewy fingers gripped Jim and held him fast.

Jim seized the arms of the other. "I've got him," he cried.

The fingers slackened. "Leggo, you fool. It's me — Sam," a voice flung at him.

Rutledge let go, willingly. "I'll watch the window. Head him off from the door," he urged.

Sam moved away. Jim heard the thud of a revolver barrel falling on flesh and a cry of pain. For the moment it was every man against his neighbor.

Through the window there came the faint light from a less intense darkness. Covering his head with his

284

arms, Jim flung himself through the frame, shattering the glass as his body crashed forward. He plowed along the ground, raised himself to hands and feet, and was off like a sprinter at the starter's pistol.

The roar of a gun pursued him. A hoarse voice shouted. Footsteps sounded. Jim raced for the hitch-rack, for any horse except the one he had ridden from town. As he heard the boots pounding behind him, Jim reached the mounts. He dragged at the slipknot, flung himself astride a saddle, and drove his heels savagely into the sides of the buckskin. A bullet whistled past his ears. Already he was flying into the night, crouched low in the saddle. A third time the revolver barked. The clash of raised voices grew louder. His enemies were in the open, heading for the horses. He put the buckskin at racing speed. The ground was very rough and broken, but he had to take his chance of a fall. Already his pursuers were on horseback and in motion.

From the cries carried to him Jim judged they were spreading out. In the darkness they did not want to miss him. The fugitives knew it was a question of speed, and before he had covered five hundred yards he began to fear that the buckskin was not fast. At least one of the outlaws was gaining on him. He could hear the hammering of the hoofs on the sunbaked soil.

Jim began to edge toward the left. If he could get beyond the outermost rider before they were too near he might slip away and let the pursuit sweep past him. But to do this he had to work his way over very gradually, for he had to keep enough distance in advance not to be seen.

It came to him presently that he was not going to make it. Would it be possible for him in the darkness to pretend he was one of the Moss outfit and gradually to let himself drop to the rear? Hardly. But it was his only chance. He slackened the pace.

Out of the darkness, over to the left, a shadowy rider began to take form.

"That you, Pete?" he called.

Then, in the winking of an eyelid, chance decided the issue. The buckskin stepped into a gopher hole, stumbled, and flung his rider headlong. Jim was dazed probably not more than a few seconds, but long enough to complete the disaster. Before he could rise a man dragged his horse to a halt, threw himself from the saddle, and ran forward with long strides. A Colt's .45 covered Jim.

An exultant whoop rang out. "I've got him." It was Clay Moss.

Almost at the same moment Devil Dave and Buck Roe arrived. Dave pushed back Roe's weapon.

"Don't push on the reins, Buck," he ordered. "We'll get that confession signed first."

"Bring a tie rope, Sam," Clay called. "No more funny business goes."

Roughly they tied the hands of their prisoner. As they jerked at his arms he judged that the fall had broken a collarbone. Just now that was of no importance. Hope had gone out of his heart. He was lost. They would never give him another opportunity to get away.

Clay mounted. Jim was hoisted to the back of the horse and his arms tied around the body of the man in the saddle.

"We've got to get this done so's we can get back to town," Sam urged.

"Soon now," the old man agreed savagely. "Soon as we get the confession."

"I'm about played out," Sam went on crossly. "Didn't know how much that wound had taken it out of me."

"You *would* come with us," Dave said curtly. "Spite of my advice to stay home."

"Think I was gonna miss the show? All I say is, let's finish an' hit the trail for town."

"Don't worry, boy. That's what we'll be doing inside of five minutes," his father promised.

They rode back to the house and dismounted. Dave Moss and Buck Roe, each gripping tightly an arm of the prisoner, led the way into the cabin.

CHAPTER
THIRTY-SIX

"High — Wide — an' Handsome."

The posse organized by Chandler Rutledge rode fast. The cattleman knew he was taking a chance in accepting the suggestion of Steve Lawson, that he was gambling on the life of his son. But the one essential was to reach the scene in time. They could not wait to follow a trail in the darkness, even if he had been sure of keeping to it. A good guess, with some reason back of it, was better than to potter along and arrive too late.

Rutledge rode beside Steve. Not once did the boy hesitate, dark though it was. What troubled him was not a doubt as to the direction but one as to his wisdom in assuming that Devil Dave was headed for the homestead. If he turned out to be wrong, Jim Rutledge was lost.

More than once the tortured father asked how much farther the cabin was. When at last they topped the slope that looked down upon the claim the thermometer of young Lawson's hope plunged down. The house was dark. The party approached from the rear.

Chandler flung himself from the saddle and strode into the house. He struck a match. One impression registered on his mind. There was a fire in the kitchen. The men he wanted had been here very recently. Another match flamed up. He saw a lamp on a shelf and lit it. A running-iron, red hot at one end, projected from the stove into the room. What was it doing there?

The other members of the posse had trooped into the house. They followed Rutledge into the parlor. What they beheld was astonishing. The room looked as though a cyclone had swept through it. Chairs were smashed and the table upset. Fragments of a shattered lamp lay scattered over the floor. A window had been demolished, the woodwork between the panes smashed violently.

"There's been one helluva scrap," Jerry Denver cried.

"Looks like," Pendleton agreed, "but I don't savvy how Jim would get a chance to fight."

Chandler Rutledge stooped and picked from the floor a piece of coarse brown paper used for wrapping parcels. Upon it was some writing. He read it, to himself, then made a comment aloud, his voice not quite steady. "Jim's handwriting."

"What's it say?" asked Garrick.

Chandler read aloud: "*I've got to the end of my rope. Tonight I killed Mamie Dugan. She wouldn't keep still about what I'd done to her and about how I stabbed Joe Shear.*"

"Good God!" cried Pendleton. "Confesses he did it."

289

"That's not all he has written," Chandler went on. "Listen. *Not a word true. Dave Moss trapped me. He says he killed both* — That's all. He broke off there."

"It don't make sense," Pendleton complained, his forehead wrinkled in a puzzled frown. "First he says he did, then he says he didn't do it."

"Don't you see? Dave Moss was dictatin' the words to him. He wrote what he was told to at first, then broke off to tell us the truth. Right then, if I guess it right, he knocked the lamp over an' went through the window." The eyes of Rutledge were shining with a hope relumed in his heart. "Maybe they didn't get him. Maybe he's still alive."

"Where is he, then? Where is the Moss outfit?" Roundtree asked.

Rutledge waved a hand. "Out there somewheres — What's that?" He stopped to listen, then blew out the lamp. "Get into those two rooms. Don't make a sound. Be ready for business but wait for me to start."

He carried the lamp back with him into the bedroom. The hot globe might betray to the outlaws that someone had been in the house. His hope was to surprise them. The sound of a laugh, followed by a ribald curse, had drifted to him, carried by the wind. It had come from over the hill. Devil Dave's riders could not have seen the light. If the horses back of the house did not betray their owners by neighing, the Moss gang would come swaggering into a trap.

There was more laughter, more profanity, as the night riders trooped into the house.

A voice, recognizable as that of Buck Roe, called out brutally and jovially, "Well, well, here we all are back in our happy home."

"Light a lamp," ordered someone harshly.

There was a sputtering of several matches. From the kitchen someone called, "Here's a lantern." Pete presently brought it in, lighted.

Devil Dave wasted no time in preliminaries. "Bring that runnin'-iron, Clay."

Jim spoke, and at the sound of his son's quiet voice, the heart of Chandler Rutledge behaved badly. The shock of joy shook his cold nerve, left him for the moment limp.

"No need to bring it," Jim said. "I'll sign no confession to the crimes you did."

"We'll see about that," old Moss replied with silken menace in his smooth tones. "Te-he! I kill. You bear the blame. It's a good joke. Laugh, young fellow. Gimme that iron, Clay."

"*Throw up yore hands.*"

Rutledge and Jerry Denver filled one doorway, with Steve Lawson craning over their shoulders. Harrison Pendleton and the other two Texans appeared in the other. Their weapons covered the outlaws, who stood staring at them, caught by complete surprise.

Devil Dave did not have a chance. He was holding the running-iron in his hands when the summons came. As he glared at Chandler Rutledge his face became convulsed with rage. He dropped the running-iron and reached for a weapon. Already Buck

Roe's .45 was sweeping up from the hip. Jim dropped to the floor and lay sprawled out.

The roar of the guns filled the room. The shapeless body of Devil Dave crashed to the floor before he could fire a shot. It was all over within a few seconds. Buck Roe spun half round, tried to recover balance, and plunged down upon one shoulder, his right arm with the revolver pinned beneath the weight of his torso. Clay had vanished through the door, Sam by way of the window. Pete still stood holding the lantern, a stupefied expression on his dark, sullen face.

"Disarm the boy," Chandler Rutledge ordered crisply.

But his eyes did not once leave the bodies on the floor. Men shot to death sometimes take a deadly revenge before their spirits pass.

From outside came the clatter of horses' hoofs. Clay and Sam Moss were galloping away with the fear of death at their heels.

Chandler moved two or three steps forward. "Get their guns," he told Jerry Denver. "I'll keep 'em covered."

Jerry collected the weapons of the prostrate men. "Anybody hurt? You all right, Jim?"

"None of us, I reckon," Pendleton said, glancing around. "Buck was a mite late. He got his before he fired an' shot wild."

"I'm all right," Jim said.

He had risen and stood looking at his father. He was a sorry sight, his hair matted with blood and his face covered by it. The color had been driven from his lips.

He leaned against Steve, half inclined to sink to the floor. The reaction of joy was almost too much for him.

"Thank God," his father said fervently.

"Busted collarbone when my horse threw me. Nothing serious, but — it's been hell." The voice of the young man threatened to break.

Chandler put an arm around his shoulder. The pressure of the strong muscles, the support flashed from the steady blue eyes, went coursing through the blood of the son like heady wine.

Jim laughed, not very steadily. "No sense playin' the baby."

Dave Moss had died instantly, riddled through and through. It was a question of minutes for Buck Roe, and he looked up at Chandler Rutledge with no weakening in the hard eyes.

"You sure got us at last, Sheriff," he said.

"You went too far, Buck," Chandler answered.

"You're right we did. It was comin' to us." He spoke faintly.

"Better come clean, Buck," the ex-sheriff advised. "We've got one of the Moss boys here, the others we'll have in a day or two. Have we got to hang them for killing this girl?"

"They didn't do it, Chan. That was old Dave's deviltry. None of us got there till after he'd done it. I'll swear that."

"And Joe Shear?"

"He did that too. Climbed through the window. Go easy on the boys. Old Dave was to blame." Buck spaced his words slowly and with difficulty.

"Anything we can do for you, Buck?"

"Not a thing. I'm ridin' to hell — high — wide — an' handsome."

They were his last words. Five minutes later he passed away. He had come to the trail's end.

CHAPTER
THIRTY-SEVEN

Jim Turns Another Page

The bodies of the dead outlaws were brought to town. It was found that the left boot of Dave Moss fitted exactly the impression labeled *Exhibit 1* that Dr. Aubrey had made of the footprints outside the Longhorn. The evidence against the dead man was overwhelming. Slim Rogers returned to town and told his story of walking in upon old Dave and his son just after one of them had washed bloodstains from his hands. The missing button, the boot track, the admission he had made to Jim Rutledge, the dying statement of Buck Roe, all tended to fasten the crime upon him. The note of Mamie Dugan to Jim, the forged letter found in Dave's pocket, the words heard by all the posse, "I kill. You bear the blame," served as contributory evidence. Under pressure, in order to exonerate his brother Sam, young Pete Moss confessed that he had recognized his father as he knifed Joe Shear and that Dave had slain Mamie Dugan to prevent her from telling what she knew of this.

Jim returned to Ellen's arms with an emotion surprising to himself. He had counted that he was a dead man, and here he was to love and be loved. For the first time since his childhood he gave himself up to mothering and could not get enough of it. The fearful nerve strain under which he had been had taken its toll of his strength. The broken collarbone served as an excuse, and he relaxed to let himself be waited on like a sick man.

And Ellen loved it. She had him back again, safe from the terrible perils he had passed through, and she made the most of it. In and out of his room she fluttered, making excuses to be with him and fuss over him. For it was only when her eyes were on him that she felt quite sure that the danger was forever past. Those were red-letter days for both of them, to be remembered the rest of their lives.

Jim discussed with his father the offer of Dane Sackville to run the Wyoming ranch for him. In the end he decided to accept it. The opportunity was too good to pass.

"Wyoming is not so far from Texas as it was son," Chandler said. "I've some notion of stocking a ranch of my own up there. Maybe after you get the lay of the land we might go into partnership, you an' I. Or we might all three form a company, we two an' Sackville. We'll see how it works out."

So Jim and Ellen went to Wyoming. They are there today, and on the Circle R, as he has named his ranch, are a swarm of young Rutledges, both boys and girls, hard riders and good ropers, brown as the suns of the great Northwest can make them. Among them moves Jim, their father, with the same light, long stride of his Texas days, still the best rider and roper of the lot.

Ellen looks at them all and smiles happily. She is still young, though a little more buxom than when she was eighteen. Life has been good to her and Jim — and still is.

ISIS publish a wide range of books in large print, from fiction to biography. Any suggestions for books you would like to see in large print or audio are always welcome. Please send to the Editorial Department at:

ISIS Publishing Limited
7 Centremead
Osney Mead
Oxford OX2 0ES

A full list of titles is available free of charge from:

Ulverscroft Large Print Books Limited

(UK)
The Green
Bradgate Road, Anstey
Leicester LE7 7FU
Tel: (0116) 236 4325

(Australia)
P.O. Box 314
St Leonards
NSW 1590
Tel: (02) 9436 2622

(USA)
P.O. Box 1230
West Seneca
N.Y. 14224-1230
Tel: (716) 674 4270

(Canada)
P.O. Box 80038
Burlington
Ontario L7L 6B1
Tel: (905) 637 8734

(New Zealand)
P.O. Box 456
Feilding
Tel: (06) 323 6828

Details of ISIS complete and unabridged audio books are also available from these offices. Alternatively, contact your local library for details of their collection of ISIS large print and unabridged audio books.